Blue Collar Love

S.A. Bierly

Copyright © 2026, By S.A. Bierly

All rights reserved.

This is a work of fiction created without the use of AI technology. All people, places, events, and ideas are elements of the author's own creation, and any resemblance to a real-life place, event, or person, living or dead, is purely coincidental.

No part of this book may be reproduced in any form or by any electronic or mechanical means, including information storage and retrieval systems, without written permission from the author, except for the use of brief quotations in a book review.

Without in any way limiting the author's exclusive rights under copyright, any use of this publication to "train" generative artificial intelligence (AI) technologies to generate text is explicitly prohibited.

This book is intended for mature audiences.

First Edition

ISBN: 979-8-9935069-1-3

Ebook ISBN: 979-8-9935069-0-6

www.authorsabierly.com

Developmental Editing by Meg Marshall, Brave New Words Editing @bravenewwordsediting

Developmental Editing by Rosemary, Heartfelt Editing @heartfeltediting

Proofreading by Cassandra Dellinger

Cover Design by Marge Turingan, Caravelle Creates @caravelle_creates

Interior Formatting by S.A. Bierly with Atticus

Blue Collar Love

S.A. Bierly

To past me.
You're gone but you'd be proud of the woman I've become.
And to my husband,
for believing in me and supporting my dreams.

CONTENT WARNING

This book contains explicit sexual content, sexual harassment, discrimination by a boss, strong language, and attempted non-consensual touching by a minor character.

Contents

Book Playlist	X
Brett	1
1. Autumn	6
2. Brett	15
3. Autumn	24
4. Brett	31
5. Autumn	37
6. Autumn	44
7. Brett	51
8. Autumn	56
9. Brett	63
10. Autumn	75
11. Autumn	84
12. Autumn	91
13. Brett	96
14. Autumn	107

15.	Autumn	115
16.	Brett	124
17.	Autumn	136
18.	Autumn	143
19.	Autumn	148
20.	Brett	157
21.	Autumn	167
22.	Brett	173
23.	Autumn	178
24.	Brett	188
25.	Autumn	197
26.	Brett	204
27.	Autumn	210
28.	Autumn	219
29.	Autumn	230
30.	Brett	236
31.	Autumn	248
32.	Brett	257
33.	Autumn	264
34.	Brett	272
35.	Autumn	278
36.	Brett	286

37. Autumn	291
38. Brett	298
39. Autumn	307
Autumn	312
Acknowledgements	316
About the Author	318

Book Playlist

1. Dirty Looks – Lainey Wilson

2. Drink Around – Ian Munsick

3. Long Hot Summer Day – Turnpike Troubadours

4. Work Boots – Cody Johnson

5. The Man – Taylor Swift

6. Single Saturday Night – Cole Swindell

7. Blue Collar Boys – Luke Combs

8. Blue Collar Town – Creed Fisher

9. Forty Hour Week (For a Livin') – Alabama

10. 9 to 5 – Dolly Parton

Brett

3 months ago

"Hey man, what the fuck!" Someone yells, standing up from their table at the bar, slopping beer on the floor. "I was watching that."

"Yeah, well, this is my bar and I'm changing the channel." Bobby slams the remote down on the bar and motions at the door. "You don't like it, get the hell out, or else sit down and shut up."

I push away the beer in front of me and shift in my seat to see that the local university graduation is now playing on the TV instead of the football game that had been on previously. The bartender, Bobby, is hyper-focused on the screen.

"My nephew is graduatin' today, Brett. Got a fancy degree in business now." Bobby turns and says to me as he wipes down the bar top. The rag he's using is clearly decades old, all brown and grimy. If that doesn't set the tone for this bar then I don't know what does.

"Oh, that's nice, Bobby," I grunt to him. My thoughts are all consumed by the knowledge that I am finally back in Mayfield. I've been away from town for several years, and for the last nine months, I'd been out running a backhoe on a pipeline job in Virginia. I haven't seen my family yet, despite parking my camper in their back field behind the barn. I had just gotten back last night, overwhelmed with the concept of being home, and what's the first thing I decide to do? Take my ass to Bobby's Bar and day drink.

I didn't have plans to return home—I wanted to keep pipelining and avoid being here—but my dad had a health scare in the form of a heart attack about a month ago, and my mom asked me to come home. I couldn't just drag up and leave, despite wanting to, for fear of something happening to my dad, so I asked for a layoff. It took some time, but I'm here now.

As I'm berating myself for being stupid, I feel my phone vibrate on the bar top. I glance down, expecting it to be my dad wondering where I'm at, but to my surprise, the screen reads *Tony Ward*.

Tony is my former boss from when I used to do jobs at the local university before everything went down with Brittany, and I transitioned to mainly pipeline work to get out of town. He's a good guy, and he would only call me if he needed something really important or had a job to offer me.

"You still out in bumfuck nowhere, Stewart?" Tony's boisterous voice rings through the phone and makes me chuckle.

"Nah, Tony. I just got back to Mayfield last night, but I'm guessing you somehow already knew that." I shake my head with the realization that Tony most definitely got a call from my handler, Benny, letting him know I was off work. I called Benny just yesterday on my drive back to Mayfield to let him know I was laid off from the job in Virginia and could be put back on the list for other work if there was anything good in the area. He mentioned a couple high high-profile jobs at the local university, so I decided to have him put my name down as available.

"Good. I got something for ya if you're willing to stick around Mayfield for a while and want to take some time off before you start. The job doesn't start 'til August." The hopefulness in his voice rings clear. Tony misses having me work for him—he'd been begging me for months to come back to Mayfield and do work at the university with him. "Whitewater is looking to put up a new building. Something for the engineering school. Job's expected to last 8-10 months for dirt work, longer for the actual building process."

I consider what he's saying for a minute. Staying in Mayfield is something I hadn't done in years. I got out of this town to hide, not to mention for the good money that comes with pipelining, and I had established myself well in the pipeliner circle. Just about everyone there is to know knows that Brett Stewart is one hell of a hoe hand. But I had also come back to watch over my family and my dad, hadn't I? So, what would it hurt to stay for this job? Work is work, and if I can spend the summer helping Adam and Dad on the farm, then start work in August, it would be perfect. I have enough saved up that I could go a couple of months without pay while I wait.

"What machines do they need hands for?" I ask, knowing this information is essential to my final decision. I'm not running a skimpy skid steer just to stick around town and make pennies a day when I could make sure my dad is good and then go somewhere else once summer is over, sit my ass in a D8 on the hillside of West Virginia, and make bank.

"As far as I know, they've got a dozer, a hoe, a couple trucks, and they want a crane operator." Tony sounds smug. He knows from all our time spent together on jobs that I refuse to get my crane certification.

"Tony, you know damn well I ain't no fuckin' crane operator," I grumble through my teeth. "But I can run a hoe, and I suppose it might be nice to stick around home and spend time with my folks for a while." When I was out doing pipeline work, I stayed out. I could always call my parents or siblings and video chat with them, so there was no real reason for me to come back to Mayfield. But with everything going on, I knew they would all appreciate being able to spend some time with me, especially if this job does go on for a while and I could be home for Christmas for the first time in four years.

"I knew I had ya when I offered the hoe!" Tony sounds cheerful on the other side of the line. I'd never known him to be a cheery guy, but I guess he just likes working with me. "It'll be good to have you back here, Stewart. No one operates quite like you do."

"Alright, bud, you can lay off. I already agreed." I chuckle and take another sip of the now warm beer in front of me. I cringe and raise it up to Bobby, signaling to him to bring me another when he gets a chance. He catches my motion and nods.

"Sounds good, man. When I get more details about the job, I'll send 'em your way. Try to enjoy your summer a little and tell your folks I said hi. Heard about your dad, hope he's doing well," Tony adds just before hanging up the phone. He's lived in Mayfield all his life, so he knows my parents quite well.

Bobby sets a cold bottle of Budweiser down on the bar in front of me and grabs the remote. He starts cranking up the volume as I see people walking across the stage.

"...in Business. Mr. Johnny Gulliver." The announcer says as a young man appears on screen, accepting the diploma being held out to him.

"That's my nephew!" Bobby starts yelling, clapping, and pointing at the TV, ensuring that every patron in the bar turns their head to watch his nephew walk across the stage. It's the next girl, however, who catches my eye.

"Master of Science in Civil Engineering, Ms. Autumn Harris." A pretty, young woman walks across the stage in heels. She so effortlessly carries herself with a sex appeal to the tens, blonde hair, and is clearly smart if she's graduating with a master's in engineering. I shake my head and clear all dirty thoughts from my mind. An engineer? That woman is going to be eaten alive on the first construction job she gets to.

Autumn

Present day

A BLARING NOISE PULLS me out of the worst sleep I've had in my life, and I couldn't be more grateful for it. I take a moment to lie in my bed, staring up at the ceiling. I am so excited for today. It is the biggest day of my career. Years of hard work finally culminate into this one singular thing.

Today is my first official day of my first assignment as an engineer. I've spent the last three months since my graduation developing the final stages of this project, and I finally get to share it with the crew that is going to bring my vision to life. Well, not just my vision. I worked with several of the sponsors for this project to design a building that would meet the goals of the University, Department, and anyone who wished to have input.

I roll over to the side of the mattress and let my feet touch the cold floor, thinking about how I am going to handle today. I'm nervous, of course, but also excited. I was told that the crew would start their meeting today at eight a.m., and I plan to be a few minutes early—although, there's always a slight chance that might not happen, as I've been notorious for pulling up exactly at the start of an event for practically my entire adult life. This morning, I had set my alarm for five in hopes of giving myself plenty of time to get ready and be early.

Quickly undressing, I jump in the shower and take a few minutes to gather my thoughts and squash my fears about today. I've practiced my presentation over a dozen times, observed every part of the blueprints I could, and practically memorized everything. I don't think there's a single question that I couldn't answer. I'd already been down several different paths with the sponsors when we were trying to come up with a vision, and I managed to answer all of those questions and navigate those conversations without fail. I think I can handle a bunch of guys who operate equipment.

After I scrub my shampoo into my hair and wash it all out, I continue down my body. Washing myself in the bath or shower has always been one of my favorite things; I find it so relaxing. If only someone else was here to wash me, that would be even more intriguing. Sadly, things on the partner-to-wash-me front have been a little slow with all my time dedicated to school and now work. Despite my desires to be washed by a man, I haven't actually ever been with one. I haven't even had a real *boyfriend* since I dated Danny Steel back in high school. I don't know if you could even call him a boyfriend—we went on a couple of dates, and our final one was to the movies, where he tried to feel me up and I decided I no longer liked being around him.

I shake the distracting thoughts of my lack of love life away, and I reach out of the shower to grab my towel off the wall.

Once my body is dry, I wrap it around me and proceed to the sink, where I can do my makeup, and blow-dry, and style my hair. I don't want to look like I'm high maintenance today—I'd certainly never been that way, and didn't want the men I am going to be working with to get the wrong impression. I have to show that I can keep up with them and work at their pace without complaint.

I swipe on light gold, sparkly eyeshadow, and some mascara, and I'm done with makeup. I dry my hair and style it in a high ponytail so it can look professional but still have it be out of my face. I hate when my hair gets in my face.

I glance down at my Apple Watch, only to realize I now only have about 30 minutes to eat breakfast before I need to leave. Fuck, how long did I spend in the shower? I lose track of time in there so easily.

In the kitchen, I grab a bagel out of the bag on the counter and pop it in the toaster. I open my fridge to grab the iced coffee I got during my grocery shopping trip yesterday and the cream cheese. When the bagel pops out of the toaster, I reach for it, pretty much burning off the ends of my fingers, and slather the cream cheese all over it. This is by far one of my favorite breakfasts to have. I sit down at my bar counter for a few minutes and try to enjoy it, but time passes all too quickly, and before I know it, I have to go.

My commute to the site is about 30 minutes, but I want to be early, so I shove the last bite of bagel in my mouth and rush out the door at 7:20 on the dot. I grab my car keys out of my purse, throw all my stuff in the back, and start my playlist on my phone. I have been curating a "First Day Jams" playlist to pump me up on my drive in for my first day.

.. ——— .♥. ——— ..

I pull up to the job site in my stark red Jeep Wrangler. I knew when I got it—a stereotypical car for a girl always trying to fit in with the guys. It feels like ever since I landed my engineering job at Arch Engineering, all I do is fight to fit in with the guys. Today is finally my chance to prove that I won't have any problems getting along with everyone and doing the job successfully.

I hop out of the driver's side, swing open my back door, and grab my bag containing my computer, which housed this morning's stellar presentation, and my armful of beautiful, glorious blueprints, all compiled by yours truly. Six years of engineering school to get my bachelor's and my master's is well worth it when I finally get to relish in the joy that I helped design plans for an entire building!

I bump the door with my hip to close it and then make my way through the job site toward the foreman's trailer. I look around and see a dozer, an excavator, and lots of mud. It rained last night, and everything is wet. Mud cakes to the bottom of my boots as I trudge my way through. I take one final calming breath, reminding myself I can do this—showing the crew the plans for the new George O. Henry building being designed here in the middle of my alma mater.

George O. Henry, whose name is always said in full length, was a professor of engineering here at Whitewater University. He was well known for being an extremely harsh critic of engineering student's design plans, always pointing out flaws and why things wouldn't work based on electrical lines, water pipes, or even just the direction of the wind. His classes were the hardest to pass, but also the hardest to get into. Every single engineering student wanted in on George O. Henry's classes. He was a hero, saving engineers from coming up with building plans that would wreck their careers.

Arguably, he was my biggest inspiration going into engineering school and I was really hoping to take one of his classes, but sadly he developed pancreatic cancer during fall semester of my freshman year and by the time spring came around, he was gone. I was devastated, as were many other students, but not just because I didn't get to take his class. George O. Henry had been my role model. His thoughts and critiques had pushed me to be the best engineer I could be, and I always spent extra time trying to think about how to ensure my plans had no flaws, no matter what. Because of his impact on engineering students, the University decided to build a brand-new building to house the growing engineering school and name it in his honor.

I push thoughts of the building's namesake from my brain, pull open the door of the foreman's trailer, and seven pairs of eyes are suddenly on me. Despite being fully clothed, I feel completely naked while standing in front of all these men, who look like they could eat me up. Immediately, fears of everything I could possibly do wrong on this job enter my brain. I stop my thoughts before they can make me turn around in fear. I am not going to let these strong, blue-collar men intimidate me out of my place here, I am an engineer dammit.

"Um, hello. My name is Autumn Harris. I'm the engineer for this project, from Arch Engineering." I nervously look around to try and figure out which one is the foreman.

"Ah, finally, Ms. Harris. Glad you could join us. An hour late..." A strong, scowly-looking man who stands toward the front speaks up.

"An hour?!" I gulp. "Mr. Matthews said we were starting at eight. If I had known, I would've been here sooner, I'm so sorry." I stumble over the words. Mr. John Matthews is the owner of Arch Engineering, and my boss. He is the last person I want to upset by getting the timing wrong and showing up late on my first day. I wonder why he would've told me eight if these guys really started at seven, unless I misheard him.

"Being late is fine today. I had to get these men through the proper training and paperwork anyway. We've only really been sitting here for about 15 minutes. I'm Tony Ward, the foreman. Please just call me Tony." The grumpy man says with a scowl and hands me a folder of what appears to be copious amounts of paper. "You'll need to fill all of this out too and go through the proper job site trainings. If you're gonna be here long term, that is."

"Yes, sir, er, Tony," I say, cringing as his scowl deepens with my calling him sir. "Is there a place I can set up my presentation for the engineering plans?" I look around the room, but, as this is a pop-up job trailer, I don't see much. There are lots of papers posted up on several bulletin boards on the walls, a large-sized table around which all the guys are sitting, taking up most of the space, and a desk in the corner with papers strewn about. This place is nothing short of a big, unorganized mess.

"Does it look like there's a place for a presentation in here, Ms. Harris? No. You're gonna have to do this the old-fashioned way, lay your plans out on the table and let my guys here look at them." Tony waves his hand over the table to show that this was my one space and apparently my only chance to show these men what I had come up with. "Best if you do minimal talking while they work."

That comment irritates me, but I know it's just the nature of the beast. The dislike for me being a woman is thick in the air, and I can feel myself slowly being choked out by it. My nerves are getting to me as I shakingly lay the plans out on the table, leaning over them as I speak my thoughts.

"These are the plans that I, under the review of Arch Engineering, have come up with for the George O. Henry building. We've designed a three-story building with a solid concrete foundation, faux brick walls that are actually concrete reinforced with steel beams, and large glass windows to let in as much natural light as possible. We had a team come a few weeks ago with 811 and lay out where the water and electrical are so that we can avoid those areas with our support system. The concrete base is going to go 12 feet into the ground to allow for a basement area."

I can feel my confidence growing back as I start to share my plans. I've been the lead junior designer on this project, under Mr. Matthews' supervision, so I know the building plans with my eyes closed, but of course I am pointing out each section as I talk about it so that the men could see what I am referring to just in case any of them have never seen blueprints before—though none of them strike me as that type.

"We also need to create an outdoor area that will be a concrete walkway around some intensive landscaping. This area will include some benches, fountains, and will need doors to access the building as well," I add.

The guys are all practically ignoring me at this point and muttering between themselves. Perhaps Tony was right, and I should've just not talked. I stand up and cross my arms. I wait for them to get their fill of observing my plans without even one glance in my direction.

I notice one of the men has taken a quick glance at the blueprints and is now leaning back in his chair with his arms crossed. He has a beautiful face, if a man could be beautiful. His rugged features included a scruffy beard that, while on the average man would look unkempt, looks perfect on his face, as if he had combed it specifically to be so messy. He has short brown hair and piercing blue eyes that are staring right at me, which makes me extremely nervous. I am beginning to sweat under his glare, but luckily the rest of the crew finally decides to stop milling over the plans and they all sit back in their chairs.

I look around at all of them and give them a look to indicate that I am waiting to hear their comments. When no one speaks up I say, "Do you all have any questions about how we're going to achieve this project? I've already had my boss coordinate with your foreman, Tony, to go ahead and order the supplies needed." I sweep my hand in Tony's direction with a smile, to see his expression has gotten a little less scowly.

I look at the men around the table again, over my blueprints, and all eyes swing to the mystery man as he clears his throat. "These are lovely plans, Ms. Harris." He gives me a smug look. "Too bad they won't work."

Brett

IF LOOKS COULD KILL, I would have murdered Autumn Harris the second she walked in the door. A scowl has not left my face since she walked in here in her tight little jeans and arms full of, what I now know are useless, blueprints. Where the hell did John get off thinking he could send us a newbie for a job as extensive as this? I'd been a part of Tony's crew several times in the past, and John had never sent us someone inexperienced like this.

Being an equipment operator, I am often moved to different jobs throughout the area, even the country if I wanted to take some of them. I'd spent the last two years doing just that, bouncing from pipeline job to pipeline job. But I grew up in Mayfield, and my parents have lived here all their lives as well. I went to Mayfield Technical School where I fell in love with operating, and I've done that work ever since. Over the years, I'd done several jobs here at Whitewater University, always under Tony's direction before a bad breakup pushed me to get out of town. Tony's a grumpy bastard, but he has always been a great foreman and really cares about his crew. Which is why I cannot believe that he let John push a newbie on us.

"What do you mean? Mr....?" Autumn eyes me nervously. She doesn't seem to have the confidence to do this. I have been working in the trades for eight years now, but she must've graduated just recently. Something about her strikes me as familiar in that sense, but I can't place my finger on it.

"Brett. Just Brett. And you've got your little "outdoor area" as you called it right over top of some serious electrical lines. You can't cover those access points; it's against code." I smirk, knowing I am right, having only taken one glance at her prints.

Her already big brown eyes get ten times bigger as she rushes forward to lean over her blueprints and observe the courtyard area. Fuck, her leaning down gives all of us a prime view right down the top of her shirt, and she doesn't even realize it. I see more than a few guys take a look and snicker to one another. "You can't be right. We had the 811 crew go through and identify all the lines; there's no way they missed anything that big."

I stand up and grab the electrical outline map that sits on Tony's desk and lay it over top of her blueprints. "Look. We had our own electrical crew go through and find the electrical points. Unfortunately, this place is loaded with them. Makes my job a lot harder than it needs to be, but that's not the point. The point here is the proposed location of your outdoor area." I sweep my pointing hand over a large area of the electrical outline that houses some of the most complicated workings. Whoever proposed putting a building here was a complete idiot. This area is covered in utilities that are going to be awful to maneuver if we can't rework these plans.

"Oh my gosh, this cannot be happening." Autumn mutters to herself quietly, thinking I won't overhear. She clears her throat and stands back up. "Okay, this is not an issue. I will need to talk with Mr. Matthews and rework the plans with the sponsors, which shouldn't take me long, maybe a few weeks?" She looks nervously at Tony, but before he can answer, I cut in.

"It won't even need to be that. Tony, I'll help her get these plans fixed, and you can start clearing the area with these guys." I point to Frank specifically, since he is set to be the dozer operator. "While I'm helping fix this fuckup, you can have Frank scrape off the top layer of dirt and get it taken out of here on the trucks. This shouldn't take more than two weeks, and I know he'll need that time just to get his slow ass in gear."

I smirk at Frank. We've worked together several times before, and there was nothing better than goading the old man into getting his panties in a bunch. Frank is a good guy, though. Even in his fifties, he can do circles around a lot of the younger guys on the crew, myself included sometimes.

Before Frank has a chance to reply with some smartass comment, Tony cuts him off by putting his hand up in front of him. "Alright, Brett. That will work. You help this girlie here fix her plans the right way, and we'll get the dirt moved outta here so when you're done, you can get your ass back to digging where it belongs. I want new plans on my desk two weeks from now *at seven*. That's your deadline."

He narrows his eyes at Autumn, and she looks away from him toward the ground. If she hadn't been late and shown up with plans that didn't work, maybe she'd get a little more respect, but as of right now, no one on this crew is a very big fan.

I take a moment to really look at her and realize she looks so young and so vulnerable at this moment. All at once, it clicks in my head that *Autumn Harris* was the woman I saw walk across the stage when I was drinking at Bobby's Bar a couple of months ago. So, she *is* a newbie. A twinge of anger and something else I can't place flashes through me. How dare John send us such an unskilled engineer for this job. Hell, she is probably just doing this job because she went to engineering school here and wants to put on a good show for the university's new engineering building. Ridiculous.

The crew all start to stand up and go outside. We have a fairly small crew for such a large job: only three operators, two laborers, our safety guy—Bob, and Tony. I lean back in my seat and cross my arms, and smirk at Autumn.

Once everyone has exited the trailer and Tony closes the door, she unleashes on me. "Who the hell do you think you are, telling me my plans won't work. Your electrical guys have to be wrong, because there's no way our guys would mess up that badly, leading me to design plans that were this wrong!" She screams at me, looking directly at my face. I swear I can see the steam coming out of her ears, and her skin has taken on this pinkish glow from her frustration. It is good to see her grow some backbone suddenly, and my cock twitches at the thought of her being a little feisty. Down boy, she's too naïve for you.

"Well, obviously they did, because our guys are never wrong, and I was out there with them myself for a few minutes, in that area specifically, so I know for a fact that there are electrical hubs in there." I stare at her with cold eyes. I am not going to let this fresh, little engineer intimidate me into thinking that my judgment is wrong. She scoffs at me. "Let's just figure out how to fix this together so we can be done and don't have to spend another minute together in this awful job trailer."

I lean forward and grab her blueprints from under the electrical map I had laid down. She grabs two pencils from the cup on Tony's desk and brings them over, offering me one with a slightly softer expression on her face. This must be her request that I forgive her for her outburst.

"You're right. I'm sorry I yelled at you. I want to prove that I can do this, and problems like this are not helping me. You have no idea what it's like to be a woman in this world." She grumbles as she sits down in the chair next to me and starts to look over her own blueprints.

Autumn has a soft face, one that looks weary, like a lot of people have taken advantage of her underlying kind nature and used it to get what they want and push her out of the way. Her big, brown doe eyes and blonde hair don't help her case at all; you know what they say about blondes. The way she wears her tight jeans and Arch Engineering polo that looks a size too small oozes sex appeal and my cock moves again at the thought of what was underneath those figure-hugging clothes. I shuffle in my seat to adjust myself. I should not be getting hard over the annoying and young, yet *deliciously sexy* engineer.

She scrunches her nose up and has a look of serious frustration on her face. "How come the people that Arch Engineering hired didn't map out that all these electrical lines and hubs were here?" She looks at me with concern all over her face.

"Well, I'm not sure, because any idiot would know they're out there. They are marked with clear caps," I say, looking at the blueprints. She has a good point—how could a company, hired specifically for this purpose, miss those? There are plates on the ground, surrounded by grass, that clearly say *Electrical*. I saw them on my way into the job trailer this morning from where I parked my truck. Any idiot should have seen those plates and known what they meant and added them to the map.

"Do you have copies of the utility maps from that company?" I ask her, thinking there was no way that these weren't missed, and she probably just didn't know how to read the utilities map.

"Uh, yeah. Let me pull them up on my laptop." She pulls a fancy MacBook laptop from her bag. So that's what she's carrying in there; no actual papers, just a computer.

Autumn opens the document on her computer and turns it around so I can see the screen. Sure enough, there are no utilities marked on these maps. "Who sent you these? What company did you hire?" I ask, moving the maps around to see if they are listed somewhere else or if there are any notes explaining why they missed a whole section of electrical lines.

"Uh, Mr. Matthews sent them to me. I don't know who he hired to have the work done. He said that kind of thing was not something junior lead engineers could do and that he would handle managing them." She looks nervous, like there's something she's hiding from me. It isn't my place to ask, so I don't. Instead, I choose to focus on the fact that this woman is a full-blown idiot.

"What are you talking about? The lead engineer on the project should always be the one to interact with the utilities companies, even if they're junior. They need to be the point of contact so that they're familiar with every aspect of the project," I snap. How does she not know this? She is so far proving to be a real shit engineer. It's almost like she didn't learn anything in engineering school.

"Mr. Matthews told me himself that he is the one who always handles the utilities for jobs, and I shouldn't worry about it. He told me to focus on making my prints because it was going to be a *difficult job*." She adds air quotes with her fingers around the last two words as she says them. "Am I really supposed to be the one leading that?"

She looks like she could break into tears any second. A part of me feels bad for her, but a bigger part of me is angry that I am stuck here with an engineer who has no confidence and isn't going to be able to complete this job. Fuck, I am going to get laid off because this project is gonna be rejected, and I already told my mother I'd be sticking around for the holidays this year because I have work at the university. If I lose this job, I can't guarantee that to her anymore.

I wipe my hands down my face in frustration as I explain the details to her, "John has never been involved in the utilities contact for any projects that he hasn't designed himself. If he told you that he would handle it, he obviously thinks you can't do the job yourself. And he was clearly right, given that you've already fucked the plans up and were late on your first day." She looks at me dejectedly.

"He's the one who told me...look, I don't know you that well, but given that you're not the one who was asked to design this project, I take it you have no idea what it's like to be an engineer, so I'm going to ask that we just move forward and I can update these plans to get the outdoor area changed. We'll likely have to do some restructuring, or we can move it over here..." she trails off and begins scanning the prints in front of her. This girl is really giving me whiplash, going from yelling at me one minute to telling me that we can work together to get the new design figured out the next.

"I told you before, my name is Brett," I say through gritted teeth. "And I'm the lead operator on this crew. Tony has a lot of trust in me, and he really values my opinion. So, if you want a shot at making it on this crew and being successful, on what I'm assuming is your first project, I wouldn't piss me off." I scowl at her. In all my life, I have never had a problem getting along with people, but this woman has already gotten underneath my skin in a way I can't explain. It's like she is a thorn that I got in my side that is working its way deeper the more we talk.

"Alright, *Brett*," she says with a strained look on her face. It seems like the feelings I have for her are mutual, and she is spitting it right back at me. Well, two can play this game, lady, and I am not afraid of a challenge. "Let's figure out how to fix these plans. What do you suggest?"

Autumn

I FLOP BACK ON the bed of my best friend's apartment. "You are really gonna break my bed if you keep doing that!" Lucy shouts. Lucy is my best friend; she has been for years. We met each other in our freshman year of college. The story is actually really funny. I was sitting in my first-ever ethics class, which was a requirement as part of our core curriculum. In walked this complete wreck of a girl. She was struggling to keep her papers in her backpack while she shoved an apple in her mouth and barely made it in the door before the professor. The only open seat was at the table next to me, so she plopped down, extended her hand, and said, "Hi! I'm Lucy, I'm a biomedical sciences major, and today is a complete wreck. Nice to meet you!"

I, of course, began to chuckle because this girl was nutso, but turns out she was super sweet and funny, and that ethics class brought us together, so I couldn't have been more grateful. Lucy always wears black clothes, has straight black hair that she dyes, a nose piercing, and is covered in tattoos. She's like my polar opposite in looks, but she's got a similar personality and is ridiculously smart.

"Luce, you have no idea. Today was seriously the worst day of my life, and I just need to curl up into a ball and cry!" I throw my arm across my face and groan. Today was hard. I did my best and was so excited for the job, and I proposed an amazing plan for the building, all for it to blow up in my face.

I was late! I still can't figure out how Mr. Matthews had the time wrong for when they started this morning. I am going to have to talk to him soon and ask if he was sure he had the time correct. But accusing him of having it wrong would not go well for me. Mr. Matthews and I haven't always seen eye-to-eye, especially after a few disagreements on how I should handle leading and working on the project. Not to mention, I keep getting this weird feeling about him when he talks to me. He stares at my chest a lot, and it always feels like he is talking through me instead of with me.

Then there was the whole issue with the blueprints. Brett made me feel like such an idiot in front of everyone, calling me out like he did. It wasn't my fault that the 811 crew didn't get the utilities right. Well, according to him, it *was* my fault because I wasn't involved in the process, but I didn't know I had to be. I'm just starting out and learning, and I went off everything that Mr. Matthews told me. He is my boss, my mentor, and I know he wants me to succeed because I represented Arch Engineering on this job. He reminds me of this all the time, always saying, "Autumn. You need to do the absolute best job you can. On the job, you are the face of this company, and what you do reflects on all of us."

Lucy pokes me in the side to get me to giggle, and it causes me to sit up and scowl at her. "C'mon, Aut. You know you're a talented engineer; you cannot let this little setback get in the way of what you've been dreaming about for years!" She's right, and she knows it, since she has that smug look on her face. Lucy is completing her PhD, and she still has at least two more years to go. I'm at least already out and about in the job world, even if it is just barely.

"If you ask me, I think Mr. Matthews is trying to sabotage you. You know he hates your guts after that fight you guys had a couple weeks ago, and it wouldn't surprise me if he gave you crap information to really mess with your first job and have a '*legitimate*' excuse to fire you." She shrugs and walks over to the desk in her room.

The *fight* that Lucy is referring to was a disagreement from mid-July when I asked for some time off to go on a family vacation and Mr. Matthews "jokingly" said that I could go but "only if I send him some pictures from the beach" which I did not like and I told him as much. He apologized and said he was only kidding and told me to have a nice vacation with my family, but I still feel like things are strained between us.

"I don't think that's it. Mr. Matthews and I don't get along, but I don't think he would purposely mess up a job like this. I am a part of Arch, and if I mess up, that looks bad for the whole company, not just me." I scroll through the now junk blueprints on my computer, and I think back to today's conversation with Brett. We had been able to actually come together in sort of a truce mode and figure out what needed to be changed. While we didn't actually make any changes yet, it was at least good to have a list of what needs to be moved.

The entire outdoor area will need to be redone. It is going to be a big job to figure out where to move everything due to the proximity of other buildings, general aesthetics, and figuring out where the actual utilities are. I will have to ask Brett or Tony if I can get a copy of their 811 prints to see where the utilities are.

It looks like our 811 company just missed the entire section completely. I don't know how I hadn't realized it before, but they just excluded that whole section of the job site where the utilities are and left it completely blank on the prints. To be honest, now that I'm looking at it with a new lens, it looks like someone just selected that whole section of the blueprints and pressed delete. Absurd, I know.

"Okay, so let's assume that Mr. *Assface* didn't intentionally try to sabotage you," Lucy starts. "How are you going to fix the issue?"

"Well, Brett, one of the main operators, and I are working together for the next two weeks to get the plans fixed. Based on our discussion today, besides being a total dick, he knows his stuff."

Brett was a total asshole to me today, embarrassing me in front of the whole crew, but he seems really smart. He was able to point out where everything was on the prints and even took me out to the site and showed me the caps that our 811 team clearly missed.

"Ooooh, is this Brett cute by chance?" Lucy presses me for information. Both of us are extremely single, and she is always trying to set me up with different guys, but I have never taken her up on her suggestions.

"He's like the most handsome guy I've ever seen," I whine in frustration. "But that is not what this is about, Lucy. I need to focus on my blueprints and fixing this mess. This is my first chance to prove to Mr. Matthews that I can do this."

Brett is extremely handsome, there's no denying that, but I can't let his attractiveness distract me from my work. Doing well at this job is the most important thing to me. I shuffle my computer on my lap and scan over the blueprints again, turning my focus to fume at the way Brett talked to me today.

"You know," I say as I slam my computer closed and slide my gaze over to my best friend, who is intently staring at a picture of a bacteria in her textbook, "Brett was, no *is*, a dick. These next two weeks are going to be so miserable."

I slide my hands down my face and groan in frustration. I have never instantly disliked someone the way I dislike this guy. He was just so irritating, and he thinks he knows the best of everything.

"Listen," Lucy closes her book and sits next to me on her bed, pushing my computer away from us. "Right now, we don't have to think about work or annoying ass guys. Because you promised me that we would have a Twilight movie marathon over the next two nights, and you know how I feel about Edward. He is *not* annoying. And now that I've finished my assignment, I'm ready for this." She pulls her blankets up and over both of us.

"Wait, I need popcorn for this." I rustle out from under the covers. "Pull up the first movie while I go make some." I wander out to her kitchen. Lucy's apartment is small compared to my house, which I was gifted by my grandparents when they passed away. Being the only grandchild had left me lonely most of my life with no cousins to play with, but it has its perks, like getting a whole house. I do miss my grandparents every day, though. Like I am with my parents, we were very close and losing them had been hard on all of us, especially my mom.

I grab a new bag of popcorn from the cabinet and place it in the microwave. My thoughts shift to the ruggedly handsome jerk face that I have to deal with at work.

It's going to be hard for me to deal with Brett at work. I have a feeling we're going to butt heads a lot. It was nice of him to offer to help me fix the prints, though, because let's be honest, it would definitely take me longer than two weeks if I had to work on them myself.

Brett has a rugged masculinity about him that I find attractive, which may cause a problem for me when I am working, but I'm sure I can push myself past that and remind myself how annoying and rude he is.

The timer for the popcorn pulls me out of my head, and I pour the freshly popped yumminess into a bowl. It's crazy how the popcorn bag was 1000 degrees when I pulled it from the microwave, but as soon as I dumped the popcorn in a bowl, it felt cold. Much like my reaction with Brett: I was fuming when he pointed out how my prints overlaid all of the electrical hubs, but as soon as everyone left and I realized he was right, that everything was a mess, I was freezing cold.

I pad across the floor back to Lucy's room and snuggle underneath the blankets beside her. Thoughts about Brett can wait until tomorrow, tonight I am going to enjoy these movies with my best friend and have sweet dreams about a tanned werewolf and not the tanned operator clouding my senses.

Brett

I PULL INTO THE lot in my black Dodge truck, and I see that no one else has arrived yet. There is something about being early to work that just calms my nerves and brings me the peace I need to take on the day.

I take a sip of my coffee and look out the windshield to see headlights pulling into the lot from what looks like a Jeep Wrangler. I'm not sure who drives it; it could be any of the guys. I continue to watch the Wrangler, but no one gets out, so it must be someone else who enjoys the peace of the morning before all chaos breaks out.

Today is set to be my first day working with Autumn on fixing the blueprints. So far, my impression of her is lacking. I'm concerned about her inability to focus and know what needs to be done. I know she's young and trying to figure out how to do this job, but man, she has done a bang-up job of showing her best work so far. I chuckle to myself. This job is going to kill me.

I look up in front of me and catch a glimpse of someone climbing out of the Wrangler. From the petite little body and luscious curves I see, I realize it is Autumn. She's here quite early today and must be looking to get set up before anyone else gets here.

I hop out of my truck and trail off after her. "Autumn!" I yell, picking up my speed so that I can catch up to her before she gets into the job trailer.

She huffs, "Good morning, Brett," and continues walking. Her tone comes across as irritated, and she looks like she is running on very little sleep.

"You sound tired," I note, trying to keep the conversation short.

She looks down at the cup in my hand, and the smallest sigh escapes her lips. "I didn't want to be late again today, so instead of taking time to stop at The Bean, I decided to skip getting coffee in the mornings. I'll be fine without it." She walks ahead without another word.

The Bean is our town's coffee shop and the place I stop at every morning to get my own cup of coffee. The very coffee I am holding in my hands and just rubbed into Autumn's face.

I shake my head and follow her, keeping a small distance between the two of us. This morning is not off to a great start already, and I'm afraid things are going to be tense for the two of us. We walk inside the job trailer, and she sets all of her stuff down on the table. I stand and watch while she lays out the blueprints she has. Based on the scribbling on the sides of the prints, it looks like she spent some time last night working on these. Good to see that she put in some effort outside of work to fix this.

"I'm just trying to restart today as if yesterday never happened. I'm ready to buckle down and get these plans fixed. Let's just focus on that." She claps her hands. "Okay, so. I was thinking about these a little bit last night and thought a good place to start would be to go back to the base. I'd like to walk around out on the site and try to map out where the electrical units are. And it would be good if I had a way to get a copy of Tony's 811 prints." She turns and looks around for something. She finally spots what she's looking for and pulls her cell phone from under the corner of one of the prints. While grabbing it, she adds, "Maybe I can just take a picture of them and reference that."

"I can get you a copy of the actual prints for your laptop from Tony." I drink the final dregs of my coffee and toss the cup in the trash. She pauses and looks at me with shock on her face, "Okay, yeah. That would be great. Then I can make edits on the file on my laptop to reprint these." She grabs a small notebook off the table and looks at me expectantly.

"C'mon, Hotshot, I'll show you around the site so you can see what we're working with." I step outside in the sun and slide my hard hat on my head. Yeah, that nickname is definitely the right fit for her. "You got one of these?" I nod at her, pointing to my hat.

"Uh, yeah. I think Tony said he set one in the trailer for me, let me grab it." She turns around and darts back up the steps into the trailer, ass on full display for all to see. A good man would've turned away and not stared. I am not a good man. I let my eyes travel her whole body.

"Alright, all set." She bounces back down with a white hard hat on her head, the same as mine, except hers is pristine, whereas mine is worn, scratched, and covered in stickers from years of work.

We walk across the job site and get to the area where the electrical utilities are.

"So, this is the spot." She unrolls the prints and looks at the spot on her paper where her proposed courtyard is currently placed, needing to be moved. "I think the best approach right now is for me to draw and make notes right here where my plans currently are."

I grunt in agreement. "Yup." I know I'm being a bit moody and short this morning, but I really don't want to get into a fight with this girl first thing again today by opening my big mouth. This monotonous task of helping her is already difficult and annoying as it is.

She starts walking around the site and making lots of little notes on her paper. I stand and watch, admiring her from a distance, where it's safe. She is so inexperienced, and I can't believe she's been trusted with such a big job. She likely doesn't know that I know she recently graduated, and I'm not sure I want to tell her. I'm sure that John is overseeing all her work. Now that I think about it, I am sure that he would have looked over her plans before she presented them to us, so why hadn't he caught that she had messed up this courtyard section? That strikes me as odd, but maybe he trusted her to do this and decided he didn't need to look over the plans.

I continue to watch Autumn as she walks around the courtyard. Despite being younger than me by four years, she is a very pretty and attractive woman. If this were any other scenario, I would say she's just my type and I'd be trying to get her into my bed. I bet she's just as shy in bed and would do anything I ask of her. My cock starts to twitch at the thought of looking down at her on her knees as I slide my cock right between her pretty little lips and...

"What is she doing?" Tony walks up beside me and brings me out of my train of thought. I realize that Autumn is now crouched down on the ground, looking over the site with her head cocked to the side.

"Fuck if I know. I thought she was just gathering information about the utilities, not doing fuckin' yoga or some shit." I snort and look at Tony.

"Well, get her done and get her off this site. Frank is gonna start clearing some dirt, and since we both can see how inexperienced she is, I don't want her walking around while the equipment is running until she's been here for a while." He turns and walks away.

"Hotshot! You done analyzing the dirt? They're gonna start the equipment up so we gotta get out of here." My tone is sharp and commanding, but I don't want her to be out here around the machines when she doesn't know what she is doing.

"You act like I've never been around equipment before, *Chief*," She saunters over and looks pissed. The nickname she hits me with really makes its mark, and I'm instantly annoyed.

"Have you?" I retort with a scowl.

"Yes, I have. We had lots of experience working on the job site around equipment in my 'On the Job site' course, my last semester of college. It's supposed to prepare you for real-world experiences, so we were out on the fields at Mayfield Tech, where the students are much worse operators than Frank." She stands in front of me and crosses her arms, standing her ground. She may be shy and unsure most of the time, but when she stands her ground and shows her confidence, it's insanely attractive.

I grunt in response and turn around to walk away.

"Can you tell me a little about what it's like to work here with this crew?" She asks, jogging beside me to catch up.

"It's fine, I guess." I shrug my shoulders. I don't want to give her details about every guy, that would bore us both to death.

"That's not what I mean, and you know it. I need to know how this crew operates and functions, and how everyone gets along. I need to know where I can fit in so I'm not looking like an idiot, like yesterday. So just tell me how I can fit in here," she mumbles the last part.

"You don't," I mutter and walk away, leaving her frozen in shock.

Autumn

SINGING AT THE TOP of my lungs to finish out the song, I turn down my radio while sitting in the parking lot. I get here early now because I want to make amends for being late the first day, but I also learned quickly that it's better to get here early so that I can get a good parking spot. Once the guys arrive, they just park wherever they want, and everything turns to chaos. Yesterday, I saw someone had parked their truck down in the ditch just to avoid being parked in.

I'm also not the only one who arrives early every day. The first morning, I barely even saw Brett's truck sitting across the way from me. It's black, and he had his lights turned off. He was just sitting there in the dark, all creepy like, with barely an early morning glow starting to appear in the sky behind him.

I have always been a morning person, so I don't have a problem with getting up early and getting here before everyone else. I just have to remind myself not to take forever in the shower or to dilly-dally when making my breakfast. Being early also gives me a few minutes of composure and peace, to relax and look over my planner of to-dos for the day. I'm skimming the list when I realize Brett isn't here yet this morning. Odd. He's always here before me.

We have been working together for almost a week now, and he actually hasn't been completely unbearable to work with. He is super smart and really knows his stuff about engineering and building things, even though he's an operator. We've been trying to figure out how to move things or to rework the courtyard so that it's not in the way of the utilities, but we have been struggling to find something that is functional and looks aesthetically appealing.

Lucky for me, I had an epiphany last night. It was at three a.m., so I need to reconsider it this morning, but I'm almost certain it could work. Once I share it with Brett, I think he'll agree.

I look up and see headlights pulling into the lot right as I try to stifle a yawn. Ah, there he was. I wonder what made him late for being early this morning.

The sun is now officially up, and the other guys are starting to pull into the lot, so I hop out and grab my computer bag off the passenger seat. I switched out my briefcase for a much more realistic laptop bag since I realized this wasn't really the place for that kind of thing. I honestly don't even take it to the main office of Arch Engineering anymore, either. This job is changing me to be more practical for what I will experience on the site for future jobs.

As I shut the door, I turn to find Brett walking toward me with two cups of coffee in his hands. I told him that I had skipped coffee the last couple of mornings because I didn't want to risk being late if I was stopping at The Bean, and coffee made at home just doesn't really hit the same once you've tasted their homebrew coffee. But I'm not too proud to admit to myself that seeing that delicious cup in his hands makes me a tad jealous of whoever the second cup is for.

"Morning." He nods his head at me and falls into step beside me. His morning voice is kind of sexy.

"Good morning, Brett," I say, trying to be nice. Although the guy was a dick at the beginning, he has been helpful this past week.

I climb up the steps to the job trailer and hold the door open for him since his hands are full. The extra coffee must be for Tony or something.

"Got this for you." He sets the coffee down in front of the chair I typically sit in.

"Oh, thanks." I pause for a moment to take in what he just said. He got me coffee? I set my bag on the chair and begin to dig through it, trying to find my pen while ignoring him. Why does his getting me coffee make me think it means more than it should? "I don't drink my coffee black, though," I say, settling into the chair.

At that moment, he drops a handful of sugar packets and creamer cups on the table next to my cup.

"I wasn't sure how you took your coffee, so I grabbed these." I look up at him in shock and a little bit of awe. He got me coffee while he got his own and didn't know how I took it, so he came prepared.

"Wow. That's so...nice...of you, actually. I was up until three last night thinking about the plans, and I have something to share today. Thank you, Brett." I sit down and begin adding two cups of the creamer and two packets of sugar to the coffee and swirl it to mix all together. I take a sip and audibly moan. "The Bean's coffee is seriously the best. Again, thank you."

"Yeah, don't mention it. So, what are we tackling today that you thought of last night?" He sits down in the seat next to me that he has been occupying for the last four days while we work on updating these plans.

"Today is all about figuring out how to draw this up so that we have a little courtyard area, here," my finger draws right over a blank area on the prints that sits between the current building standing and the new proposed building, "that connects the two buildings and allows us to have everything I envisioned."

That afternoon, we decide to take a stab at thinking about how the hardscaping could be readjusted to fit a courtyard instead of just sidewalks between the two buildings. Working together, we come up with some pretty good ideas for walkways and even a fountain in the middle.

As I share my ideas with Brett, it feels like the first moment where I really have been able to show him that I do truly know what I'm doing. Brett is very supportive of my decisions and even points out that the pipes for the fountain would run right past the center, and it wouldn't be too hard to add a joint in there. The university would just have to shut the water off to the building for maybe a day at the most.

"Okay, so this could work." I look down at my scribbles of notes on my notepad. I know they won't make sense to anyone else, but they make sense to me, and that's what's important. Brett looks over my shoulder at my notes.

"Wow. How do you even know what that says?" He asks, clearly shocked at my horrid handwriting and child-like drawings for the flowers, shrubs, and sidewalks. I'd seen his handwriting a few times, and it was like calligraphy, so beautiful. Too beautiful for the rugged man in front of me.

"Hey!" I yank my notepad to the side, away from his eyes. "I don't judge your work! Anymore," I mumble the last word.

"Okay, Hotshot. Well, it looks like you've got some ideas there that just might work." He stands up and walks to the small refrigerator over by the wall. As he grabs a water bottle, he continues, "So what do you say we go out and look at the shading on the site and see if your landscape will work in the sun?"

He walks towards the door, expecting me to follow. And like the good girl I am, I walk right behind him. Brett has been growing on me the last few days. Once I got past him being a total jerk at the beginning, I kind of realized that he just wants everyone involved in the work to do a good job. That's just the kind of guy he is. I saw him a couple of different times, talking with Enrique and James, and he pointed out to them better ways to do the work they were doing and how to be a better team—laborer and operator. He's actually very nice to them. And I can't forget how, at the end of the day yesterday, he looked all sweaty and dirty from when he walked around the site with me to triple-check the electrical plans. That's something I put in my Rolodex for private times later.

I rub my hand down my face in an attempt to remove all dirty thoughts of Brett from my head when I catch him saying something I was not expecting.

"You see how that patch of shade from the building covers the area right there? If you plant those patches of blanket flowers there, they won't do well. Those need full sun and…" He turns around to finally look at me instead of the space in front of him and stops short. "Uh, Autumn. You might want to fix your face." He looks at me with a concerned expression on his face. Brett may be getting nicer to me, but he is still extremely blunt.

"What's wrong with my face?" I question while I brush the flyaways of my hair back out of my eyes.

"Well, it's all scrunched up, you look like you're in pain. Are you okay?" He looks genuinely concerned and reaches out to touch my shoulder.

I shrug him off and say, "I'm just shocked that someone as grumpy as you would know flowers. Let alone flowers native to Mayfield." While I'd been dreaming about how sexy and dirty Brett looks, he's going on about shade versus sun and just mentioned putting butterfly milkweed here because the flower is native to Mayfield and an attractant for butterflies.

"My mama owns *Becca's*, the flower shop in town, and she always had this big flowerbed in our backyard while I was growing up. She planted everything in there from Coneflower to Bluebells and would tell me and my brother and sisters about how they could be used and how they were beneficial to the insects." He says all of this with a light in his eyes that I hadn't seen before. I'm not sure if it is a secret passion for the flowers or his true love for his mama coming out.

"Wow, Brett. I would've never pegged you as the type to care about flowers." I joke and poke him in the shoulder as I chuckle and look up into his eyes.

They glaze over, and that warmth I had seen moments ago disappears. "You don't know anything about me, Autumn."

Autumn

"Cheers to you, smarty-pants!" I hold up my beer and clink it against the side of Lucy's margarita for the fifth or sixth time tonight. She has never been a beer drinker, no matter how hard I try to expose her to the world of beer. You'd think she would be against fruity drinks, too, given how colorful they are, but they're her favorite. I guess she makes up for her all-black outfits and style with her colorful drinks. We've been cheers-ing each other every time we get a new round of drinks.

We are out celebrating because Lucy's project was accepted for an oral presentation at the World Bacteria Conference next October. She has been working on this project for months and finally got the data completed on time to apply.

"Thanks for coming out and celebrating with me, Aut." She takes a sip of her drink through the tiny straw.

"You know I always have to support you in everything you do. I'm happy to be here." I settle into my chair and swirl my beer with a sigh. I finally feel immense relief that things are looking up for both of us—she got her project accepted, and

I got my plans sorted out. We are turning into a pair of real successful women.

Suddenly, I feel like I'm being watched. I know there are tons of people in this bar, and the idea is absurd because, of course, someone was bound to be looking at me, but this feeling is like a distinct tingling on the back of my neck.

I turn around and instantly see him. He saunters up to the bar with his sexy, rugged masculinity—wait, did I just think *sexy*!? I remind myself to pull it together; I cannot be having these thoughts. Brett Stewart is not sexy, despite the way his forearms flex and his muscles bulge underneath his gray t-shirt.

I find myself leaning on the bar, daydreaming and staring, when his eyes connect with mine. I see them widen and flare a bit as he takes in my appearance. I'm dressed far differently than I usually am for work, so I'm sure seeing me in a sundress and flats is a bit of a shock to him. I also have my hair down, which reveals just how long and straight it is.

I know I've had a fair amount to drink already, but celebrating with Lucy is essential for this achievement of hers. I pull my eyes away from him and turn to Lucy. "You will never guess who just walked in here."

"Is it Riley Green?! Because if it's not Riley Green, I'm inclined not to care, Aut." She takes another drink of her margarita and laughs at me.

"Pfft. I wish it were Riley Green," I sigh. "But no, it's Brett from work."

"OH EM GEE! The Brett?!" Lucy slurs a bit. Maybe we should slow down just a tad—it's only eleven p.m. and we still want to do a couple more hours of partying. We agreed to leave by one a.m. since it's Friday and she finally doesn't have any lab work scheduled for tomorrow. "I have to meet him so I can find out what makes him so hateable. Where is he?" She starts scanning the bar, as she tries to find out which one of the guys in here is the notorious Brett, whom I'd told her so much about.

"Stop it, you're embarrassing me. He's already seen me!" I swat her on the shoulder and draw her attention back to me.

"Girl, if you do that again, I'm gonna smack you back. I want to know what he looks like so I can tell you if all your frustration is valid or if it's just pent-up sexual tension." She chuckles and takes another sip, wiggling her eyebrows at me. "Which I'm thinking is the case because I know you've never had a roll in the sack, and he could be just the man to finally bring you over to the dark side."

This makes me roll my eyes at her. "Lucille Maria. I do not have pent-up sexual frustration toward my coworker."

"Oh yes, you do!" She chides me. "Now pleaseeee tell me which one is Brett."

"Fine. He's the one over there in the gray shirt that says, 'Stewart Farms' on the back." I nod my head in his direction, not wanting to outright point.

She looks around and must quickly spot him because her eyes open wide, and she gets the biggest smile on her face. "Autumn! He's SO sexy. Wow, girl, you definitely have some sexual frustration over that one. How can you not want to ride that face?"

Lucy is a lot more experienced in the sexual department than I am. She's had several boyfriends during her time in college and grad school, while I had none during my schooling. I haven't even been any further than second base with someone. This means she's always open to making inappropriate jokes or pushing me toward all the men she considers hot.

Of course, the moment Lucy says that is the moment someone decides to step into our conversation. As soon as he talks, though, I realize he's someone Lucy and I are both familiar with.

"If you ladies are looking for a face to ride, I'm right here," I remember Jeremy from high school, but it had been a long time since I'd seen him. I'd heard once before that he frequents Bobby's, but Lucy and I had never interacted with him, only seen him a few times from a distance.

"Whoa, bucko. We're not riding any faces tonight," Lucy looks at him with a disgusted face. She made me promise to keep her away from all men at the start of the night. She said she wanted to focus on celebrating herself for once. I, however, did not necessarily share the same sentiment and hadn't told her to hold me back. I don't want to go home with anyone, but I'm not opposed to dancing with someone. Especially since Brett is now here—a little distraction with someone else wouldn't hurt.

"It's okay, little mama, I just wanted to see if I could buy you ladies a drink and chat with you, it's been a while, and who knows, I might have you changing your mind before the night is over." He leans onto the bar top next to me.

"No thanks, Jeremy. We have plenty of abilities to buy our own drinks, thanks. I wouldn't be opposed to a dance, though." I turn and hand my drink to Lucy and grab his hand to pull him to the dance floor as one of my favorite dance songs is being played by the band.

"Are you sure, Autumn?" Lucy reaches out to stop me before I can walk away. She looks at Jeremy like she's unsure of whether she can trust him.

"Luce, it's okay. I'll be fine. It's just a dance." I reassure her and walk toward the dance floor with Jeremy in tow.

Settling in to dance next to him, I begin to move my body to the beat. "How have you been, Autumn? It's been a while, and you look great." He leans back to admire my body while he reaches out to grab me and places his hands a little lower on my hips than I like, but I leave it.

Ignoring his comment about my appearance, I respond to his question. "Not bad, Jeremy. How are things going for you? Did you go to college somewhere or start work in Mayfield?"

"I joined my dad's auto shop down on First Street and stuck around."

"Ah, got it." At that, I turn around to dance with him a little bit more scandalously. Jeremy was well known but unpopular in high school. He now had a unique appearance about him that made him intriguing. He still had a boyish charm and barely any muscle, but his face was well structured, showing off a cutting jawline that gave him a sculpted appearance. No facial hair adorned his face, but this didn't make him seem younger.

I wouldn't normally dance like this, but I've had a bit too much to drink, so maybe my judgment is clouded, but I don't really care anymore. Life is looking up for me in my career, finally, so maybe I can live a little for once and really let go to have a good time.

Before I know it, Jeremy's hands are moving all over my body. It's not what I wanted, but with all the alcohol flowing through my system, I'm slightly enjoying it. It doesn't necessarily give me that overly excited feeling, but a man is paying me attention, and that's a plus for me.

At that moment, when I'm finally settling into what is happening, I happen to look up and lock eyes with Brett. His gaze is like a bucket of cold water over my whole body, and suddenly, I really begin to hate the way Jeremy's hands feel on my body because they're not *his*.

I shudder and pull away from Jeremy. I want to leave the dance floor and go back to Lucy at the bar; the mood now killed for me, but he grabs me by the hips and tugs me back into him.

"Could you let me go? I'd like to go back to Lucy at the bar." I glance over to where she had been standing before, but realize she's not there. She must be in the restroom. I hope she isn't breaking her promise and dancing with someone. "This was nice, Jeremy, but I'm done dancing." I try to peel his arms off me, but his grip tightens.

"I'm afraid I can't do that, Autumn. You and me, we're gonna have some fun tonight." Jeremy whispers in my ear while his hands start to roam my body.

I feel sick. I need to get out of here. This is not what I had in mind for this evening, and I can feel myself panicking. I wanted to have some fun tonight, but this is too much. I need someone to respect my boundaries if I'm going to do anything, let alone sleep with them. I'm nervous, and I cannot be with someone so brash.

I try to pull away, but he just won't let go. "Jeremy, let me go," I say with some sternness and wriggle harder to get out of his grip that keeps getting tighter and tighter. This man is taking advantage of my drunken and vulnerable state, and I'm beginning to feel unsafe.

"I don't want you to touch me like this. *Stop.*" It seems like my firmness finally gets to him as he releases me, and I stumble forward a bit, only to be caught by strong, firm arms that, despite not having touched before, I would know anywhere just by the look.

"I think it's best you leave, pal. The lady said stop."

I stand up on my own and find myself chest to chest with none other than Brett himself.

Brett

As soon as I walk in the door, I spot her. My eyes are instantly drawn to her body like a moth to a flame. Tonight, she's wearing a pretty, blue sundress that doesn't leave a whole lot to the imagination. It just proves that her legs are just as appealing as I imagined them to be in her tight jeans that she wears to work.

I do my best to ignore her. I came in here tonight to have a drink and catch up with some buddies I haven't seen in a while. I have to deal with her annoying ass all day at work. The last thing I want is to see her in the evening, but here she is, sitting across the way from me in Bobby's.

The guys and I have been chatting about work going on and coming up in the area, when I see her get up and head to the dance floor with Jeremy in tow. I don't know him personally, but I know the guy has quite the reputation here with bothering women. She must know him from school. They are about the same age, I believe, around 25 or 26—several years younger than me, at the ripe old age of 30. I'm by no means old, but I feel it daily with my weary muscles and sore back from sitting in a bouncing excavator for hours every day.

I keep watch on the two of them out of the corner of my eye. There is absolutely no reason for me to do it, but something about Autumn just makes me act defensively. Like I will do anything she needs if she just asks—I *hate* that thought.

Next thing I know, Autumn's eyes catch mine. The look that crosses her face is one of shock and confusion, and I know she saw me watching her. It's the same look she gets whenever I catch her studying me at work.

I take a drink of my beer and try to focus on my conversation with the guys, but it's no use. She's captured my attention, and now I want to watch her dance. I glance back over at her, but instead of dancing, it looks like she's trying to back away from Jeremy. This puts me on alert, and I set my beer down on the table in front of me.

He grabs her by the waist and yanks her back into him, hard. She seems visibly uncomfortable and completely shaken. Before my brain catches up with me, I'm instantly on the move, ready to set this man on fire.

"I don't want you to touch me like this. *Stop.*" Her voice is laced with fear, and I know I've chosen the right moment to intervene.

He smirks at me and lets her go, so she stumbles forward. My arms instantly reach out to catch her before she falls face-first on the floor. "I think it's best you leave, pal. The lady said stop."

She looks up into my eyes. I see a refreshing calm cross her eyes that instantly turns into anger, and she turns around and shakes her head at both of us before she points directly at Jeremy.

"Get the fuck away from me." Without a word or glance in my direction, she turns and storms out of the bar. I know Autumn isn't a huge fan of me and probably doesn't want to interact with me after work, but every nerve in my body is telling me to go after her. I follow her to do the only thing my brain wants to do right now—make sure she's okay.

"Autumn..." I'm a few steps behind her when I see her stop in the alley beside of the bar. She rests her hands on the brick exterior and is bent over to either breathe or cry, I'm not sure which.

She looks up at me with tears in her eyes. "What the fuck was that in there?" Her eyes are a swirl of emotions: anger, helplessness, and perhaps even an underlying hint of lust. Interesting.

"That guy was being a dick, Autumn. I just did what any man should do." I look at her and shrug my shoulders.

"Everything in there just ruined my night. I was having a good time with Jeremy and was looking forward to seeing where things could have gone, and before I knew it, I was looking up at you, and suddenly, I didn't want anything to do with Jeremy!" She blurts out and slaps her hand over her mouth. I know she's had a lot of alcohol because her words are slightly slurred, so I don't think she meant to admit that seeing me was the one thing to bring her out of her good time spent with Jeremy. "Ugh, this night is going to shit." She lets her head fall back and stares up at the sky. I can see a glistening tear roll down the side of her face.

"Autumn, I've been coming to this bar for a long time. That guy has a reputation, and you don't want to be part of it." My voice comes out a bit exasperated, and I know I'm all but begging her not to be angry at me. I'm also going to just ignore what she said about seeing me and then not wanting anything to do with him, for now. I can think more about that later.

"I don't care, Brett. I'm looking for some fun tonight. Lucy and I are celebrating, we're out to have a good time. Even though she didn't want to, I just wanted to have a little fun. Maybe I could've gone home with someone and finally done something that I haven't been able to do before!" She's shaking with sobs at this point, her words coming out a little muffled as the tears roll across her cheeks and into her mouth. I know everything she's admitting to me is because her filter has been removed with the alcohol consumption.

My expression turns dark, and I take a step toward her, close enough that I can talk quietly but still far enough back that she doesn't feel caged. Especially after what just happened. "Are you saying you've never been with a man, Hotshot?" She looks up at me and backs up against the side of the bar. She sniffles as her cheeks turn even more noticeably red from her blush.

No one can see us here; we're out of the streetlight just enough that we can see each other, but we're hidden in the shadows if someone were to walk by. We look like just another drunk couple having a discussion outside the bar. She looks so shy and reserved at this moment, but at least her tears have finally stopped.

She nods her head ever so slightly. "Mmhmm." Her admitting this little fact makes me want to protect her more. I need to get her back inside to her friend so that she can head home. I knew she'd had too much to drink, and I'm thinking thoughts that shouldn't cross my mind right now.

"Alright, Hotshot. Let's get you back inside to your friend." I place my hand on the small of her back and guide her back inside. I push all my inappropriate thoughts about my coworker into a box and lock them away. She doesn't need that right now, and there's just something about this woman that makes me want to be a better man.

Autumn

My brain has been going one thousand miles per hour all weekend. As soon as Brett walked me back to Lucy at the bar, she took one look at my face, and we hightailed it out of there so I wouldn't have to be around anyone with the shame I had been feeling. We spent the night at her house, and on Saturday, we went to the library to do some reading, which was followed by some retail therapy a couple of towns over, where all the good shops are.

It's now Sunday afternoon, and I've been trying to distract myself all day by reorganizing things in my house, but it has proven futile. No matter how much I scrub the flooring in my kitchen, I cannot stop thinking about the way Brett had looked at me with shock and awe when I confirmed that I hadn't slept with anyone before.

He already thought I was young, dumb, and naïve before; now what is he going to think? I throw the rag I am using to scrub into my wash bucket and lean up against the cabinets. Usually, cleaning helps me work through my thoughts, but sometimes I just need to have some floor time to try and bring things back into perspective.

I bring my knees up to my chest and wrap my arms around them. Reaching out, I start to pick at a piece of dirt that is on my floor as I try to wrap my brain around what happened on Friday. I wanted to have a good time out with Lucy, but of course, every single time I go out, something always happens that ruins the whole night for me. It's why I'm such a "stay inside and hang out with myself" kind of person. I really only ever go out when I'm with Lucy.

I love to do movie nights and go out shopping and doing things with her, but I like to hang out by myself more than anything. When you're by yourself, you can't be heard by idiotic people, and you don't have to worry about what anyone else thinks or does. You can just be content with yourself. It's one of my favorite things about living in this house alone.

I know I'm an introverted person, and I always have been, but it's been further emphasized for me every single time I try to go out. Readjusting, I stretch my legs out in front of me in a "V" shape and continue to let my thoughts roll out of my brain.

Another thing pops into my head: why was Brett there on Friday night? I mean, yeah, of course he's allowed to go to the bar whenever he wants, he's a grown man—but why was he there that night of all nights? I mean, it was a Friday night, so he was bound to be there, honestly. There aren't many places in Mayfield for single people to really go and do things in the evening. All we really had in this town was The Barrel, the library, and The Bean, the last of which is closed daily by four p.m.

I suppose there's also the campground you could go and hang out at if you have some friends who want to maybe play in the lake, but that's mostly reserved for parents with young children, and typically only during the daytime. There's Becca's, the flower shop, which he told me his mom owns, but it's designed for quick trips in and out while you pick out the most beautiful flower bouquets I've ever seen. I didn't know that he was even related to Becca, the owner of the flower shop, but I guess I should've put that together since they have the same last name.

But people do always say, in a small town, there are a lot of people with the same last name who aren't related, so it's hard to just assume that people are related if they have the same last name. Typically, they are around Mayfield, though.

I am glad that Brett came to my rescue, although it was his fault that everything happened the way it did. Despite his forwardness, I was having a decent time while dancing with Jeremy. Then of course I looked at Brett and well, everything changed for me. Why? Oh, just because it wasn't Brett that was there touching me, it was Jeremy. I wanted it to be Brett so bad, but of course, that's not something I really should be considering. Like at all. I have to work with him every day, so I shouldn't entertain the idea that I find my coworker very, very attractive.

It's just easier to pretend that he hasn't been the reason for my fantasies the last two days and to just keep working side by side with him. Since we're both working on the plans, we are stuck together for another week, and even then, we are still on this job for another seven to nine months together, so he can help finish the dirt work. He's also the *lead* operator, so we're going to be working together quite a bit, and the last thing I want is for us to do something stupid together that results in complete awkwardness or completely ruins my job.

I throw the piece of dirt across my kitchen floor. I laugh to myself. No matter how much I wipe or clean, there's always going to be dirt inside. It's a side effect of my job, unfortunately. I clap my hands together and stand up.

I know that I should get started on putting away the laundry that has been sitting in my basket for a week now. I need some clean shirts for work tomorrow. All of my Arch Engineering shirts are either dirty or hidden in that basket. I also need to make sure that I have work pants and underwear that I can wear this week because going commando on a job site with all men is not ideal.

I walk back to the bedroom and grab the basket off the floor, setting it on the unmade bed. As I fold a pair of pajama bottoms, I continue to think about this insane scenario that I've found myself in—lusting after my coworker, unsure if I'm reading into his actions wrong. The way Brett came over and saved me from Jeremy—it was a real damsel in distress/knight in shining armor moment. Not that I needed him to be my knight in shining armor. I'm a tough woman and can save myself in most situations, but it's always nice to have someone come to your defense on occasion.

Plus, he kept looking at Jeremy like he wanted to murder him and at me like he wanted to fuck me. If that was really how he felt, I wish he had just told me. I likely wouldn't act on that revelation of feelings, especially now that he knew that I'd never had sex with anyone before, but I would at least know what his intentions are. He's definitely not going to try to put any moves on me after I admitted that. Brett is probably a very experienced guy who only wants to have sex with very experienced women. He probably wouldn't even have time for a shy, nervous ball of nerves like me. I wonder if he intervened with Jeremy just because he knows me from work. It's probably for the best that this all happened because I really don't think that anything should happen between us.

I'm sitting next to Brett in my work chair, and I'm suffocating today. Thank goodness we have the door open, and a breeze is blowing in. Even though I'm pretty sure he can still see my armpits sweating and the flush of my cheeks.

"You good today, Hotshot?" Brett eyes me with a smug expression. It's like he's totally unfazed by what went down at the bar Friday night. Well, if he wants to forget what happened, then so will I.

"Yep. All good here, Chief." I take a sip of my coffee. The coffee he has been bringing me every morning. After he saw how I prepared it the first morning, he's been getting it with two creams, two sugars every morning since. I won't deny that I'm grateful for it.

"Good. Wouldn't want you to be too tired and hungover after having fun over the weekend." His words go right to my core. Did he think I went home with someone that night? Surely not, he saw Lucy and me leave the bar while he was still there. Maybe he's just referring to the alcohol I drank because the only thing I did that night was go back and have a nice cold shower in Lucy's apartment to try and drown out everything that had happened. For some reason, though, I'm feeling spicy today, and I feel the need to see if I can make him jealous.

"Oh yeah. Someone kept me up super late Friday night." I smirk at him, hoping not to give myself away that the someone was Lucy, trying to coax me into telling her what went wrong. I was a steel fortress, though, and refused to tell her. I just wanted to be in my own sadness for a while, and I didn't want to ruin her fun night more than I already had.

He grunts in response and looks down at the plans in front of us. Veering away from our current conversation, he asks, "What do we have left yet? We present these updated plans to Tony on Friday, so we gotta make sure they're done."

I let it slide that he's changed the subject, and I look down at my to-do list, where I've crossed off all the things we have managed to complete in the last week: moved the sidewalks, remapped the electricals, and determined the amount of dirt needed. There are only a handful of items left to be completed yet. "Well, I guess we should probably start figuring out the layout for getting water to the fountain in the middle of the courtyard. It's a good plan, but if we can't get it to fit there with the size we've come up with, then it can't go there. I'm thinking it needs to be in proportion with the building. If it doesn't work out, we might not be able to include it at all." I start shuffling around my papers, looking for the details I had printed about the fountain.

Brett has been essential in helping figure out the layout and where things would look best. I bet if there wasn't so much schooling involved with the process, he would have been a hell of an engineer. Not that his talents are wasted on operating—I'd only seen him run the hoe one time, and he was better and faster than anyone I'd ever seen.

Brett

I PULL INTO THE job site and park my truck in the lot. Today is going to be a big day. I'm pretty sure we have several things to talk about with Tony, and I know there are some trucks coming in. Not to mention, we need to do a lot of dirt work today. I look around the parking lot, and I don't see Autumn's vehicle yet. I know it's early yet, even for her, so I decide to just hang tight and wait for her to arrive.

Working with Autumn has been extremely difficult. I get really stressed around her, and she drives me nuts. I know she's just trying to learn how to do her job, and the least I can do is help her get her footing, but man, I haven't worked with a newbie in a long time. Usually, when I work with someone new, I just pass them off to someone else.

As I'm just scrolling through my phone on social media, I see Tony pull into the lot. He's early this morning, so I guess I can go out to shoot the shit with him for a little while. I unplug my phone from the charger cord, throw it in the middle compartment, grab my lunch box, and slam the door after stepping down. I walk over to Tony's work truck. He drives a little white sedan to the main office for jobs that he manages around Mayfield, which works for him because it saves him on gas. There, he always grabs his work truck, which is what he drives around all day for any errands he might have to run, heading down to the hardware store or to grab lunch from The Barrel. When we were on bigger jobs, he would usually drive the work truck to his camper or hotel so that he could fill up the fuel tank that sits in the bed at the yard in the morning, before coming to the site.

"Mornin' Tony. How ya doing?" I say as I walk up next to his truck. He's still sitting in the driver's seat and watches me as he drinks his coffee.

"Mornin', Brett. I ain't ready for today. You ready?"

"Yeah, I'm ready. I don't think there's anything that can't be handled today." I laugh.

"Well, we got them trucks coming, and I think Pam's coming with them. I ain't ready to see her." He chuckles, taking another drink while shaking his head.

"Oh boy. Good ole Pam. She's the greatest." I smile, thinking of my memories with the woman.

Pam's an older lady who drives truck for the company, and she is a handful. She always teases me about being an attractive young man and says how if she weren't 20 years older than me, she'd be all over me. I chuckle to myself. There's nobody quite like her.

"Well, I haven't seen her in a while, so it'll be good to catch up. Although she'll probably pinch my ass." I say laughing out loud.

I hear the crunch of dirt and look up to see Autumn's Wrangler pull in.

"Well, gotta grab my coffee out of the vehicle and make sure Hotshot over there gets hers." He gives me a look; one I take as confusion. I've shown nothing but animosity toward her, so I'm sure he's wondering why I buy her coffee. Some mornings, I wonder too. I slap the windowsill of his car and walk back to my truck to grab our coffees.

With one in each hand, I walk over to Autumn's Jeep as she's climbing out and grabbing her lunchbox.

"Morning, Hotshot," I say to her and hold out the coffees so she can grab hers. I make sure to get it with milk and cream now since that's what she likes. The Bean is on my way into work, so it's just easy for me to grab coffee for both of us.

I remembered her saying early on that she couldn't make coffee in the morning sometimes because she runs behind when she takes too long getting ready. Thinking about Autumn getting ready and being in the shower is not something I should be doing, but I find myself doing it anyway. I imagine the water running down her smooth, silky body, glistening in the light, throwing her hair back with her full, perky breasts exposed, nipples peaked and ready to be sucked on.

I shake my head to clear the thoughts of Autumn in the shower. She starts talking and pulls me out of my head.

"Thanks, Brett! I really need this this morning. There was this guy on the way in, and he was just riding my ass the whole time, and I had his headlights blinding me in my rearview mirror, and it was just really awful and—" She stops short. "You probably don't need to hear about my journey in this morning, but anyway, thank you for the coffee."

I chuckle to myself. Now that I have gotten to know her and she seems more comfortable around me, Autumn is always going off on tangents, telling stories that are way longer than they need to be, and she just can't stop talking sometimes. But it's okay. That's just part of her quirky personality, and it makes her who she is.

"What's on the agenda today, Chief?" She asks me, taking a sip of her coffee and looking at me expectantly while leaning on the door of her Jeep.

"Well, today Tony's got some trucks coming, there's some trenches that need to be dug, and I think Frank's gonna be scraping off some dirt again into that pile." I point to the large dirt pile we've accumulated almost in the middle of the site. "I think that pile has to be moved, and so he's going to be working with James on making sure that it gets done."

"All right! Well, cool then. I guess I'll just stay in the trailer today and probably just get some much-needed emails sent and plot out some stuff. I was informed today about a potential new project that Mr. Matthews would like me to start working on plans for a bid on, so I want to make sure that I get a jump on that. Although it's not for something that's starting relatively soon, so I'm not sure why he has me working on it. I think it will overlap with this job toward the end…oh well, whatever." She shrugs.

With that, she turns and starts to walk towards the job trailer. My eyes act on their own and immediately go to her ass as she saunters off.

.. ——— .♥. ——— ..

"James! Do you think you could fuck it up anymore? That's the worst operating I've ever seen!" I yell, giving him shit. James has been in my hoe, and he's been working on digging a trench for some of the footers we needed to pour tomorrow. It's not completely messed up, but he has been fucking off this whole time. I think he's on his phone talking with people and doing a bunch of shit he shouldn't be, and it's causing him to make mistakes. I know he can do better than that.

I'm going to have to talk to him with Tony, I just know it. Sometimes being the lead operator on the job is overwhelming because it's my responsibility to keep the guys in line and make sure they're getting their work done to the best of their ability. I feel like I'm constantly yelling at laborers to get off their phones and pay attention so that accidents don't happen on the job. Bob, our safety guy, is always talking with the whole crew about how important safety is and how we don't want anyone to get hurt. Hell, we have a brief safety meeting every morning, and everyone has to sign in on the iPad to make sure they're both in attendance and paying attention.

"Sorry, man!" James calls down to me through the walkie-talkies we use on the job site. It is always so loud here, so it's nearly impossible to hear anyone speak if you're anywhere near a running machine. Walkies are at least right in your ear, attached to the front of your vest, so you can hear it crackle and beep.

I shake my head at him, pointing to the trench as an indication for him to focus and get the job done. I need to go to the bathroom, and watching this guy to make sure he doesn't have any fuckups is really delaying me.

I look to my left and see a familiar head of blonde hair in a white hard hat pop out of the job trailer and look around. When she spots Tony, she smiles and jogs over to him. I'm not sure what the two of them are talking about, but I know it can't be good. Anytime Autumn and Tony talk, plans change.

Instead of watching James dig his trench, my eyes are glued to the two of them. Autumn speaks with her hands, waving them through the air while Tony stands there with his arms crossed, nodding occasionally when she must say something he agrees with. I have to hand it to the woman; she may be new and nervous, but she talks to Tony about her plans with a confidence that I wish more people had. Before I look away, she spots me watching her. Her gaze locks with mine, and she waves at me, smiling.

My body feels out of my own control when I wave back. This woman is going to get me in so much trouble.

That evening, I'm walking down the cereal aisle of the grocery store looking for my favorite frosted flakes. I have these for breakfast every single morning. I know it's a bad habit, but it's my guilty pleasure.

I grab the box and toss it in my cart, looking down at my list to see what items I need yet. As I turn the corner into the next aisle to look for juice, I almost run my cart into none other than Ms. Beverly.

I don't know her last name, but everybody just calls her "Bev" anyway. She's the sweet old lady I've known from growing up in the area, and she is always so kind to me. She often helps my mom at the flower shop.

She clearly isn't paying attention and—*wham!*

"Oh, Brett!" She presses her hand against her chest, clearly startled. "I'm so sorry! I did not mean to crash my cart into yours."

I chuckle. "It's okay, Bev. Don't worry about it. It's just a small crash, and it didn't hurt me none as long as it didn't hurt you."

She swats me away and says, "Ha! You know me. I'm tough as nails. But I wouldn't mind you helping out a little old lady with getting her groceries, so I can get some of the stuff off the higher shelves that's better quality."

"Sure, Bev. I wouldn't mind walking around with you. You know it's good luck to be seen with such a beautiful woman." I add, trying to charm her and make her laugh. We come around the end of the aisle, and I look across the vegetable section.

Bev begins chatting about some event she is going to next weekend with her other old lady friends that involves yarn. I've been diligently listening until I make eye contact with Autumn across the stand of tomatoes laid out in front of me. She's in the melon section, grabbing some pumpkins.

Her cart looks to be filled with a lot of premade meals that you can just pop in the microwave and eat. I know she has those in her lunch at work, I just hope she makes herself actual meals during the evening. Having well-balanced meals is really important for your health, and something I take pride in is making sure I cook every evening. She takes me in and then switches her gaze to Bev. Seeing her, she smiles and waves to just Bev, I'm assuming, or maybe it's both of us. She also knows Bev since she grew up in Mayfield as well. I may not have been familiar with Autumn before this job, because of our age difference, but I do know her dad and know she's from this area.

Bev knows everybody in town, so she waves back, turns to me, and says, "Do you know her? That's Miss Autumn Harris. Her mom is proud of her because she graduated with her master's degree in engineering. I heard she's working on some big project. Do you know what that's about?"

"Yeah, Bev. She's working on the same project I'm working on. She's the engineer for the building over on campus." I say as I place some onions in my cart. These will be great for my homemade fajitas later this week.

"No way. I had no idea she was working on that building. I didn't even know you were working on that building. That must explain what you're doing back in town then, since you're normally not around." She smiles at me as she pushes her cart into the next aisle. As I said, she spends some time helping my mom, so of course she would hint at the fact that I'm never around. I'm sure she and my mom have talked about it many times.

"Yep. That's why I'm here. I'm helping out Tony on that job. He called for me specifically. It seems like he really needs the help." We continue to push our carts side-by-side as we go, talking and walking right past Autumn so that Bev can grab some bell peppers for her stuffed pepper soup that she claimed she was going to be making.

Stuffed pepper soup made by Bev is one of the town's favorites. She makes it every year for the soup competition during the Fall Festival, and I always eat more than my fair share of it when she wins. But it's always so good, full of flavor, and made with lots of extra "old lady love." Thinking about the Fall Fest, I realize it's coming up in a couple of weeks. My mom had mentioned it to me a few days ago, asking for help with the stand for her flower shop. The Fall Fest is the highlight of the town during the fall season, and you can see everybody there. It would be a great way for me to catch up with a lot of folks I haven't seen in a long time. I'll have to make sure to wander around once I'm done helping mom set up her stand for the flower shop.

I wonder if Autumn is going to be making anything for the Fall Festival baked goods table. Based on Autumn's age and how long she told me she was in school, I think this will be the first time that she isn't in school during the Festival, so she might be able to attend more of it around work. Maybe I will get to see her there. My heart flutters a little at the prospect of continuing to see Autumn outside of work, but I will it to stop and focus my attention back on grocery shopping. I need to focus on work and not any women at work. That did me no good in the past.

Bev and I make our way to the checkout, where I help her load up all her groceries into her bags. She always brings reusable bags because she is just a saint, always trying to save the world one grocery bag at a time.

I, however, don't have the luxury of reusable grocery bags, so I stuff all my groceries in the little plastic ones they provide. We walk out to her car, and I load everything inside the back for her.

"You're the best boy, Brett. Thank you for helping me with my groceries. I'll be sure to let your mother know she raised a good son." She kisses me on the cheek as a thank you. I help hold her door while she climbs into her car and watch her drive off.

I head over to my truck and load all my groceries in the bed, transferring all my cold groceries to the cooler I keep stocked with ice-cold drinks. I'm just glad there's enough space in there to fit everything. I don't like leaving cold food out to the warm air, even on just a drive home. Food safety is important to me.

When I climb into the front seat, my phone starts ringing. I see it's Enrique, one of the laborers on the crew, calling.

"Hey, man, what's up?" I ask, concerned that something might be wrong at the site for him to be calling me this long after work.

"Hey! We're going out to *The Barrel*. You want to come with us? I know it's a little late notice, but it'll be a late supper tonight. I think maybe 7:30," Enrique invites me to go along with them with joy in his voice.

The Barrel is what all the local people call *The Broken Barrel*, the only restaurant in town. It has a rustic charm featuring down-home American cuisine, a dartboard for games, and all the beer that a bunch of rowdy construction workers can drink.

I laugh and glance at the clock on the dash: 7:00. This is exactly why I put my cold groceries in a cooler on ice. "Yeah, I could probably make it."

"Sweet. I suggested going to Texas Roadhouse, over in Pikeville, but you know, James has to hit on Katie again." Enrique's laugh is loud and fits perfectly with his boisterous personality.

I chuckle to myself. James is so much trouble. "Alright, yeah. I can be there." I start my truck and put it in drive.

As I'm leaving the parking lot, I see Autumn coming out to her car. Part of me thinks I should stop and see if she wants to come along, but she's got her phone to her ear, so I just keep driving. There's a pang in my heart realizing that this night would be a lot more fun with the company of a certain blonde.

Autumn

TODAY IS OUR LAST day of finalizing all the plans before we share them with Tony tomorrow. I'm extremely nervous about this, but we're going to get it done. We've been doing everything we can to come up with all the right pieces and parts, and making sure that everything is going to work based on the correct 811 map Brett shared with me from Tony's computer. We've come up with the perfect plan to move the courtyard just a little bit over to the left, around the side of the building, and it's still going to allow us to have a beautiful space in between both buildings where students can play, sit, relax, and enjoy the landscape.

Brett even helped come up with some of the flowers that are native to Mayfield to fit in here. He's also surprisingly good at hardscape as well, coming up with the best places to put in retaining walls, concrete walkways, even a water fountain, which we were able to figure out how to run pipes to from underneath. I'm not sure Tony is going to approve, but I'm hoping he does.

Focusing on today's goal of finalizing the plans helps me remove the image of Brett at the grocery store last night from my head. He was helping Bev get her groceries, and I was enamored by how nice he was being to her. Seeing Brett step in between me and Jeremy at the bar, and now helping Bev, makes me think he's a lot sweeter on the inside than he lets on.

We're sitting at the table in the job trailer, looking over the final plans. Brett brought me my usual morning coffee, as he has been for the last week. I'm not sure which it is, but after the first day, when he saw me put in the perfect amount of cream and sugar—two and two—he's brought me a perfect coffee every morning from the coffee shop in town.

I'm pretty sure it's on his way into work, and they're open at like four in the morning. God bless Louann, the owner of The Bean, for opening that early and being able to get me a good coffee. I could probably tell Brett that I want some super fancy coffee and he would get it for me, but I'm just gonna pick my battles and go easy on him with this one. After everything that's gone on between the two of us, I haven't been pushing my luck because I don't want to get things too messed up between us.

"Alright, Autumn, do you think we're ready to show these plans to Tony? I think we have everything we need. Looks like we've got all the landscaping, hardscaping listed. We've got all the new plans and new layouts, the new maps, we've got all the supplies needed—any extras—well, actually, it isn't really extra, because we're just moving things, and we're actually saving pipe on this fountain since it's going to be right there and we don't need to add extra pipe to work it over to the spot we had previously planned."

I look at him with a little bit of awe; he just keeps saying *"we—we planned this, we planned that."* Technically, it's all on me, but Brett has never let me feel like I'm alone in remaking these plans. After the fiasco that happened, we've talked about it multiple times, and he's convinced that someone deleted the 811 map that Mr. Matthews sent me, but I don't know if that's really the case. I mean, it's possible someone deleted it, but I don't know who would or why. There's no reason for that.

"Yeah, I think we've got everything we need, and I'm feeling pretty confident as long as we can finish up today and make sure we have a good presentation."

He chuckles.

"What?"

"I don't think we need to worry about a presentation for Tony. We just gotta show him the plans and be like, 'This is what we're going to do, and this is what we've come up with,' and I think he'll be okay with it, honestly. He's not a big presentation kind of guy. Don't you remember the first day you walked in here and you were thinking about doing yours, and it ended up just being, 'Let's look at the plans here on the table?'"

I try not to think about the first day that I came in here. I was late, Brett was rude, everyone was staring at me, and it was kind of a shitty day. I look at him.

"Well, I don't remember the first day very well because I tried to block it from my memory. Trauma, you know." I smile at him. He smiles back, and we move on.

"Well, all right, that's fair enough, but I don't think we need to worry about a big presentation. We just need to show Tony the plans, and I think he'll go forward with them."

"Okay, if that's what you think, then I'm fine with doing that. We'll just lay the plans out on the table, and we'll go from there. You know Tony better than I do. You've worked with him for years, so you get it. I'm probably gonna head over to the office and show these to Mr. Matthews just to make sure he's okay with them."

I click save on the file on my computer so that everything we have is permanently saved, transferred over to the hard drive that I have externally, where I've been saving all my documents and important information, because I have this crazy fear that my computer is going to just crash—which wouldn't surprise me because it happened in school—so I panicked a little bit and I don't want to lose anything that's important for this job.

Brett stands up, throws his coffee cup in the trash, and says, "All right, well, since we're good here, I'm gonna go out and work with some of the guys and see what we can get done. I'm glad we could fix those plans and that they're finally finished."

"Yes, thanks, Brett. I really appreciate your help. You know, I may have been really hard on you at the beginning because you were kind of an ass, but you're actually a pretty good guy, so I really appreciate the help."

He smiles at me and says, "No problem, Autumn. You know, you're a lot smarter than I gave you credit for at first. I think this job is a little much, but you're just learning, you're just figuring things out, and you're getting started, and that's honestly the best way to learn—to just get in there and do it. So, I applaud you for that. Glad we could get this figured out. We'll see what Tony says tomorrow."

Before he can leave, I add, "Sorry for hating you when we first started. I know we both were kind of at each other's throats pretty quickly."

He looks me right in the eyes and says, "I never once hated you, Autumn. I just thought you were in over your head." He walks out the door without a look back.

I'm left alone, sitting at the table, looking over everything in front of me. How did I end up at this point? How did I get this far? I'm really nervous about this job. I've been doing it for a couple of weeks now, and it's so far been disastrous. I'm really hoping that things can get better and go forward from here. Hopefully everything goes okay tomorrow, and Tony likes the plans we came up with. I'm nervous, but I think it'll be okay.

As I'm sitting there, lost in thought, Tony comes into the job trailer. "Good morning, Autumn."

"Oh, hey Tony, how are you?" I ask, smiling up at him and taking a sip of my coffee.

"I'm just fine. You getting those plans ready? I saw Brett outside with the guys." Tony raises his coffee mug up to point out toward the site.

"Yeah, we finished up on the plans this morning, so he's out talking with the guys to figure some stuff out today—what they want to do and how they want to handle some of the things we came across. Then we're going to be ready for tomorrow. I think we're going to do one last chat and look over the plans again this afternoon before the end of the day. Then we'll make a plan for tomorrow, and we'll be ready to show them to you. I think we need to finalize one last list of supplies and make sure that we can get everything ordered in time."

Tony nods at me in confirmation. "Well, alright, that sounds like a good plan. I'll go out and yak with Brett and see how he's doing and check out the dirt work coming along with Frank. He's been in charge, and it's been a bit of a disaster," he laughs.

"Alright, that sounds good, Tony. I'll talk to you later. Actually, I might end up going into Arch's office so that I can back up my files and grab some stuff from there. I also need to chat with Mr. Matthews a bit about the drawing of the plans, if that's okay with you." I say, playing with my pencil in my hands.

"Yeah, Autumn, that's fine. You do whatever you got to do. If that means going in and talking to John, then that's what needs done. Just let Brett know if you're gonna be going off the site, okay?"

"Can do, Tony. I really appreciate it. Thanks," I say to him as he walks out the door. I start packing up my items to head to the office. I need to chat with Mr. Matthews about supplies, the final plans, and make sure that he approves everything before I go and present it all to Tony. If he doesn't approve something, it's going to be a bit of a disaster, because then I have to change it, even though our deadline is tomorrow. Fingers crossed he agrees with what we've come up with and doesn't try to screw me over for once.

・・ ——— ・♥・ ——— ・・

Mr. Matthews isn't in his office, so I have to settle for working at my desk for a little while until he gets here. Colin, one of my coworkers who works in the cubicle next to me, lets me know that he stepped out for a meeting and he would be back in an hour or two, or so he claims.

I'm hoping he's back before that because I was hoping to go back to the job site since I accidentally left my lunch there. If not, I guess I'll be eating a late lunch this afternoon.

After spending an hour or so updating all of my files on my computer, uploading them to the Arch Engineering software website cloud platform so that they're accessible for the entire company and backed up with the firm, Mr. Matthews stops by my cubicle and knocks on the wall. "Hey Autumn, Colin let me know you wanted to chat with me."

"Oh, yes, Mr. Matthews. Hi. I did, yeah. Do you mind if I come by your office? I want to show you the plans that the operator and I came up with for the job over at the university." I stand and grab the papers in front of me.

"Sure, come on in. I'll let you share these with me." He sounds exasperated and annoyed, but that's usually just his standard tone when talking with me. I don't know if it's me, or if it's the job, or if he's just constantly tired.

Following behind him, I sit down once we reach his office and open my laptop. I haven't printed the plans out yet on the big, blue paper, but I have them on my computer and some small sketches in my notebook.

"Okay, so what we were thinking was moving the courtyard over here into this space where there's no electrical wires to worry about and actually makes it easier to run water pipes for the fountain and—" He cuts me off.

"Whoa, who came up with these plans? Was it you, or was it the operator? Because I would like to know. If the operator's doing your job, we need to have a discussion."

"Well, we kind of came up with the plans together. Both of us were in charge of doing so per Tony's recommendation, so we've been working on this together for the last week. I've been drawing everything, he's been throwing out suggestions for things that may or may not work, but mostly it's been my ideas." I say, trying to scramble and save myself, even though Brett and I probably had equal support. I need Mr. Matthews to realize that I can do this and that I know what I'm doing, so I may stretch it a little bit and say that this was mostly my idea. Brett will be okay. He would understand, and how would he even know anyway?

"Okay, well, as long as it's you coming up with the ideas and not that operator, then that's fine. But he would probably know a thing or two because he's been there longer, so I hope you listened to him when he gave suggestions."

The shock flutters across my face, but I try to hide it quickly. "Oh, yeah, I listened to him, you know, for a lot of his ideas that he shared, or feedback that he gave me on things I had thrown out. He was pretty helpful, and he definitely knows what he's talking about. He knows the area well, and he knows Tony well, which was helpful."

I finish showing Mr. Matthews all the plans and my drawings, and let him know that I'm going to be printing them out on the blue paper so that I can show Tony the next day.

"All right, Autumn, that sounds fine. Don't be late in showing Tony and make sure that you present to him well. Remember, you're representing the firm."

"Yes, Mr. Matthews. I understand completely."

With that, I'm dismissed by a flick of his wrist, and I go to the print room to print out my plans.

Autumn

I walk into the job trailer with the blueprints in my hands. I'm extremely nervous today. I was up super early; I couldn't sleep all night, and I'm jittery even without having any coffee yet. Today is a big day, and what happens determines how the rest of this job goes.

Brett is the only one in the job trailer once I get inside, which is nice. I can have a moment to just breathe and chat with him before Tony comes in. We're both early this morning, which I knew we would be. It's right around 6:15 a.m., which is long before anyone else will show up.

"Morning, Autumn. You're here early." He smiles up at me, holding his coffee in his hands. The other cup, the one for me, sits in front of my unofficial seat next to him.

"Well, I could say the same to you, Brett." I laugh, setting the blueprints down on the table.

"Yeah, that's a good point. I thought you'd want to get here early, so I made sure I got here *earlier* with your coffee. I thought it would be the least I could do today. It's probably a stressful enough day for you anyway." He gestures toward the cup.

"Yeah, today's extremely stressful, but I really appreciate the coffee. Thanks, as always, Brett." I take a big drink of the coffee, nearly burning my tongue off. Waving my hand over my mouth, I say, "You know, one of these times I'm gonna ask you to get me something fancy. Do you think you can order that?"

He looks at me with a confused expression. "Well, it depends on what you're getting and if you text it to me or not. Then I could just show it to the barista."

"Well, I couldn't text you my order because I don't have your number." I look at him nervously.

"I thought you got my number from Tony. Usually, everyone on the job site shares numbers on, like, the first day or so." I worry I'm about to be berated again for not doing something correctly.

"Uh, I only have Tony's number. I haven't gotten anyone else's phone number, so if I ever need something, I always just have to call him, and he'll direct me or he'll talk to the person I need to." I'm nervous about saying this to Brett. I don't want him to think that, yet again, I don't have a clue how to handle myself on the job site.

"Oh, well, you ought to have his phone number, my phone number, and James's phone number at least. Although maybe not James—he'll probably hit you up at times you don't want to be talked to. But you ought to have Frank's phone number. And even Pam, she's the truck driver." He keeps adding people to the list of numbers that I should have, as he thinks.

"Hmm. I don't have anyone's phone number, so..." I shuffle around the papers on the table nervously, trying to lay out the blueprints so that they can be seen by Tony.

"Here, give me your phone. I'll put my number in it, and then you can call me whenever you need something or text me if you want a fancy, flavored coffee in the morning."

Smiling at him, I hand over my phone, and Brett puts his number in, texting himself so that he has my number as well. I take a sip of the coffee he's given me, letting the warm liquid hit my throat, giving me the energy I need. It'll take a minute, but this should kick in by the time Tony gets here at seven.

Brett and I sit down at the table in the job trailer, looking over the plans one last time. Once he's done scanning, he looks at me. "I think I'm gonna let you take the lead, obviously. These are your plans, and all I did was help provide input from what I know and what I have experienced, but this is your show, Autumn. You know these plans. You're the engineer, and you're going to be expected to handle this on any future job, so I'm making sure you know that you're in charge here. You give the feedback to Tony. You tell him the plans, and any input you want from me, you can explicitly ask me."

I hold the cup in front of me with both hands, looking at it nervously, stressed out of my mind. "Yeah, that's fine with me, Brett. This is my first time correcting a mistake officially, so I know that I need to own up to this, and that I need to do this my way and be professional."

We're all set up, waiting for Tony to arrive, and he comes in right at seven on the dot. He looks at both Brett and me sitting here. I know he knows what today is, but it doesn't seem like he's in a rush to find out about our plans. He sits down and pours himself a cup of coffee from his thermos.

Once he's finally good and ready, he starts. "Well, you two. I guess you've been working hard to fix these plans these last two weeks. Why don't you go ahead and tell me what you got?"

Brett looks at me, and I look at him nervously and begin sharing details. "Okay, so we've been correcting these plans, and I'm going to present them to you, ensuring that this will work and that you're okay with the decisions we've made. I presented these to Mr. Matthews yesterday. He was okay with the decisions based on the fact that Brett ensured that everything we were doing would be sufficient with you. Obviously, we need your input on that for sure, but Brett was pretty confident, and Mr. Matthews seemed pretty confident in that decision."

Brett looks at me with skepticism, like he didn't understand what I was saying. I hadn't told him that Mr. Matthews was skeptical of my plans until I assured him that Brett had said they would work. Brett may believe in me, but that doesn't mean that everyone else does, and I need him in my corner to prove to both Mr. Matthews and Tony that these plans are good and that they will work.

Tony nods and looks at me with determination. He's listening intently to every word I say, and I really appreciate it. Most folks don't listen to what I have to say with that type of intention, especially not at a meeting where I've presented these plans before and already messed up. His giving me a clean slate provides me with a small boost of confidence.

"So, what we've proposed is transitioning the courtyard that we had outside out back to the other side of the building, so that way it is between the new building we're putting up and the current engineering building. This gives students a walkway to move from building to building through a little courtyard with sidewalks, landscaping, even a fountain that we've been able to put in for a justifiable price since the water pipes run directly underneath it already, and it would simply be a matter of cutting into the pipe, adding a connector, and diverting the water to the fountain. Brett helped come up with the landscaping and budget. He even said that his mom could probably get us stuff from the local flower shop, which would be cool to bring in a local aspect. I know on a job this big, typically that stuff doesn't matter, but I think it would be a really cute touch that the university itself would really like, and it doesn't affect our budget much at all. So ultimately, what we've proposed is sidewalks here, here, and here."

I point to the locations on the blueprints to display the fan of walkways that we've created around the fountain. We've created a circular walk around the middle fountain and five shoots coming out from equidistant sides around the circle that are pathways students can walk on to get from one building to another or from one sidewalk to another.

Brett helped me come up with this idea, and I thought it was clever—doing the fan and the five offshoots from the circle—because it resembles the five schools of the university, even though this isn't something that they would probably even realize. It's something we came up with that we thought was clever and a cute little touch.

"So, as you can see, these are the plans that we've come up with to try and fix this 811 disaster situation. Now, we won't affect any electrical spots in the ground underneath, and everything should be fine."

Tony looks over my plans thoughtfully, scratching his beard, and sits back in his chair. "Well, I think you guys have come up with a fairly decent set of plans here. I think it'll work as long as it's been approved by John. The budget isn't really affected, and if Brett thinks he can do this dirt work—then that's fine by me. Full speed ahead."

"Yes!" I jump up and shout, clapping my hands. Both men turn and look at me. "Sorry, I just got a little excited." Trying to be a little more professional, I collect myself, clear my throat, and straighten my shirt.

"All right, great. We'll go ahead and get started on these. Brett, you can start on doing whatever dirt work it is you need to do. You know the plans intimately now, so you know the next steps we need to take. Direct the guys to whatever they need, and I'll just be meandering around, making sure that things go as planned. Please let me know if you have any questions about this," I say, looking at Brett as he stands up.

"Great job, Autumn." He smiles at me, proudly. "I'll go ahead and talk with James and Frank to see what we can do next." He walks out, leaving me in the job trailer with Tony.

"Listen, kid, you're doing a pretty good job. I know your first job can be intimidating, and Brett explained to me a little bit about what was going on with the plans and how he thinks they've been messed up. Hopefully, that's not really the case, but we'll get to the bottom of it for you." Tony seems sincere in his comments and I appreciate the sentiment.

"Oh, Tony, you don't have to do that," I say, waving him off. "I think I've already figured it out. It's not a big deal. It was more than likely an error on my part. I found the plans online on our Arch Engineering server after Brett sent me yours, and they were completely together, so it was probably just something that I missed on the plans Mr. Matthews emailed to me, or I printed out an incomplete version. It's totally my fault; don't worry about it."

Tony looks skeptical but nods as he walks out of the job trailer. I sit down in my chair, fall backward, and I feel the weight lift off my body. The pressure and stress that I've been carrying for a week now are suddenly relieved, and I honestly could cry. But I pull myself together because I've got a job to do. We've got to finish up the day's work because tonight is game night at Lucy's.

Autumn

"Ha ha!" I shout as I place my last pieces on the Scrabble board. I just played the word pencil and scored ten points, earning me the win against Lucy. Usually, she wins, and she's an incredible player at Scrabble. She uses these fancy science words that I don't know and scores tons of points against me, so it's nice to finally win.

We've been having our monthly board game night, and we've been playing a wide variety of games. First it was Battleship, then we played Sorry, then Connect 4, and now we're on Scrabble. This one's usually our longest and the one we end with because we take our time to think about big words and do what we can to get the best scores. It's been neck and neck, with each of us having our own wins as the night goes on. I also won Battleship, but Lucy won Sorry and Connect 4, so now we're tied—and that's no surprise because that's exactly what happens every week for every month that we play. We always end up tying.

You'd think we'd add in a fifth game so that we could split our ties and actually have a winner, but it's more fun for both of us to come out winners in the end, and then we get to have a good laugh about it. It'll be a great time when one of us finally edges the other out because we have a standing bet that whoever loses has to fund a $250 shopping spree for the other at a location of their choice.

It's nice that we take this time to spend together because Lucy's classes are starting to pick back up. She's getting busy with her lab work all the time, working on complex bacterial cultures that she has to check every 12 hours or so, so she's got a lot going on. It's good to take a break so that she can relax a little, and I just selfishly love having time with my best friend.

"So how are things going with the research?" I ask.

"It's going okay. My colonies are being difficult, but Dr. Imani says that we can try one more different method, and then we need to give up on this one. At that point, we'll probably have to move on to a completely different idea because what we're trying isn't working. It's super frustrating because I spent months trying to perfect these colonies so that I could do this sequencing and synthesis, but it's just not working."

Lucy has always tried to explain her work to me, but it goes a bit over my head, just like when I explain engineering concepts to her, she doesn't understand them either.

"Dang, that sucks. I'm so sorry to hear that." I'm sincere in feeling her pain. I've been watching her struggle with this experiment for a long time, so her failures feel like my failures.

"Yeah. It is what it is," she shrugs and takes a drink of her cocktail and falls back into the beanbag chair she's sitting in. "So, you gotta give me all the details on how it went today."

I'm surprised it took her this long to ask. She's been desperate in wanting to know how my presentation to Tony went today.

"Unlike your experiment, it went great! I feel so relieved. He seemed to be totally on board, which was great. I'm glad it was that easy, especially after all of the struggles that I had at the start. He even told me that I was doing a good job, which was nice to hear." I smile, thinking back on my conversation with Tony earlier.

"And?" Lucy prompts. "How did Brett do? How did things go with him?"

"Things with him were fine," I laugh, knowing this is what she really wants to talk about. "He let me lead and provided support, which was cool. He did add some explanations where appropriate to get Tony to really understand things that maybe I wasn't explaining well, but overall, it really worked out great in the end."

"See! He's not a bad guy!" Lucy shouts.

"I know. I never really thought he was a *bad* guy; we just got off on the wrong foot. Yeah, also he was kind of a dick, but things are better now. We've been working together really well, and he was a really big help with everything." I pop some M&M's in my mouth, enjoying the crunch. They're easily my favorite candy, and Lucy always keeps them stocked in her apartment just for me. Now that's true love.

She bites off a piece of the Twix bar in her hand and starts talking with her mouth full. "Personally, I really think that there could be a friendship, if not more, between you two. The way he came to your rescue at the bar the other week, hot girl. HOT."

"Shut up," I say, tossing a red M&M at her head. "Nothing is going on between the two of us. I'd be lying if I said I don't think he's attractive, but I'm almost certain he thinks about me as more of like a little sister than anything."

"Oh, step-sis!" Lucy moans teasingly, laughing and throwing her head back.

"Lucille! That is not appropriate. I need to focus on work; you know this job is important to me. But maybe I wouldn't mind spending some time with him at the bar or something outside of work. It has to be completely unrelated to work, though." I say, burying my head in my hands.

If I feel safe admitting my tiny crush on Brett to anyone, of course, it's Lucy. She would never judge me, only try to push me in the direction to go after what my heart wants. She's always been supportive of me making my own decisions, but she does try to influence me sometimes.

Lucy throws her head back in laughter, and I smile. It's these moments that I'm grateful for her and everything that she does for me. She understands me even when I don't understand myself, and she gets me to admit what I usually don't want to say out loud, but that I'm shouting loud and clear internally.

Lucy makes me a better person, and spending time with her is no doubt my favorite thing to do.

And these game nights? They're a cathartic release, and it's so nice to spend some time with my best friend on a Friday night, relaxing instead of going to the bar like we usually do.

We made our own little drinks that we could have in her apartment, but the snacks are obviously the best part.

Finally, after cleaning up the board games, the snacks, and the drinks, Lucy hits me with a yawn.

"I think I'm ready for bed, dude."

"I'm right there behind you," I add, and we make our way back to the bathroom. We brush our teeth, change into our PJs, and she climbs into bed.

"Goodnight, Luce, love ya," I whisper as I walk out her door to head to the couch.

"Night, Aut, love you too," I hear in response.

It doesn't take long for me to realize that I'm about to fall asleep. The last thing I think about is how Brett went to bat for me, how he really cares, and how he was helpful with this whole project. He truly is a good guy, and I wish I had given him the benefit of the doubt.

Before I nod off, I grab my phone and send one quick text message:

Autumn:

> hey brett thank you for your help today I really appreciate you and all you did for me goodnight

Brett

I STARED AT HER text message all weekend, not having a clue how to answer it. She was extending me an olive branch and being kind, and I was being an idiot. I don't know what I should do with this information. I think Autumn is nice and she's super attractive, but she's young and she doesn't know what she's doing. Her desire to be good at her job at whatever cost is admirable, but it also worries me. I do think she's very hardworking, but the world gives her shit cards to play with, so I'm being cautious. I don't want to be hurt again.

This morning, I'm sitting in my excavator, and my brain is going 10,000 miles an hour. I'm trying to focus on the work in front of me—getting these dirt piles moved out of here—but of course I can't stop thinking about her and that text. And I can't stop wondering what she's doing right now.

I know she's in the job trailer with Tony and they're discussing ordering some things, but I want to know what she's doing every second of every day. I think I'm starting to become obsessed with her. Getting to see her every morning because I bring her coffee is the highlight of my day. Seeing her helps me believe I can face whatever shitshow the day will bring.

At first, I brought her coffee as an apology for being a jerk because my mother would ring my neck for the way I talked to her. Now it's because I like her and I like seeing the look on her face when she takes that first sip in the morning.

As it always happens, I finish the work in front of me all too quickly. Pausing my machine, I look around and try to decide what I need to do next when I hear some yelling. I don't like it when people on my crew are upset, so I am immediately attuned to it and need to know what's going on. Being lead operator, the crew depends on me to make sure that everything runs smoothly. Obviously, everyone answers to Tony, but he chats with me daily, and we meet every morning to discuss what we're going to do for the day. Hell, we even meet at the end of the day to discuss what we did and what we're going to do tomorrow. If there are any parts we need to order, if we need to call the mechanic, if we need to get some trucks, whatever, it goes between Tony and me.

Walking over towards the cause of the commotion, I look and see a familiar figure. I would recognize that girl anywhere—from the back side, front side, left side, right side, you name it—I would know her. She's currently being berated by one of the labor foremen, Johnny, and I feel my blood start to boil. Putting a lid on my anger, I continue to walk up to them, needing to know what's going on right now.

"—The confusing ass email you sent. This isn't gonna be right, Autumn. You need to fix this right now!" I hear him yelling at her, just catching the tail end of their conversation. She looks mortified and nervous.

Obviously, after being yelled at by me at the start of this job, telling her that her plans wouldn't work, Autumn might have a somewhat traumatic response when it comes to being yelled at, and she might be experiencing something similar again. She looks nervous, but she starts rifling through some papers and apologizing profusely.

"I'm sorry. I'm so sorry, Johnny. I don't know how you received that email. I'm sorry. I will work to fix this, and I will get you the right information. I can have you contact my boss if you'd like, and you can talk directly to him if you prefe—" He cuts her off.

"Yeah, that's probably the best. You know, I know John, and it would be just a lot easier if I could just talk to him and get this sorted out."

"I totally understand. I'll give you his phone number here, unless you already have it," she pauses, and he shakes his head no. "And then you can just call him." She's blubbering and trying to pull up her contacts and figure out what's going on.

"Everything okay here, guys?" I ask, finally making my presence known.

"Not really, Brett. The newbie here sent me all these gibberish notes via e-mail, and now I'm supposed to figure out how I'm supposed to get my guys over here and what I'm supposed to be doing with them. I asked her about it, and now she's saying she gave me the wrong information. I wish she had just talked to me directly, and we would have organized this better because now I don't have enough hands to get this work done." Johnny complains to me, throwing his arms in the air before crossing them.

"Okay. You said she emailed you information?" I ask, confused why Autumn would be emailing someone information after we talked about getting phone numbers so she could call directly.

"Yup." He says, popping the "p" in irritation. "She sent me an e-mail late last night with some details about what my crew needed to be doing, and I was confused because it was just random notes, and usually we talk about this stuff here, but I didn't know because she was new. I thought maybe she wasn't informed."

"Well, Tony knows to talk to Autumn and Autumn knows to talk to Tony, so I'm not sure exactly how an e-mail was sent to you. Autumn, did you send an e-mail to him last night?" I have a hard time believing that she would have sent an email to him, unsure how she would have even gotten his email address, since I believe she's only talked to Johnny once.

She looks up at me, really confused. "I don't remember sending an e-mail last night, but I know I write stuff up in my e-mail drafts that I need to remember to tell people. I'll sometimes put the sender's name in because then I know the person that I need to talk to. I don't know, maybe I accidentally hit send, and then he got this e-mail that was just like my blubbering thoughts. I'm really sorry, guys. I never intended to do this, and if I wrote anything down, I knew that I was going to talk to you about it this morning, which is why I came out here in the first place to find you, because I knew we needed to talk about today's plan."

She looks so nervous, and she's so cute. Her cheeks are tinged pink, and she just looks so precious and adorable, but I need to stop thinking about her like this. She's my coworker for Pete's sake, and she's smarter than I give her credit for. She knows what she's doing, and she's trying to find her own system in this crazy job world. I know first-hand how hard it can be to remember everything you need to know. It's impossible to write everything down, but if she did send an e-mail accidentally to the labor foreman and now, he's confused about what's going on and doesn't have enough people, then that's on her.

It's not a very good look, but he doesn't need to be giving her the third degree because she made a mistake. She's learning, and we've only been on this job for two weeks, so he needs to chill the fuck out.

"It sounds like Autumn made a mistake. She didn't mean to send you that e-mail. Clearly, it wasn't intentional, and she had every intention of coming over here and meeting with you this morning to discuss what was going on. Even if she had sent you an e-mail last night, she had the intention of coming over and clearing up. You're the one who jumped the gun and told the guys they didn't need to come today. So, let's think about this for a second and calm the fuck down, Johnny, because this is not appropriate. You can't berate someone on the job just because you're in a piss poor mood and you don't understand what's going on, or things aren't working out for you. That's not how this job works, and you know it. So, for right now, what we're all going to do is take 15 minutes to get our shit together. Autumn's going to figure out what she needs to talk to you about, you will forget the e-mail that she sent to you, and you will take everything she says with a clean slate. Are we good?" I hold out my hands, palms facing outward, directing to both of them, making sure that they are understanding what I'm saying and that everything's going to work out.

"Alright, yeah. Sorry Brett. I'll grab my information and come back out here and try to clear things up with Johnny. This is totally my fault. Let me go grab my papers." She turns and stalks back to the job trailer.

I turned to face Johnny. "Man, what the fuck! You cannot be so rude to her. She is just startin' out on this job, on any job for that matter, and she's figuring it all out." I'm pissed off on her behalf for Johnny looking at her like she's less than him just because she's a woman.

"I heard she fucked up those other plans, too, so I wouldn't be surprised if she doesn't know what she's doing. She's messed up this job a bunch of times now already. She sent me a stupid e-mail with a bunch of misinformation and garbage. I'm not surprised. She clearly doesn't know what she's doing, and she shouldn't even be on this job. She is a hazard to it, and somebody's going to get hurt from her mismanagement. I thought women were supposed to be organized." Johnny complains, pulling his phone out of his pocket and starting to turn away from me.

My mom raised me to treat everyone with respect, especially women, and I don't tolerate people talking shit about others behind their back. Grabbing his shoulder to stop him from turning away, I squeeze to make sure he's listening to me. "Dude, she's trying. You have some fucking nerve. Cut her some slack. This is her first job out in the real world. I've gotten to know her these past two weeks when I was helping her fix those plans. The ones that, yes, she messed up, but there was some kind of crazy error. It looked like the plans she got weren't even complete, like somebody had just cut the file. I don't know. Maybe somebody is trying to sabotage her, and they hacked into her e-mail and sent you her draft that she never intended to send. Maybe she did it on purpose, maybe she just doesn't know. Either way, you need to cut her some slack and be nicer.

I don't like it when people on my crew whine, and I especially don't like it when people on my crew are assholes. So, if you're going to stick around here and be the labor foreman and look after these guys that you're supposed to take care of, you gotta give a little respect. Remember, as foreman, you need to go to bat for these guys, and so yes, you gotta make sure shit goes right, but you also need to hear people out, and if there's confusion or miscommunication, you gotta fucking talk to the person or you come to me or Tony so we can discuss what's going on." My speech must hit home because he puts his phone away and apologizes.

"Alright, Brett. Sorry, I didn't realize that you and she were so close, and I apologize for being a jerk."

"It doesn't matter how close we are or not. It's about respect for the people on your crew that you work beside every day. And it's not me that you need to apologize to." I look at him sternly. "It's her. When she comes back, you'd better tell Autumn that you're sorry and that you will listen to her from now on."

I'll have to have a talk with her and Tony later about the e-mail situation because she doesn't need to be emailing anyone information without a clear explanation, and there absolutely should be face-to-face in-person communication for all important notes. Having said my piece, I turn around and start to walk away.

"Hey Brett, thanks, and I'll talk nice with your girl from now on." Johnny throws at me with a smug look.

I keep my face stern, but my heart flutters in response to hearing her referred to as my girl. "Not my girl, asshole."

I walk over to the job trailer, and I find Autumn inside.

"Hey. You okay? I talked with Johnny and he's good now. He's calming down, and you guys can go back out and have a meeting. You can explain to him whatever it is that's going on that you talked with Tony about. Do you want to tell me what it's about?"

She's sitting in a chair, and she looks distraught. I know she struggles with not feeling good enough for this job and not feeling like she's getting out what she's putting into it. I know she tries her hardest, but sometimes things still get messed up.

"Brett, I am so sorry. I have no idea how that e-mail got sent. Like I said, I write all my notes down, and I don't ever try to send them. I usually just keep them in my draft folder, and sometimes I'll even like mess the e-mail up just a tad so I can't accidentally send it. I'm pretty sure I did that with this one, but oh, I don't know how it got sent." She hides her head in her hands. "I don't remember hitting send at all, but maybe I did…I don't know. I was working on it last night in the office, and I was kind of late typing things out. I left my computer up and had to go talk to Mr. Matthews, but he wasn't around. But anyway, it doesn't matter. My life's kind of a mess right now. I apologize, and I'm going to go back out and talk to Johnny and chat with him and try to get this all sorted out." She shakes her head and looks down at her papers in front of her.

"It's okay, you know. We'll figure this out, and we'll go from there. Do you know where Tony is? I need to go chat with him about some stuff." I ask her, trying to distract her from the situation and get back into the groove of work. "I heard he said dirt trucks were coming, but I haven't seen anyone around the job trailer today, not even Pam."

"Oh yeah, I saw him earlier. He said he was going to find James. Something about those same dirt trucks, I think, so yeah," she chuckles nervously and grabs her papers. "Well,

I gotta go talk to Johnny and explain to him that these guys are definitely going to have to do a lot more digging than they initially thought. Turns out there are a lot of live wires, and you guys can't get within two feet of them with the machines, so they're going to have to do a lot of hand digging. Hopefully Tony can find room in the budget to hire a couple more laborers because if not, it's going to be so much on Enrique and Rick." She looks stressed about this news, and I know it's going to be hard for her to break that to Johnny. He's not going to like hearing this.

"Oh shit. Well damn, yeah, hopefully we can get that sorted out because that would suck if Enrique had to do all that digging by himself. He's way too lazy for that shit." My comment makes her laugh as she heads out the door.

"See you later, Chief." She smiles at me with a wave. I swear I can feel my heart flutter in my chest from her smile. It's so genuine and pure despite being faced with challenge after challenge.

"See you later, Hotshot." I smile and wave back at her. I watch her go, knowing that girl is a powerhouse, and I really applaud her for taking her moments to apologize and regroup herself. I also think about what she said about working on the e-mail late last night and not accidentally sending it. I wonder if somebody in her office might have gotten on her computer and sent it. It would make sense, especially since I'm already leaning towards the idea that somebody sabotaged the plans that she received.

I wonder if Autumn has any trouble with people at her office. I'm going to have to ask her and find out because if somebody's sabotaging her, I'm going to get to the bottom of it.

Autumn

"Hey, hey. There's the little boss lady!" James calls, jumping down from the skid steer he was running to move pallets.

"Morning, James, how are things going today?" I ask, walking up to him while fighting with my vest that got turned inside out while in the job trailer. I know I'm not supposed to be on the job site without it on, but I've only come a few steps out of the trailer before running into some of the crew.

Enrique and Rick are also with him; they've been the ones stacking the pallets that James has been moving. "Hey there, Miss Autumn," Rick adds, reaching up to tip down the brim of his hard hat while nodding at me. Rick is an older gentleman, and he's always been very respectful.

"Well, things are much brighter now that you're here on the job site, shining on us with your glowy skin!" James is the definition of a Title IX violation in the way he talks, but I know that, truly, he would stop if I asked and he would never hurt a fly.

"You're so full of shit, man," Enrique laughs at him, throwing a shovel full of dirt at his legs.

"Hey! These are my good jeans. If I get them too dirty, my ma is gonna kill me. I shouldn't have even worn them today, but I forgot to take my laundry to her on Monday." James jumps back, yelling while trying to brush and shake the dirt off his pant legs.

"You mean you don't do your own laundry?" I ask him, laughing and tucking my clipboard under my arm. I originally came out here to check on the number of pallets of Qwikrete we had left, but since the guys are stacking them up, I assume that number is zero.

"I've never done my own laundry a day in my life!" James looks at me, smiling.

"Uh, I don't think that's something to be proud of?" I give him a confused look and hear Rick and Enrique chuckling while they get back to work, stacking the last pallet on top of the pile.

"You guys are only laughing because your moms don't love you enough to do your laundry." James retorts, but he really sounds like a little boy begging for his mom's help.

"Yeah, yeah. Not all of us are lucky enough to have a mom like you. Hey, maybe I'll come over and she can do my laundry too!" Rick jokes, punching James in the arm.

Watching these guys interact like this and knowing they're now comfortable enough to joke and laugh in front of me gives me a warm feeling inside. I'm doing my very best to fit in with this crew and just be one of them. Being let in on their banter feels like a big moment, and I hate to ruin it by asking about real work, but I have to know if my assumptions about the Qwikrete are right.

"Hate to break up the party planning for the night at James's house, but do we have any bags of Qwikrete left, or did we use them all?" I ask, pulling my clipboard out and flipping up the page to get to where I have my weekly order written down.

"Let me clue you in on a little secret, Aut. When the pallets are all stacked up like this, you know there's none left." James jokes and pokes at my clipboard. "Jot that note down on your little clipboard, so you know for next time."

"Oh, yeah, okay. Thanks." I say, my nerves getting the best of me. I thought things were going okay, and we were all joking around, but James made it seem like I should know that fact about the pallets, and I had no clue.

"Hey," he turns to look at me with genuine concern on his face. "I don't mean that to be rude. That really is the note of how we let the person doing the ordering know we're out. We stack all the pallets up like this. Just how we've always done it. You'll get the hang of this little Aut." James pats me on the shoulder and turns to walk away.

"Thank you!" I yell after him as James and Enrique begin pushing and shoving at one another as they walk. Neither of them touches Rick. I wonder if that's another unspoken rule.

Laughing at the goofiness of these guys on the crew, I jot down the note about the pallets and turn toward my next inventory task—checking the whole job site for Tony so I can talk to him about how to place this order.

I stop at the office after work to gather some paperwork and get some quick things done. I have my own desk at Arch Engineering's main office in town, and sometimes I come here before going to the job site, or I'll stop here during the day at some point and do some work. This is where my main computer is, and it is where I back up all my documents for the blueprints and everything that's needed for the job. This is where I was late last night when I was working to come up with the details needed to talk to Johnny about the labor situation—needing to dig into other options because the machines can't get as close to the underground power and water lines as they could on some other jobs.

I look at my desk to make sure that nothing's out of place and that I didn't leave it logged in last night or something freaky that could have happened. Everything looks normal, so maybe someone hacked my computer and pulled the email out of my drafts and sent it to Johnny.

I vividly remember that I had messed up his e-mail address with one letter, putting an "n" instead of an "m" in the ".com" so that it wouldn't accidentally send.

I do that with all my contacts for this job every time I'm writing up one of these drafts for the person I need to talk to. I always replace at least one letter in their e-mail address, so it doesn't send. I don't know what happened or how he got that e-mail with all my gibberish stuff that didn't make sense to him. No wonder he was so confused and upset this morning.

Since it's the end of the day, I'm just here to grab some stuff before I head over to my parents for a quick dinner. I grab the USB drive out of my drawer, throw it in my bag, and walk out the door.

It looks like Colin, one of the other employees who started around the same time I did and was also in my graduating class at Whitewater U, is here doing some late-night work.

"Hey Colin, have a good evening," I say to him as I walk out the door.

"Hey, Autumn. You look nice today." He comments with a smile.

"Uh, thanks?" I question. "Have a good night, Colin," I say awkwardly, looking down at my clothes covered in mud, and I know that I am very sweaty and very smelly. Yeah, I definitely need to shower before I go to my parents.

"For sure! Have a great night, Autumn. Enjoy your time doing whatever it is you're doing." I wave to him and walk out the door without another word.

I don't really like Colin, he's kind of weird, and he's always eyeing me up and doesn't even try to hide it. It creeps me out and prevents me from wanting to work with him. I've never had the guts to say anything to Mr. Matthews about it, because he's never really done anything other than be overly nice.

I drive my Jeep home singing country music at the top of my lungs, trying to put myself in a better mood before I head over to my parents' house. Pulling into my driveway, I get a text message on my phone.

Brett:
> Hey. Sorry about today. I hope you're okay.

Autumn:
> yeah im doing okay thanks for stepping in and kind of mitigating the situation I didnt really know how to get it under control

Brett:
> No problem. Johnny can be a bit of a hardass.

Autumn:
> yeah you got that right

Brett:
> Well, have a good night, Autumn. Enjoy dinner with your parents tonight.

I don't remember telling him that I was going to dinner with my parents, but I must have slipped it into one of our conversations. We've been talking a lot more on and off throughout the day now. We get along now, and Brett is starting to feel like my safe space on the crew.

He's the one I can go to, and I know he won't judge me because he already has—in the worst way in front of everyone else—and we worked through it. He worked with me and has since sincerely apologized, so I know that he cares about me as a person, and I know that he wants me to succeed in this job. He told me himself that he thought I was in over my head, which, in all honesty, I probably was.

I didn't know what I was getting into with this job, and it was tough at the beginning, but luckily, now I've gotten my confidence, and I feel a lot better. Brett has been there to guide me every step of the way, too. He's been nice.

We text what feels like all the time now about random things, and he always brings me my coffee in the morning. Usually, he'll even come into the job trailer for lunch if he's not super busy, and we'll have lunch together. He, with his fancy put-together sandwich, fruit, and veggies, and me, with whatever microwaveable meal I could find in the store for cheap.

Brett's funny, and he makes me laugh. He's got a lot of jokes and a lot of stories to tell about past jobs that he's been on. He likes to talk about his time on the pipeline, and I'll admit I don't know a lot about that stuff, but it sounds cool.

The way he talks about it, it sounds like a job that he really likes to do. He travels and gets to see the country. It's awesome, and it almost makes me wish I was able to do that and do engineering, but unfortunately, a lot of engineering jobs keep you confined to one place, especially if you work for a firm like I do. Brett did mention to me once in passing that there are engineers on all the pipeline jobs he does. They have to manage the layout of the site, ensure the safety of the crew, and make sure that the job is getting done, so I will admit that piqued my interest. The idea of being able to still be in the same construction-operating-pipeline realm that I'm in now and do my engineering while seeing the country and meeting tons of new people all the time? I mean, who wouldn't want to do that? It sounds like a lot of fun.

Autumn

AFTER A SHOWER AND a change of clothes, I drive the 10 minutes to my parents' place. They have a large, cute colonial-style home, white with navy blue shutters, big bay windows, and gorgeous landscaping. My mom and dad can afford to have a landscaping crew come out once a week to make sure the house always looks perfect. In the summer, this place is full of pops of color from all the flowers my mom makes sure are ordered and planted.

They live in Mayfield in the same childhood home that I grew up in, and they probably will live here forever. This is a small town, and my dad and mom both love it here. Both of their parents moved here when they were young adults, fell in love, and raised my parents here, so my family has been in this area a long time. My grandparents are no longer around, since I own their house now, but my parents and I try to have dinner when we can.

I walk in the door and yell. "Hey Mom! Hey Dad! I'm here!" Taking my shoes off in the front foyer, I'm greeted by

Finn, my parents' sweet old Golden Retriever, and my childhood dog before I can make it any further.

"And how are you, my handsome man?" I ask, bending down to give him kisses and hugs. Coming to see Finn is one of the best parts about visiting with my parents all the time. I miss having a dog companion, and Finn was my best bud. We did everything together when I was growing up. My parents got him when I was sixteen, so he was with me through some of my most impressionable teenage years.

No one listens better than a dog when you can't stand the world around you.

Standing up and walking my way into the kitchen, I find the two of them in there singing, dancing, and cooking together. Cooking is one of the things that they love to do together now that they're both retired. Dad's the worst cook in the world, and Mom is the best, so it's mostly her cooking and him getting her whatever she needs, but it works for them.

My mom is a former middle school teacher turned substitute on occasional days for the local school district, and my dad used to be the principal at the very same school my mom taught at. Hence, they met, fell in love, and got married. It was fun having my mom as my teacher and my dad as my principal when I was younger, but I was a straight-A student, so I was basically *the definition* of teacher's pet for many years.

Both of my parents now spend their days outside as much as they can, either growing vegetables in their garden, taking short hikes on the local trails with Finn to keep him active, or spending a lot of time at their permanent site they have at the local campground—Finn's favorite place to be besides my bed in my old room. The owners of the campground are my mom's best friend and her husband, so she and my mom can often be found at the lakefront beach, if you want to call it that, or helping out in the food concession stand.

"Hi, Sweetie!" Mom says. She comes in for a hug. "Oh, we're so glad you made it here! How are things going with your work?" My mom steps back and smiles at me, bracing my shoulders.

"Things are actually going pretty well now. We got the plans figured out, and the lead operator, Brett, has been really helpful for me while I'm figuring out how to do this job." I laugh, going in to hug my dad next.

"Honey, that's great. I'm so happy for you. And it sounds like Brett is a real nice gentleman." My mom winks, smiling at me.

I put my hands up to stop her. "It's not like that. I mean, he's nice, but we just work together. He's just a lot more seasoned and has tons of experience. I'm sure he's just being nice, honestly, because I don't know what I'm doing in this job. I made that clear on the very first day." I stop and laugh at myself.

While Brett has been super nice to me, I don't think he's actually taking pity on me. He's never given me that impression, but I have to keep my mother at bay. She's been playing matchmaker for me ever since I graduated, and I've had several men thrown at me in the last few months. Needless to say, I've just been trying to focus on my job.

"Well, if he's so nice and you guys are getting along, then that's great," my dad chimes in, stopping my mother from being her overbearing self. She means well, but she can be a bit much sometimes, and Dad knows exactly how she is. "I'm glad you aren't alone on that job, and you have someone to help you when you need help. God knows that that wiener head over at Arch Engineering wouldn't help even though he's your supervisor."

My dad has disliked John Matthews since high school. They both graduated together, and Dad says that Mr. Matthews was always a jerk. He was always a player, taking advantage and hitting on women, doing things he shouldn't be doing, but then my dad went off to college out of state and had stopped thinking of him. Both dad and Mr. Matthews came back, and Mr. Matthews started Arch Engineering, but dad didn't give him much thought; even then, he just avoided him around town. But lo and behold, 26 years later, I started working for him, which brought all of my dad's old feelings back out. I can't help it, though, because he's the only engineering firm in the area, and Dad knows I'm not ready to start out on my own, so I need to get the experience if I want to stick around here.

Conversation flows casually between the three of us, catching up on the last couple of weeks while I help my mom set the table with plates.

"So, honey, the fall festival is coming up next weekend," my mom mentions as she stirs the pot of pasta on the stovetop.

We're having spaghetti tonight, one of my favorite childhood meals, and some garlic knots that my dad mixed up himself with his own recipe. Dad's cooking skills, while improving, still aren't that great, so hopefully they're good, but there's a fifty percent chance they'll be hard as rocks.

"Yeah, I'm super excited! Do you still want to go all together?" I ask her, laying the last piece of silverware next to Dad's plate on the table.

"We'd love to go with you if you'll still have us. Have you asked Lucy what she is doing?" My parents love Lucy like their second daughter. I'm an only child; my mom never wanted more kids of her own, but Lucy came home with me one day to work on a project, and my parents fell in love with her instantly. She comes over as often as her schedule with classes and research allows, and sometimes, I'll even come over and find her already here hanging out with my parents without me.

"She said that she is working on a bacterial growth experiment, and it may take up her time, but she's going to try and plate things in the morning so that she can be around in the afternoon on Saturday or Sunday. So hopefully she can come, but I told her not to stress. She's been trying to redo this bacterial growth for weeks now with little success, so she needs to focus." I said, moving around to turn off the timer on the oven as it signaled Dad's garlic knots were done.

"My knots!" My dad shouts, running back into the kitchen from down the hallway. He grabs some mittens off the counter and pulls the tray out of the oven.

The knots look delicious, perfectly golden brown, and they smell amazing. Here's to hoping they're soft and fluffy and taste as good as they look.

"I'm gonna go wash up in the bathroom and then I'll be ready to eat whenever you guys are," I say to my parents and walk back to the hallway bathroom just as my phone buzzes.

Brett:
> Need you to settle a debate for me: Michelob Ultra or Yuengling Light?

Autumn:
> michelob ultra obv thats literally all I drink

Brett:
> Cool, thanks Hotshot.

Autumn:
> are you out at bobbys?

Brett:
> Nah, me and my brother are together at my place working on some stuff.

Autumn:
> ah, have fun with him

Brett:
> Ha, yeah. Do you have any siblings?

Autumn:
> nope only child so I dont know what its like to have to suffer in sibling debates

Brett:
> Dang. You're missing out. It's actually fun.

I smile and stick my phone back in my pocket. I'm not going to be texting him anymore. Tonight, I'm focusing on my parents. I walk back out to the dinner table, and we all sit down to eat.

After dinner, I'm helping my mom with the dishes. She washes, I dry and put away. "So, Honey. I know you aren't looking, and I know you don't want a man, but tell me about this Brett you work with. You seem to really like him, and you get a sparkle in your eye when you talk about him," she nudges me with her elbow while I dry a plate before placing it on top of the stack.

"Mom, it's not like that. Like I said, he just really helped me when I was down on my luck, and you know how important my job is to me. This is my first big role outside of university, and I want to make a good impression on Mr. Matthews and everything, so I need this to go well, and he's been really helpful." I reach for the silverware drawer to place three forks inside.

"I see. Okay, well, I won't push you about it anymore, but if you do want to bring him around for anything at any point, I'm sure your father and I would love to meet him." My mom says sweetly with intent in her voice. I roll my eyes at her and put the last plate in the cupboard before finally closing the door.

"Yeah, yeah, Mom, whatever you say," I say, smiling at her. All the dishes are dried and put away, so we head into the living room. Once I sit down on the couch, the tiredness hits me, though, and I decide I should probably head home before I'm too tired to drive.

"I'm really tired, so I think I'm gonna go home," I announce to my parents, who are both getting comfortable side by side on the loveseat. They're snuggled up together anyway, so they probably won't miss me.

After saying my goodbyes, I drive the short distance back to my house, pull into my driveway, and sit in my Jeep for a minute. My mom's words are stuck in my head, and I can't stop going over them.

Just how much do I like Brett? Is he more than just a friend? He's been really helpful, but am I confusing help for something else? He's been really nice to me, and I'll admit, it feels good to get along with someone the way we do now. But does he like me? He texts me, but that doesn't necessarily mean he wants something more with me than just friends at work. I don't know, maybe he does, but maybe he doesn't. There's a part of me that would love to have the attention of a man like Brett. He's powerful, he's sexy, he's masculine, yet he's really kind and smart as well. But for now, I just need to focus on work and get through this job. Who knows, maybe if it were another life, then Brett and I could work out, but we're both really dedicated to our jobs, and that comes first to us. There might not ever be anything more between us, despite how much I might want there to be.

I grab my phone out of the middle console, hop out of my Jeep, and walk into my house. While I plug it into the charger on the kitchen counter, I see that I have a missed text:

Brett:
> I'm out here looking at the stars from my parents' porch, and I can't stop thinking about you, Hotshot. Tell me—do you think about me?

I feel the blush creep across my face. Okay, well, maybe it is more than friends for both of us.

Brett

I LIFT THE BOX of vases and set it on the table in front of me. Texting her last weekend was a dumb move. She hasn't responded. Maybe I was too forward with her, or I scared her off. I just wanted her to know I was thinking of her and that I enjoy talking to her. Autumn is fun to spend time with, and I'd love to get to know her outside of work.

"Brett, honey. Pay attention. I need those vases to go over here. Set them out so that people can grab one to put their arrangements in." My mom, Rebecca herself, knocks me out of my thoughts with her instructions.

"Shit, sorry, mom," I say, moving over to the other table she had pointed to.

"Don't curse. Especially not here. Gosh, one of these old ladies hears you, and they'll say I let you and your brother do whatever you want." She scolds me jokingly, bending back down to pick more cut flowers out of her cooler of water.

I chuckle to myself, knowing she's absolutely right. If any of these older women parading around here heard me swearing, they'd have my hide, especially Bev. As I place the vases on the table, I see her over in the soup tent stirring her pot and tasting it to ensure that things are cooking just as expected.

I'm helping my mom set up her flower stand for the fall festival this morning. The festival starts today and ends tomorrow. So, while it's short, it will be jam-packed with everyone from town.

The fall festival happens every year, and it's a full schedule of all of the fall-themed small-town events you can think of. There is a corn maze, pumpkin picking, apple bobbing, and all kinds of fall food. There are pies to purchase by the slice or whole. There's every kind of apple treat or meal you can imagine. And there's the famous soup contest. The entire town comes by to celebrate the changing of the seasons. Even the farmers around stop their harvest for one day to make a pit stop at the fall fest. Dad has crops to cut down, but Mom is here with her stand, so he's going to make an effort to come by at least for a couple of hours. I think Adam is stopping by before he does the nighttime feeding as well.

Mom's stand is for her flower shop, and it gives people the opportunity to stop by and either build their own bouquet or buy a premade bouquet of all the fall flowers—sunflowers, dahlias, even wheat stalks if you want to add them.

As I set the last vase on the table, ensuring that none of them are going to get knocked over or fall if a breeze blows through, I see Bev walking our way.

"Hi, Rebecca. Hi Brett. It's lovely to see both of you here. I'm sure that you're having a wonderful time with your son back in town, aren't you, Rebecca?" Bev asks my mom, smiling and coming up to hug me.

Even though my mom named her flower shop *Becca's* and everyone calls her Becca, Bev has always been formal and calls my mom by her full name.

"Oh yes, Bev, it is fantastic to have Brett back. I have missed him so much, and he's been a big help around the house and here with the fall festival—getting my flowers and vases here, setting up my tent and my tables. I've barely had to lift a finger, definitely nothing heavy." My mom places her hand on my shoulder, smiling at Bev.

"That's great, Rebecca. I'm so happy for you. Speaking of setting up things for the fall festival—we've got everything over at the soup tent all set up, and it looks like we have about 20 entries this year, which I think is a record for the soup contest. But one of our judges, Mr. Radford, just called my daughter to let me know that he is ill and isn't going to be making it to the festival, which brings me to my question. Brett, honey, would you be willing to be a fill-in judge for the soup contest?" Bev asks, smiling brightly at me.

She knows I won't say no to her because she's the sweetest woman ever and because I'm always willing to lend a helping hand. As long as mom doesn't need my help, I'm free and don't have anything else planned.

I was hoping I would run into Autumn here, but if she's not coming, or without confirmation of plans, it's kind of just up in the air on whether or not I'll see her. Keeping myself busy may be just the thing to distract me from thinking about her and looking for her in the crowd.

I look down at Bev. "Well, I think I can do that. What time do you need me at the tent?"

"Oh, perfect, that's just wonderful, dearie. Thank you so much. The soup contest begins right at 3:00." She hands me a card that I'm assuming is my judge's name tag. How she already had it made up, I'll never know, but I suspect she knew I wouldn't say no. It's a little piece of paper stuck in a plastic badge with the magnet on the back that I assume clips on my shirt.

"Okay, I just put this on and show up to the tent at 3:00, and someone will guide me the right way?" I ask, trying to gather all the details I can. I don't know exactly what I'm getting myself into.

"Yes, that's exactly what you do, sweetie. My daughter will be over there, and she helps guide all the judges. Mrs. Smith and Mr. Porter—because we can't have a tie—we have to have three judges. You'll likely be the tiebreaker because Mr. Smith and Mr. Porter never agree on anything. I guess that's what happens when you have a brother and sister judge the contest."

I smirk, knowing that Mr. Porter and Mrs. Smith have always judged the soup contest. They are siblings from the Porter family, one of the well-known families of this small town. Everybody knows a Porter in some way or another, and usually everybody's related to a Porter in some way or another. Now the Smiths are related because Sarah married Jeremiah Smith.

"Okay, Bev, I can do that. I'll help my mom finish up here and make sure that she's all set to go, and then I'll make my way over before long."

Glancing down at my watch, I see that it's noon and the fall fest is officially open. Folks will start parading through, looking at stands, buying knick-knacks, all the food they can eat, and partaking in all the fun fall festivities. There's a photo booth with some fall-themed backgrounds—straw bales stacked up with corn stalks, pumpkins, and mums sitting around. It's the perfect backdrop for couple photos, family photos, and everything like that. It happens to be right next to mom's stand because flowers make the most sense for additional display items, and often people will purchase their very own bouquets and go over and take a photo with them. It just works out.

I'm helping my mom load the last of the empty coolers into her truck bed so that she can focus on all the flowers in front of her and the customers that come through, when I see a familiar face walking through a crowd with her parents on either side of her. She's laughing, and her smile is gorgeous. It lights up her whole face, and it's a side of Autumn I haven't seen at work. She is happy, don't get me wrong, but she's never truly this happy. Her parents really bring her a lot of joy; that's clear to see. I imagine she's close to them, considering she's here with them instead of with a friend or group of friends.

They make their way over to my mom's stand, looking at all of the bouquets. Autumn motions to her mom that they should make their own bouquet, so they slide their way down to the other side of the booth. She starts grabbing flowers as I stand there leaning against my momma's tailgate and watch her.

Her golden hair, normally captured back in a ponytail or braid to keep out of her face, is flowing freely around her shoulders. It's perfectly straight, and it makes her look stunning in the afternoon sunshine.

She still has yet to notice me, although I'm sure she knows that Becca is my momma—everybody knows that around town—and her parents would definitely know that her mom was my middle school teacher when I was younger and her dad my principal. They are familiar with me and my family. I don't know them well, but I know of them, and I know her mom only in the capacity of a teacher. Since I left shortly after high school, I didn't really have a lot of time to get to know everyone in the area as an adult.

Finally finding the courage to walk over to her rather than just stare at her from a distance like a creep, I find myself on the other side of the table right across from her. She's reaching for a sunflower, and before she can grab it, I pick it up and hold it out to her.

She looks up at me and makes eye contact, slight shock fluttering across her features before settling. "Brett. Hi. I didn't know you would be here." She says, looking slightly nervous.

"Hey, Hotshot. I'm just here helping my mom. This is her stand, as you probably are aware."

She blushes, taking the flower from me, and decides to put it in the middle of her bouquet.

"That's a really nice bouquet you've made there. I can't make bouquets at all, so that's why I leave it to my mom. She does a great job. But it looks like you've got a knack for it too. That's really pretty."

She smiles and says, "Thank you."

Her mom calls her from a distance. "Autumn, we're gonna take a picture now. Are you ready? Did you finish your bouquet?"

She turns to look at her parents and then back to me. "Well, I'm going to go enjoy the rest of the fall festival and go get a picture with my parents, but I'll see you around, I'm sure. If you plan on hanging around anyway."

I shoot her a smile in return and laugh. "Oh yeah. I got suckered into being a judge for the soup contest, so I'll be here. If you want to stick around, that's at 3:00, and they give out soup samples afterward for anyone to try—especially the winning soup, which is usually Bev's, and it's pretty good. Is this your first time at the fall festival or have you been here before?"

She pushes her hair behind her ear before looking at me, holding her bouquet. "I've been here before, technically, but it's been a lot of years. Usually, I've been in school or college, so I haven't really taken the time to come. This is the first time in a long time that I've been here, so it's nice to enjoy it as an adult and get to see the different events and actually partake in things. Although, as a kid, this was a lot of fun—going through the corn maze and convincing your parents to buy you all kinds of apple-flavored sweets so you're up all night." She laughs, reminiscing over some of her childhood memories, I assume.

"Oh, well, yeah, you're right, it is a lot of fun as a kid. I've been here every year of my life, except for the ones that I was gone, and I was out pipelining. So, it's been a while since I've been here, too. But I'll catch you around. Have fun with your parents."

She gives me one last glance and a little wave, and she's off. I watch her walk away over to the photo booth area and see her smiling with her parents. She's having a great time, and the glow in her face is incredible. Seeing this different side of Autumn shows me that she carries herself with a lot of confidence outside of work. Maybe I can help her bring that confidence into what she does at work. She's a smart woman. She just needs that extra push to get there.

·· ☐☐☐☐ ·☐· ☐☐☐☐ ··

I placed the spoon with creamy goodness into my mouth for what feels like the millionth time. This is the last soup. There were twenty-two entries in total, so there are a lot of decisions to be made.

This one is butternut squash, pumpkin cream bisque made by Mrs. Johnston, following what she called her great-great-grandmother's recipe from when she lived in southern Louisiana. I wasn't expecting it, but there's spice in here.

The kick makes me cough, slapping my chest to contain the heat burning across my tongue.

"Wow, that is a unique flavor, Mrs. Johnston."

I clear my throat. "Well, it was very good. The pumpkin and the butternut squash really complement each other very well. The spice is unexpected, but it's not terrible."

"Oh, thank you for that."

I make a note on my little pad that that one is last for me. I don't mind spicy foods, but a warning is definitely nice, and I know that no one else around town is probably going to like that, so I doubt that she should be the winner. The flavor just isn't quite right.

I think back on all the soups I've tried and review my notes down on the pad in front of me, walking back over to the judge's table to sit down and converse with Mrs. Smith and Mr. Porter.

"Well, have you made a decision, Brett?" Mrs. Smith looks up and asks me.

"I believe I have actually. Uh, do you guys have opinions on what you think?"

"Well, I tell you, that spicy bisque we just had was the worst thing I've ever tried. Should be disqualified from the competition," Mr. Porter complains.

People around here don't really like change, and so every time there's something new, it's hard for them to get on board. Mrs. Johnston just moved into the area last year, according to my mother, and so her entering the contest is a change. And she's providing everyone with a new soup they're definitely not used to.

People really like the consistency of plain chili and stuffed pepper soup. Not that it's bad, but a little change can be good sometimes. I know because a little change is good for me. Coming back to Mayfield wasn't something I wanted to do, but I feel reenergized here, like my cup is filling back up, and it's been great to spend time with my family and to spend time in the town that I grew up in and love. I am reminded often of the things that happened between me and Brittany and the work that I did here, but I'm getting better at pushing that aside. Time really, truly does heal all wounds.

"Well, I think I would like to give it to Bev with her stuffed pepper soup. She always does so well, you know that's the best soup we have here every year," Mrs. Smith says.

She's always been a huge proponent of Bev's stuffed pepper soup, and that's why Bev wins every year. Again, back to the refusal to change around here.

"I was actually thinking we could maybe give it to Mr. Tanner and his venison chili recipe. That was by far the best thing I tasted here, and it didn't have any spice. It was very delicious—nothing more than the typical chili powder," I say, giving my opinion.

A chili has never won our soup contest, but it was probably the best chili I ever had, and it was definitely the best soup that was here, if you could call chili soup. Obviously, the people around here allow it because it was entered in the competition, but not everyone would feel that way, so I'm treading a fine line by trying to push out a bit. Not that her soup wasn't good—it was delicious—but I liked the chili.

"Well, typically we give the win to Bev, but I think you might be right, Brett. Actually, the chili was very good, and using venison instead of beef was a really unique move. I liked that. It really made the flavor quite different."

Mr. Porter agrees with me. Mrs. Smith is a little bit harder to convince. After a little bit of back and forth, she finally concedes, and we agreed to give Mr. Tanner the win with his venison chili.

I stand up at the table and call everyone's attention to announce the winner. Holding the small trophy in front of me, I say, "Well, the votes are in, folks, and we have convened. We've decided that this year's winner for the soup contest is going to be Mr. Tanner with his venison chili recipe. Congratulations, Mr. Tanner. Very well done."

He comes walking up, shakes my hand, and I hand him the trophy, smiling at him. "Venison was a good move, man. I love venison," I say to him.

"Thank you, Brett, this is very appreciated."

As he walks back to his stand, I clap my hands and say, "Now the soup contest is over. Any available soup can be taste-tested by anyone who wants to, and there will be bowls of the winner's soup as well. Please know that the soup will go fast, so if you want some, you better get it now."

I say, drawing a crowd, watching as people line up quickly in front of folks with their favorite types of soup. The line for Mr. Tanner's venison chili builds quickly, and I know that it will probably be gone before they even get to the end of that line. Luckily, I had my fill already.

Smiling at everybody, I see Autumn and her mom and dad walk over to Bev and get their little bowls of soup. She looks up at me, smiles and waves, and I smile and wave back. There's something about that girl that is really intriguing to me.

Autumn

I'M BACK AT THE Fall Festival today, but this time with Lucy. She wasn't able to go yesterday because she had an experiment in the lab, but today she wanted to stop by and get some food before they close up. We're here near the end of the day, and a lot of people have already packed up and left, but there are a few stands remaining. We've been lucky enough to already devour our fair share of apple-flavored donuts, apple-flavored ice cream, and a piece of pumpkin pie for each of us with some very delicious cinnamon-flavored whipped cream on top.

I see that the apple funnel cake stand is still open, and there's an apple cider stand selling the last remnants of their gallons poured into cups. They're even warming some of them up because it's an unseasonably cold day today.

Mayfield doesn't get a lot of cold weather in the fall, but today is enough to warrant wearing a jacket and a beanie, and it has a lot of folks looking for a warm drink. We're typically used to warmer weather longer in the year, being in the south, but we still get cool days and some snow, usually in December and January. Today is a little bit of a colder day with the temps at about 55°F. It's nothing too crazy, but it's cold for this area and has a lot of us locals freezing.

"So, how was it yesterday? Was it lively here? Were there a lot of competitors in the soup contest? I can't believe I missed it for the first time in 4 years. Who won?" Lucy is asking me a lot of questions today, trying to get a recap of everything that happened yesterday while I was here with my parents. "Was it Bev? She always wins, but her soup is to die for!"

Lucy didn't grow up in Mayfield, but she's made sure to come to the Fall Festival every single year around her classes and work. She hasn't missed it like I have, and so she's very obsessed with the soup contest. When she's here, she tries every single one, just like a judge.

"Actually, no, it was Mr. Tanner. He made this venison chili, and it was delicious! Mom and Dad both loved it," I answer her thousandth question.

I've always tried to come, but with classes and homework during school time, it's been hard for me to get here. I know Lucy usually makes it work, so it's been a little bit of an excuse. I kept telling my parents that I was too focused on homework or that I had too much backlog going on already, so they let me slide.

I'm really glad I came this year, though, because the Fall Festival is fun and I got to catch up with a lot of people. I even got to see Brett, which was nice. It was good to see him outside of work, and I enjoyed talking with him. I just wish we could've spent some more time together.

There's something about him that calms my racing heart and draws me toward him. Even though I knew I didn't like him at the beginning of the job, spending time with him and being around him has really grown on me.

It helps that he's extremely attractive. I love watching him from a distance when he's working on stuff. Man, his muscles flex, and it is everything I could ever dream.

Lucy and I are walking through the stands, and I see that Brett's mom's stand is still here. I see him helping her pack up some stuff into boxes and load them into the truck parked there.

I hope she had a good time with the Fall Festival and that she sold lots of flowers. She had a really cute setup with building your own bouquets and taking pictures in front of the display stand she had created. It was really cute.

Mom loved the photos that we took so much that she's going to get one printed and put it up on the wall in the living room already.

"Ooh, is that Brett over there?" Lucy points. I reach out and shove her arm down immediately.

"Lucy, do not point at people!" I say, trying to hide her from his view so that she can't make a scene. There aren't a lot of people here, but I still don't want the whole town knowing anything is going on between Brett and me, even as just friends. Rumors spread like wildfire in a small town. "Yes, that is Brett. He's helping his mom with her stand. Stop being obsessed with him. Sometimes I think you're more obsessed with him than I am." I chuckle and then slap my hand over my mouth. I did not mean to say that out loud.

Lucy looks at me in shock, grabbing me by the shoulders. "Oh my God! Finally, you've admitted it! You are obsessed with him, and it's okay because he is obsession-worthy. Listen, let's go get some apple cider, and you can get some for him and take it over there and talk to him. It looks like he could use a warm drink."

I look over at him again and see that he's got his ball cap with a beanie over top, a flannel jacket on, and he's slapping the tailgate on his mom's truck with her in the driver's seat. Probably to let her know that she's all loaded up and can go.

"Okay, let's get something quick and head over there." I agree with her, just wanting to talk to him some more and feeling my heart race with excitement at the thought. It doesn't take us very long to grab the apple cider, simply because there's no one else around. We're lucky enough to get the last three cups from the stand, and the guy throws in free cinnamon sticks for each drink, too, since he's cleaning up. I turn to head over towards Brett.

"I'm actually gonna go grab a funnel cake," Lucy says, jerking her thumb over toward the stand. "I'll meet you over there once I have that."

That sneaky little bitch. I know exactly what she's doing. She just wants to give me alone time with Brett, but thankfully, I'm grateful for her getting me the way she does and letting me have this moment. I'm walking up to the stand, and I can see that Brett is folding up a table. I call out to him to get his attention.

"Hey, Chief." His eyes dart up at me in surprise, and I hold out the two cups of apple cider that are in my hand. "I got you some hot apple cider. It's a little chilly out today, so I thought that maybe it would be good."

I hand the cup to him as he abandons his table breakdown duties so that he can chat with me. "Hey Autumn! Thank you, that's kind of you," he says, taking a sip. "Did you have a good time at the festival?" He asks me, knowing I had been here yesterday.

"Yeah, it was great and I got to see a bunch of people that I haven't seen in a long time and hang out with my parents, so that was a lot of fun." I sigh, leaning up against the one table that's still standing.

"That's awesome," he replies, smiling at me. We're being friendly, and it's nice. I wonder if he likes spending time with me as much as I do with him. I won't admit this to him or Lucy yet, but seeing him at work every day really brightens my day and makes my time there a lot better. I want him to know that I'm grateful for all the times he's brought me coffee by returning the favor with this apple cider. I know it's only one time, but sometimes that's all it takes for someone. Maybe the things that are going on between us are a two-way street, but I'm still too scared to talk them into existence for fear that I've read into him wrong.

"Are you waiting on someone since you're here, or is there something else going on? Just trying to figure out why you're still here after everybody's pretty much packed up and gone," he asks me, curiosity laced into his tone.

"Yeah, you remember my friend Lucy? She wanted to stop by and get some last-minute food. She's been kind of trapped in the lab at the university all weekend, so I told her we'd come by and see what was left. No surprise, it isn't much, but she's over there in line now waiting on her apple funnel cake to finish cooking, and I think that's the last of the food. We're going to get going after that." I say, pointing over to where Lucy stands beside the funnel cake stand. All of the food trucks here usually go around to local county fairs all summer with their regular food items, and then they come up with a fall-themed menu just for this Festival.

"I gotcha. Yeah, the apple funnel cakes were a big hit this year, so that was cool to see, but pretty much everyone packed up and left at around 4:00 today." He looks down at his watch on his wrist. "Looks like it's 5:00 now, so prime dinner time. But I imagine everyone remaining will leave before long, wanting to get home for the evening and put stuff away before work tomorrow."

"Yeah, that's okay. I honestly thought we'd get here and there would be nothing left, but Lucy wanted to come by and see. We're lucky that we got here at a decent time; otherwise, we would have gotten nothing." I laugh, knowing that I had to rush Lucy out the door so we could get here on time.

I look over to see Lucy—fully decked out in her typical black clothing with her straight, long, black hair and very gothic appearance, walking our way. She's got all the witchy vibes that are fit for October. She always wears this similar style, and honestly, it works so well for her.

"Hi Brett, thanks for keeping Autumn company while I waited for my apple funnel cake to finish. Gosh, those things take forever to cook, but they're so good. You ready to go out? We gotta get back to my place so we can hang out before I have to go back to the lab and move those colonies around." She turns over to Brett and laughs. "I'm growing bacteria."

He gives her a quizzical look, hoping she'll explain more, but all she adds is, "Not on me! I should specify that I'm growing them in the lab."

She throws her head back in laughter, and Brett and I both chuckle, joining in with her.

"I gotcha. Okay, well, it was good seeing you, Autumn, and thanks again for the apple cider, appreciate it." Brett smiles at me and Lucy, and I turn and walk away. That interaction went so well, I am extremely excited to see him at work tomorrow.

Autumn

Working on this job isn't as bad as it was at the start. Things are getting better. The guys are starting to accept me a little bit more and I'm starting to get the hang of everything I need to do on a daily basis: paperwork, making sure that things are all filled out, making sure that orders are placed correctly, making sure that Tony knows what's going on, making sure that all safety requirements are being met, you know just stuff like that. I finally feel like I'm starting to fit in around here a little bit more.

I'm getting along with mostly everyone now, but especially Brett. He brings me my coffee every morning, which I'm so grateful for continuously, and he always has some teasing comment about my hair looking good or my pants fitting me just right. I know it's borderline sexual harassment but with Brett it just feels like a genuine compliment, and he doesn't mean it to be pushy or inappropriate. I also like it because it's really a confidence boost and I know he would never be mean to me, so I let him keep going. If it gets too far, I'll stop him, but for now I'll just take the little comments. He's not hurting my feelings, if anything, he's stroking my ego.

This morning I'm in the job trailer, filling out paperwork for some of the new laborers that we've hired because of the extra digging. As I predicted, Johnny was not happy about having to hire some more guys. But he's done it, so I'm just making sure their paperwork is filled out, making sure they understand safety protocols, and ensuring that all I's are dotted and T's are crossed before sending them out on the job site.

I'm not really going to be managing these guys in any sense, but I'm happy to help fill out paperwork and do a little bit of grunt work. It doesn't hurt and it gives me something to do and something to make Tony like me a little bit more if I can take some of the stuff he doesn't like to do off of his plate.

"Alright, guys so it looks like your paperwork is all set, so you're going to go out and find Johnny, and he'll direct you. I think he's over by the large stone pile." I smile at them, tapping their papers on the table in front of me to even them out so they can be paperclipped and placed on Tony's desk.

"Great, thank you, ma'am," the one gentleman nods at me, holding his hat in his hands as he walks out the door, placing it on his head. The other man nods and follows suit without saying a word. Both of them seem super nice, and they're a lot older, probably in their 50s, actually, but I'm sure they can work circles around some of these other guys.

Rick will give them a run for their money, but he's just a shoveling machine, honestly, and he's pretty funny. He's been the one guy on this crew who's been so nice to me since the very beginning. He's never given me any issues. He's nothing like

James, the other operator who works with Brett and Frank. He's been a handful. He's really tough with the safety protocols and following what we need to do to a T, but he's always throwing teasing remarks everybody's way, including me, and he really gives it to everyone on the crew.

Tony says he's full of himself and that he thinks he's an amazing operator, but he doesn't really know what he's doing half the time. I've watched him a few times, though, and he seems to know what he's doing pretty well. Now, of course, he's no Brett, but he definitely knows how to operate equipment.

All of the guys on the crew are really funny, and they get along really well, so I'm glad to see them all working together. Seeing them be so chummy with one another makes me glad that they're finally starting to like me and let me into their circle a little bit. It's been really tough working here with them keeping me on the outside.

Finally, looking back down at the papers in front of me, instead of staring off into space thinking about all the folks on this crew, I'm writing some notes down for Tony to know this is the new hire paperwork when I hear a knock at the job trailer door.

"Hey, hey," and in walks James, Tony, and Brett.

"Hi, James. How are you?" I chuckle at him and smile his way.

"Great little boss lady. How are you doing?" James always talks with a little bit of flair, and I think it complements his flirty, quirky personality extremely well. He also always calls me some version of "little boss lady," and I have to admit, the nickname is funny.

"I'm doing okay. Just working on some new hire paperwork." I add as he sits down in the chair across from me.

Brett leans up against the wall, catches my eye, smirks, and nods at me. I smile his way, feeling the blush creep across my cheeks.

"We've been talkin' and we got to get those stones in here so that we got the pile of 'em on standby and then we can dig that final dirt off. Then we can lay everything out and get that foundation poured soon." Tony starts telling me what's going on while Brett and James listen in to gather important details.

"Okay, yeah. That sounds fine. Do we need to scrape off where the courtyard's going, also? I think we talked about putting stone underneath that section as well, and then some dirt on top just for proper drainage for the plants and the concrete walks and stuff." I throw out to the group to get feedback.

I look up at them while I'm talking, finally portraying confidence because I know exactly what I'm talking about, and I'm feeling a lot more confident in the words I'm saying and in the decisions I'm making. It's been a huge change in me in just a couple of weeks, but it's amazing how fast you get into the groove.

"Yup, I think that'll work. I'm going to go actually make that call now and get those trucks ordered to get that here. Brett, you said we need probably 10 or 12?" He looks over to him for confirmation.

"Yeah, I'd go ahead and just order a dozen just in case. It's better to have extra than not enough." Brett confirms.

"Got it," Tony adds as he nods and walks out of the trailer, pulling out his cell phone to make a phone call to the stone quarry a couple of towns over.

"Hey Autumn," James says, leaning forward, placing his forearms on his knees, his coffee mug in between his hands. "We're going to the restaurant tonight. Why don't you come with us? It'll be a really fun time." Brett's eyes grow wide as he looks from James to me, and I smile big at James.

"Hell yeah! I would love to come with you guys. I haven't been to the restaurant in ages, and I think it would be a good time. Thanks for the invitation, James." I place the papers in front of me in a folder and close it. I can feel Brett's gaze burning through me. I just hope it's because he's excited for me to come along and not that he's angry I've encroached on their dinner plans. Either way, I'm overdue for a good time with some good people. Man, I hope that this day passes quickly because tonight should be a lot of fun.

Autumn

The glass door shuts behind me as I walk into the restaurant and swivel my head around looking for the guys. I find them all in the back corner at a big, long table that they must have pushed together to make for all of us. I mean, there are seven of us or something like that, so there's a big group, and I imagine they probably get rowdy. They do serve beer here with dinner. It's classic American meals, but the real fun is the dartboard that they're positioned near.

I walk over to the table and see that the only seat remaining open is next to Brett, so I scoot in next to him and smile at him. It actually comforts me a little bit that he's the one I'm sitting next to because he's the one I'm most familiar with on this crew and the one I know the best. Across the table from me is Tony, also a reassuring face, and next to him sits Enrique. He is probably the funniest guy I've ever met. Down the table further, we have James, rowdy as ever, with four empty beer bottles in front of him already. And across from him is Frank, who is sitting on the other side of Brett.

So, it's only part of the crew that we have here. I overheard James invite Todd, but I guess he decided not to come or just didn't show up. Classic. At lunch today, Brett was telling me a little about these dinners, and he said that Todd always says he'll come but then never actually shows up.

Katie, our waitress, comes over to me. She is in her early 20s and working here while she attends Whitewater University. She's from Mayfield, so I've seen her around town before, and I saw her a few times in school because she's just a couple of years younger than me, but we aren't all that familiar with one another. She's been working here, dealing with these guys all the time. God bless her.

"What can I get for you, girly?" She asks me politely, holding her notepad to jot down whatever I order. She makes eye contact with me and her smile brightens. You have to be pretty tough to put up with this rowdy bunch here all the time, for sure.

"For now, I'll just have a Michelob Ultra, please," I say to her, smiling.

"Got it. And any appetizers I can get you?" She takes a note of my beer and looks back at me.

"Oh yeah! I'll start with the three pretzel sticks. With the beer cheese, please." I smile, not even needing to look at the menu on the table in front of me.

I've lived here all my life, and since this is the only restaurant in town, I've come here many times with my family, and therefore I know exactly what's good on the menu and exactly what to order. I'm going to get the mushroom swiss burger and the sweet potato fries. It's seriously the best meal ever, following perfectly after their delicious Bavarian pretzel sticks. The beer cheese is so good. I do like their mustard dip, but it's a little bit spicy for me. I can handle a little heat sometimes, but I'm pretty sensitive to spicy foods.

Conversation picks back up around the table with the guys mostly just talking about what they did at work today because that's all they ever talk about, and I add details where it feels important. The conversation flows pretty smoothly between everyone while we hang out.

Of course, James constantly throws out teasing remarks, and when Katie brings me my beer and pretzels, he has to say some stupid comment, and she just laughs and smacks him on the shoulder. Clearly, she's very familiar with James and his flirtatious attitude.

Everyone starts to place their order for their meals. I get the mushroom swiss burger as promised, and Brett surprises me by also getting a burger—the American burger. A very classic burger with cheddar cheese, lettuce, tomato, and bacon. I really thought he would get a steak or something super filling, you know, meat-and-potato type variety, but he doesn't. In fact, he also gets a side salad with his burger instead of chips or fries, which really throws me off, but hey, whatever he likes to eat.

I've seen his lunch, and he always has a really well put together sandwich with fruit and veggies on the side, so he must like to eat healthy or take care of his body. He's not super fit, but he's not out of shape either, so he definitely cares about how he looks. He's always cleaned up and presented well, which I admire about him, because a lot of these guys just come in here and they look really scruffy and don't even wash their hands. They don't care about anything like that, so I'm glad that he has a little bit of cleanliness to him. It makes him more attractive than he already is. I won't deny that I find Brett attractive; anyone with eyes would be able to see he's a good-looking man.

Dinner conversation flows casually, talking about all kinds of crazy things—tools, machines, equipment, trucks, snowmobiles, you name it, the conversation goes there. No topic is untouched, including wives, kids, even single people and their boring lives, aka Brett, me, and James. Although, based on conversation, James' life isn't as boring as mine or Brett's, and he actually goes out and looks for people to spend time with. We don't.

Before long, more beers are brought to the table. Katie offers us dessert, but we all turn it down. I'm thinking the night is ending when Enrique speaks up.

"Hey Autumn, would you like to try your hand at darts? Are you any good?" He looks smug, but clearly, they must not know that the restaurant has a wall of names for everyone who's gotten high scores at darts here, and if you look back on that board, you will find my name from when I was in high school. I used to play here almost every week with friends from high school, but didn't get my name on the board until I came here with my parents, and we decided to have a dart contest between the three of us. My parents knew I came here, but they didn't know I played darts regularly. When we played that game, they did so horribly, and I played so well that I got a high score. Second-highest on the whole wall. I'm obviously not going to tell them this, though, so I keep it to myself and smile, playing innocent.

"Oh. I've played a couple of times. I think I know what I'm doing, so that would be fun. Let's give it a shot, Enrique." I say standing up. It's been a few years since I've played any darts, but, like riding a bike, it comes back to you pretty quickly. Enrique throws a couple of shots, showing that he's pretty good. I throw a couple shots to start that aren't that great, just to kind of get myself back in the groove, and then I let go, and all of a sudden, I am kicking his ass.

We play three or four different games, and I win every single one. As I throw my last dart on our last game, the guys all around are whooping and hollering and very excited to see that Enrique, who apparently is the popular dart player of this group, is getting his ass kicked by a woman.

James tries to take me on, but he also loses. Tony doesn't even acknowledge that he is being told he should play. He just nods at me, raises his beer, knowing he would lose, and continues to watch everyone get their asses handed to them.

Brett has been sitting at the table watching me, drinking his beer, and not saying a word to Tony. He's just sitting there watching me like he can't keep his eyes off me. I feel his gaze on my body, and I know he likes what he sees. He looks so smug about it, too, and so maybe I do throw a little wiggle in my walk when I walk back to the dart board, and maybe I do try to puff up my chest a little bit whenever I can. So what if I make myself look attractive to Brett? We are both single, and as far as I know, neither of us has anyone we're talking to, so what's it hurt if I flirt and show off a little bit? I kind of like having his attention on me. It makes me feel sexy.

Enrique finally gives up and decides that he doesn't want to lose at darts anymore, and we all sit back down at the table. Katie brings a final round of beers for us, and we decide that we've been here long enough, so we ask for our checks.

As she walks around the table scanning everybody's cards, taking tip money, and chatting away with us, Brett leans over to me and whispers in my ear.

"Wow, I didn't know you were so good at darts." He smiles at me, and I swear I see a gleam of pride in his eyes. "I hope you had a good time tonight." I walk back over to him to whisper in response so that only he can hear this next part.

"Don't tell anyone, but my name is on the award board back behind the bar. I used to play darts here pretty regularly when I was in high school. I won a lot of games here, including against my own parents, when I got my name on the board." I smile knowingly and feel him tense up a little at my admission. "But thanks. I did have a good time tonight, and I'm glad that I got to come out with you guys. I know it's hard to include me in the stuff that you do, but I really appreciate it." Brett looks at me, confused.

"It's not hard to include you, Autumn. I'm happy to invite you to be part of anything we do, and I'm happy to give it to the guys who don't want you to be there. They're just assholes." I've had enough beer to feel a little buzz, but nowhere near drunk, and his words are shooting right to my heart. He basically just said he'd defend me against anyone who talks shit. And hasn't he already proven that when he came to my rescue with Johnny? What a man. I feel myself warm to his presence.

"Haha, well, thanks, Brett." I chuckle, nervously wringing my hands in my lap, looking down at them. I'm trying to rein in my thoughts of him to a reasonable level before I look at him again. After a couple of seconds, I look up. "I really do appreciate being able to come out with you guys, and I appreciate you coming to my defense like that, so thank you." I stand up and grab my purse, and start making my way to the door, saying goodbye to everyone, letting them know I'll see them tomorrow at work, and head off towards the door.

Brett is following right beside me, and he walks me all the way to my Jeep, opening my car door for me, which I think is so sweet. I set my purse inside and lean on the door, turning to face him.

"Thanks again, Brett. I had a good night. I guess I'll see you tomorrow morning." I say, looking up at him, locking my eyes with his. He takes a step closer to me, and he's hovering over me. His eyes are full of lust, and they're a piercing blue color going right into my soul. He's very close to me now, and I can feel his breath on my face. It's warm and hot and smells like beer, and it's very tempting to lean up and let our faces connect.

"Brett." My voice comes out breathy, and I clearly want this moment to go somewhere.

"Autumn. I'm glad you were here tonight. Even if it was impossible for me to take my eyes off of you." He cages me in by placing his arms on both sides of my body and moves so that only a few inches separate our lips. He places his fingers under my chin and tilts my head up so he can look at me.

He looks sexy as hell, and subconsciously, my tongue darts out across my bottom lip before I suck it in and whimper a little. I know we've both been drinking all night, but I feel zero effects from the alcohol I've consumed and all of the effects from this man in front of me. My body is responding to him in a way it never has to anyone ever before.

He looks down at my lips and then back to capture my eyes before he utters the words that wreck my self-control, "Fuck this."

He loses it and lets his mouth crash into mine. At first, I am shocked, but then I loosen up, and I'm more desperate for this than he is. Our tongues dance against one another quickly, and I feel my body relax and push forward against his.

He tastes like beer and the one glass of whiskey he had at the end of dinner, and I know we should stop, but it's a flavor that's so addicting, I'll never forget it. His lips are soft and move with grace, but his stubble is scratching against my cheeks and lips in the absolute best way. The sparks shooting through my body should be enough to electrocute me to death, but this moment is sending me straight to heaven. Brett and I may have started out disliking one another, and I may fight him like a bull daily, but we kiss like we're meant to set the world on fire.

The sound of a truck starting its engine rips us apart, and I look up at him through blurry vision. "You should get going. Goodnight, Autumn." He takes a step back and turns to walk back to his truck. I stand there watching him go, and all I can think about is the taste of beer and whiskey on my lips.

Brett

This morning, there is supposed to be a big safety meeting. Todd went and cut off his toe with one of the circular saws, and now we all have to have a discussion about workplace safety. So now the guys from the crew are all standing around, waiting for this to get started. But instead of paying attention to what's going on around me, all I can think about is two nights ago when I kissed Autumn's perfect, soft lips.

She tasted like beer and honey and a little bit of cheese from her dinner that she had. Everything about that kiss was perfect. There was electricity running through my body, and it was like no kiss I've ever had before. She molded perfectly into me, and when she leaned forward and brought her hands up to clutch at the back of my neck, I just lost it. I knew I had no control left. When I just let it all go and I kissed her, I thought she wouldn't want me to, but maybe she did because she kissed me back with just as much fervor as I kissed her.

Things have definitely changed between us now. I didn't get to talk to her all day yesterday I was so swamped with work, getting countless phone calls from Tony, and organizing trucks coming to collect dirt and haul it out of the site, so that I missed my chance to talk with her. We didn't even send any text messages yesterday. I don't know what she did for the day and I worry that not following up the next day after kissing her was a dick move on my part. And of course, today we're at this big safety meeting. I look around me and see all the guys, but I don't see Autumn anywhere. Surely a notification went out, and she knew we had this meeting this morning.

I take a sip of my coffee, and I keep looking around, watching for that familiar head of blonde hair to pop out and stand next to me, already gearing up to make fun of the guys around us, but I don't see her anywhere. I do see, however, Mr. John Matthews walking my way. He knew about the meeting, apparently.

He's never here on the job site; he sends Autumn in his stead, but for something like this, he obviously has to be here. He has to know what Autumn's getting into, and he has to make sure that he's being responsible for her while she's on this job site. That's his job.

He comes up to stand beside Tony, a few yards away from me, and they start chit-chatting. They shake hands, and he's laughing without a care in the world that his employee isn't here. If she's not here, that's on him since he's the one who should have told her about this meeting as her direct supervisor. He's the one who would have known about this meeting and would have been the one responsible for making sure that she was here.

I pull out my phone to check the time quickly and to see if I have any text messages from Autumn, but I don't. Just a blank screen and the time 6:57 a.m. blinks back at me. Don't panic, Brett, so Autumn is not here, and this meeting is about to start. I need to think logically about what I need to do and what is going on. Where could she be? Is something wrong? Did she have an accident?

"What is going on, Stewart?" Tony looks at me and gives me a look to say, 'Where's your girl at?' I see John has left him to go talk with someone else. I shrug at him and hold up my phone, pointing at it, signaling that I'm going to give her a call and see if I can find her.

I walk away from the group so I can place the call in private and hit the dial button on her contact. She picks up on the third ring.

"Hello?" She asks, sounding calm.

"Autumn, where are you?" I whisper-yell into the phone.

"What do you mean, Brett? I'm at the office at Arch. I had to grab some papers this morning before I came in. I didn't think it would be a problem?" She sounds confused on the phone.

"Are you not aware of the super important mandatory safety meeting we have this morning? You know the one that we have to have in response to Todd cutting off his toe yesterday? Even your boss, John, is attending. He's here and you're not. Where are you?" I start to get nervous for her. I don't understand why she's not here, and if she's not here, she's going to get in trouble, and this time it's not just going to be with me. It's going to be with Tony and Mr. Matthews, probably also Bob, our safety coordinator.

"Fuck fuck fuck. I didn't know! No one told me about this meeting. What should I—I didn't know this was a thing." She yammers on into the phone, obviously extremely nervous and freaking out. Trying to keep her calm, I respond with a steady voice.

"You need to get over here as soon as you can. I'll try to stall for as long as possible, or let Tony know what's going on, but you need to be here, Autumn." I try to push her to understand the importance of this meeting.

"Okay, yeah. I'll be right there. I'll leave right now and come back to get this stuff later." I hear her running in the background, and her breathing is labored. "I'll see you soon, bye!"

She hangs up the phone without me saying bye. I know she's trying to rush out to her vehicle and get over here. It'll take her 10 minutes to get here, so I can try to stall, but I'm not sure that'll happen. Sometimes they bring breakfast sandwiches to these things, and it looks like there's a table of them, so maybe we can use that as a tactic to put the meeting off until she gets here. We do have to sign in on the iPad that Tony uses to acknowledge that we're here, and I can't sign for her.

Sticking my phone in my pocket, I walk back over to Tony and try to pull him away from our safety guy.

"Hey. Autumn didn't know about this meeting for some reason, and she stopped by the engineering office to grab some papers for today. She said she's gonna be here in a few minutes, but she's probably going to be late. Is there any way we can stall with the breakfast sandwiches to get this started so she has time to sign in?" I look at him with slight desperation in my eyes.

I need to save this girl. She already has a hard enough time with the guys after everything that went down in the first couple of weeks with her new plans. I know it's not my job to save her, but I feel like I need to. We're starting to become friends, or more now since we've kissed, and I really like her. I want to defend her. I want her to be my girl, and that means that I need to show up for her when she needs it.

"Yeah, we could probably try to stall for a little bit with the sandwiches, but I don't know if it's gonna hold Bob off forever. He's really up in arms about this meeting. I mean, a guy lost a toe for fuck's sake, so I'm not sure, but I'll try. Let me go talk to him." Tony walks off trying to find the safety guy so that he can talk about this meeting and get the breakfast sandwiches going, which will hopefully put the pause on getting this started until she can get here.

I run my hands through my hair in exasperation and put my hard hat back on. I was holding it while on the phone with Autumn, and I know I need to put it back on, otherwise Bob will be on my case about wearing my hard hat on the site and hard hat safety. Not to mention the equipment handling safety talk we're about to get.

I'm standing there looking around, trying to see what's happening between Bob and Tony, when none other than John Matthews walks up beside me.

"How you doing there, Brett? I heard you had some run-ins with my employee here on the job." He holds out his hand for me to shake. I take it and nod at him.

"I'm good, John." I chuckle and add. "Yeah, Autumn had some issues with her plans when she first started, but it's all worked out now, and we're doing great. She's fitting into the crew really well, so I'm glad to see that." I boast, showing my pride in her fitting in here. He must misjudge it for arrogance because his next comment isn't one I approve of.

"Yeah, she's a bit of a scatterbrain, that one. She tries to stay organized but misses details and, of course, misses important information. Like this morning's meeting, apparently, since she's not here, even though I clearly sent her a text message." He holds up his phone to show me proof of a text message that was sent to a contact named "Autumn Harris."

All of the text messages are one-sided, with him sending them to her with no response. This strikes me as odd because Autumn is always one to respond to text messages. It seems unlike her not to respond to her boss with at least some form of acknowledgment, but maybe she's trying to keep it professional with him. Still odd though.

"Weird that she didn't respond to you about it. But I just gave her a call and let her know to get over here, so she's on her way now. She might be a minute or two late, but she'll be here."

I try to reassure him that his employee is, in fact, on her way and that this isn't like her.

"Well, at least someone's looking out for her, I guess. I'd hate to see something happen to her on this job, but she's only got so many mess-ups before I'll have to remove her. This is getting to be a bit of a handful, and I can't keep cleaning up after her." He shakes his head in disbelief. "Well, I gotta get going over there. I'm gonna be helping deliver this safety meeting with Bob. Bob and John." He chuckles to himself and starts walking away. I nod after him and raise my arm, waving him away.

"Okay, everybody, we're going to go ahead and get this meeting started." Bob stands in front of the whole crew and claps his hands to get our attention. "We have some breakfast sandwiches that we'll go ahead and let everybody grab some here, real quick, if you want to get something. You will also need to sign up on the iPad at the end of the table. Please remember to put your signature on the line next to your printed name so we can measure your attendance, making sure you're at this meeting, which, as a reminder, is mandatory. So go ahead and form a line, we'll get sandwiches handed out and get this sheet filled out, and then once everybody's done with their sandwiches, we'll get started."

Bob yells above the crowd, and everybody starts to line up in front of a table. There aren't too many of us, so it won't take long to get through, but hopefully it's enough for Autumn to get here in time. I'm just about to grab some sandwiches off the table when I hear a vehicle pull in the lot. I look up to see that it is Autumn. She's jumping out fast as lightning, slamming her door, and running over to us all with her hair blowing in the wind. Her face is flushed from exertion, and she looks exasperated. She clearly sped over here and has been stressing about it the entire way, but she's made it on time.

"Autumn. Nice of you to finally join us." I hear her boss say to her as she comes up.

"Sorry, Sir. I totally didn't know this meeting was happening. I apologize I'm here now." She puts her head down and grabs a sandwich next to me, hopping in line behind me. She signs her name on the form, and we both go stand next to one another in the crowd.

John starts talking about safety—how you need to operate equipment properly, and have all the proper PPE, making sure you have steel-toed boots and are wearing your safety glasses. He goes over, in great detail, all of the classic safety precautions of operating hand saws, large equipment, and anything else he thought of that we could possibly work with on the job site. I'm listening for the most part, paying attention like a good studious employee, when I nudge Autumn in the shoulder with my elbow. She's partially standing in front of me, so I lean down behind her and whisper in her ear.

"Did you get a text message from John about this?" Autumn looks back up at me; confusion clearly spreads across her face before turning back to face forward, acting like she's paying attention. She leans back ever so slightly and responds.

"Uh, no. I did not get a text message from him. I would have known about it if I did, and I would have been here much earlier."

"Huh," I sigh and look back up to pay attention. John showed me the text message on his phone that he sent to a contact named *Autumn Harris*, but Autumn is saying she didn't get the text message from him. Something is not adding up here, and I'm not sure I am liking what I'm smelling. I'm going to have to keep track of this one. I know Autumn's missed a few other things by now that are important at work, and emails have been sent out from her work e-mail account that she never intended to send. She missed a major part of the 811 blueprints, and I'm starting to wonder if something here is leaning towards sabotage.

I don't think that John would have any reason not to like Autumn or the work she does, but I can't figure out what is going on. I might know a guy who can get to the bottom of it though, maybe. I'll have to reach out.

After the safety meeting is done, Autumn and I part ways, with Mr. Matthews calling her over wanting to talk, while I head toward my machine. Pulling out my phone, I send a text message to the one guy that I know might be able to help me figure out what's going on between the two of them:

Brett:

Hey. Do you still do that hacking and gathering information stuff?

Knox:
> Yup.

Brett:
> Then I got a job for you, man.

Autumn

It's been a little over a week since I've been berated by Mr. Matthews for almost missing the big safety meeting. He claims to have texted me, but I have no text from him on my phone anywhere. I don't know what happened, but it is what it is. Luckily, Brett came to my rescue yet again and called me. I got there on time; it just sucks to be yelled at by your boss. Especially in front of the entire crew that I'm working to impress.

I'm trying to embrace a new attitude by moving forward and trying to be a little more organized. I felt like I was pretty organized already, but I'm now also trying to sync my calendar with Mr. Matthews anytime I can, making sure that I get any important invitations through there.

I've also asked Tony to add me to their group chat so that I can get all of the updates that are important from a separate source. He's been really kind about the whole situation and added me, but of course, it's just been totally silent so far. But at least if important information comes through, I'll get it. On the job, they mainly use walkie-talkies for most of the stuff, but sometimes people can't answer or they need to get a hold of Tony and he's farther than the walkie-talkie range, so the occasional "bring me water" text will come through.

Brett and I have been getting along so well, which is nice. And I can't stop thinking about the kiss we shared after our dinner at the restaurant. It was incredible, and he is an amazing kisser. He continues to bring me coffee every morning, unless I text him that I'm not going to be there for some reason, like if I plan to spend all morning at the office. I'm so grateful for him, and I'm loving the crew now. I've even started bringing in cookies for the guys.

In the evening I usually have some free time, so I make cookies and other baked goods that I bring in and set in the job trailer. James eats a lot, but I always have a special bag for Brett because he's clearly my favorite. I even have an extra special treat for him today; he just doesn't know it yet.

I'm not scared to admit my feelings, especially now that I've kissed him. It feels like he peeled me open and brought me alive in a way that no man has before. It was seriously the best kiss of my life, and I haven't been able to stop thinking about it, even though that was two weeks ago now. It's been put in my Rolodex for fun times with my vibrator every night this past week.

Despite not having talked directly about it, Brett has been less nervous, and he'll give me the occasional touch, placing his hand on my back when we walk somewhere, or resting his hand on my leg while we have lunch in the job trailer, and I let him. It's comforting to know that he doesn't regret what we did, and his touches confirm with me that he'd like to keep exploring whatever this is between us. I hope that by letting him, he knows that's what I want too.

This morning, I'm sitting in the job trailer working on ordering paperwork. Tony has asked me to help him with this, and I obliged. I didn't really have much else that I was planning to do today, so this gives me a task to help with.

Anywhere I'm needed, I try to jump in. Obviously, I can't really operate equipment, and there are limits to what I can do on the job since I don't have all the necessary skills, so I just try to help when I can, and if that means doing paperwork, then that means doing paperwork. Being an engineer is a lot of paperwork anyway, so I'm kind of used to it, and it doesn't hurt.

I have the doors open to the job trailer pretty much every day that I'm in here because it is blisteringly hot. At least there's a nice breeze blowing through today, and I think it's supposed to rain this afternoon, so we might get an early day. Every time it rains, we get what's called a rainout, and that means we don't work either for that day or that afternoon. We do get paid for it, and how much depends on what time it is when we leave. If it's first thing in the morning, we get a couple of hours; if it's later in the afternoon, we might get a whole day. It all depends on what's going on and the weather.

Looking at the paper in front of me, I hear a knock on the door and look up to see my favorite person on this job site.

"Hey, Chief. What's up?" I look at him and smile, tucking a piece of my hair behind my ear. I don't wear my hard hat in here, so I let my hair down.

"Hey, Hotshot. Just coming in to eat lunch together. It is that time, you know," he laughs, looking at my mess of papers strewn around me, clearly not ready for lunch. I looked down at the watch on my wrist.

"Dang! I wasn't even paying attention to the time. Yeah, we can absolutely eat lunch together. That would be nice." Brett doesn't come in here every day, but he does come in here a lot to have lunch. On this job, the guys are forced to take a mandatory lunch even though a lot of them complain about it, especially Brett. He's used to being able to work right through lunch on the pipeline jobs he does, but it's good for him to take a break sometimes, and it's nice to be able to take a break from my monotonous work and chat with some actual people.

He comes in and sits down in the chair next to me and starts digging his lunch out of his lunch box. "How's it going in here? I know it's a hot one today." We're having a string of unseasonably warm weather for mid-November. It's been hanging at around 75°F today.

"Yeah, it's pretty warm, but I'm just working on some paperwork for Tony," I respond while I pull my own lunch out of my lunch box. Today, it is microwavable macaroni and cheese.

I stand up and walk over to the microwave that we have on the small table in the corner, pop my lunch in, then I turn around and look at him leaning back in his chair in a kind of sexy way. I think I'm ovulating this week, so everything is really getting to me, and he looks good despite being covered in dirt and totally sweaty. During college and my job site training class, when I got to watch real operators work, I realized this is how I like my men. Brett is a perfect example of this, and I love staring at him.

"I see. So, um, do you think we could finally talk about that night at the restaurant?" Brett asks, looking at me while opening what looks like a Tupperware of macaroni salad. It's the first time he's brought it up at all since it's happened, and my face heats.

"Oh. Uh. Yeah. What about that night?" I look at him, extremely nervous. I don't want him to say he regrets it, and I really wish we could do more. I'd love to be able to kiss him every day if he'd let me.

"I'd like to do that more often if you'd like to. I don't want to pressure you into anything since I know you said you haven't ever been with anyone before, but I'd like to kiss you more, Autumn. If you'll let me." He looks me dead in the eye with a firmness and confidence that I wish I could carry. I look down at my feet, and I know my face blushes even more, but relief rushes through me.

"Yeah, yeah, yes. I would love that, actually. That would be great." I stammer out. He stands, places his sandwich on the table, and walks over to me. He towers above me as he looks down and grabs my chin with his hand, pulling my face up to look at him.

"That is such a relief, Hotshot. Because I was really worried you were gonna say no and I was gonna be crushed." He leans down and places a gentle kiss right on my lips. My eyes open wide in shock, and then I settle into the kiss. It's just a quick peck, but it's enough to make me woozy on my feet, and it sends heat racing straight to my core.

"Brett. Whoa, I didn't really mean right here at work right now, but I mean okay," I laugh nervously. I'm clearly acting shy, but he is patient with me, and he's comforting; he wraps his arm around me in a hug.

"That's alright. I don't have to kiss you here if you're not comfortable with it, but I would like to, maybe in the mornings or at the end of the day. I would like to do a lot more than kiss you, but we'll take it slow." He continues to hold me until I lean back and look up at him.

"I appreciate that." I smile, thankful that he's aware of what I told him at the bar when he saved me from Jeremy. Before I think about that too much, my mind turns to the treat I have for him today. "Oh! I have something for you!"

I turn to grab my lunchbox and pull out the surprise I've been hiding all morning for him. "Close your eyes," I say. He does, and then I spin around and hold out the cupcake on the plate in front of him.

"Surprise! Happy birthday, Brett," I say with a smile.

Brett

I OPEN MY EYES to see a chocolate cupcake with sprinkles on a plate in front of me, being held by the woman who never fails to make my day better. "How did you find out about my birthday?" I ask her, confused and not remembering if I ever mentioned it to her.

"Well, I may have peeked into your records in Tony's paperwork and saw your birthday on one of your files. I only did it because I wanted to be able to surprise you! Birthdays are a huge deal to me." She says nervously, obviously afraid that she peeked into my file.

I chuckle and take the plate from her, placing it on the table beside us. "Thank you, Autumn. I haven't celebrated my birthday in years because I've always been out of town. This is nice." I reach my arms around her and pull her into a tight hug. My mom used to always cook me a birthday meal, and she is later tonight, but I missed being treated special on my birthday. Letting her go, I step back.

"Originally, I was going to get you a candle and do the whole song and everything, but then I thought that might not be a good idea at the job site, so I just went with a simple cupcake. I picked this up from the grocery store last night." She smiles at me. "Go ahead, have a bite." Motioning toward the cupcake on the table, she sits in her seat, and I do the same next to her.

I grab the cupcake, taking a big bite. It's been a long time since I've had a cupcake, and this one is chocolate with vanilla icing. It's perfect. I smile at Autumn, and she gives me her biggest grin right back before diving into her microwaved macaroni she brought for lunch. Her eyes twinkle with excitement, and I know the things I'm feeling for this girl are starting to be very real. There's a fire growing between us. I just hope I don't get burned again.

·· ☐☐☐☐ ·☐· ☐☐☐☐ ··

The end of the day rolls around, and all I can think about is how Autumn treated me to a birthday surprise at lunch. None of the guys on this crew even mentioned my birthday, and that's pretty much how every job has been. Today was seriously the best birthday I've had in a long time. I've been stealing glances at Autumn all afternoon while she's out wandering the job site, hoping for any chance at a smile. Of course, every time we make eye contact, she gives me a big one and sometimes a little wave, but nothing too crazy since we're just starting out, whatever this is we're starting. I don't want to push her too hard.

Tony asked us all to meet before we head out today, so we're all gathered around the trucks waiting for him to show his ass up to tell us what's going on. He comes walking through the crowd, breaking all of our impatience, finally.

"Okay, everybody. I just wanted to let you know that next week, as you know, is Thanksgiving, and so management above me has decided that we're going to be off Thanksgiving and the Friday & Saturday after, so you'll have four days off work, including Sunday. I still expect your asses to be back here on Monday, bright-eyed and bushy-tailed. You should be well rested with four days off." He announces to the whole crew, clapping his hands together as he finishes.

"Tony, this could have been a text message!" James says sarcastically and sounding frustrated at the same time. The guys talked about going to the bar tonight, and I think they finally decided to, but I said I wasn't going. I have some things I need to take care of at the farm, and hopefully that also includes texting Autumn a lot.

"Yeah, yeah. I guess it could have been, but it's easier to tell you guys shit in person. Alright, well, everybody have a good rest of your night and I'll see you all tomorrow." He says, dismissing us all.

Choruses of "have a good night, Tony" echo from the crowd as he waves us all off and goes to climb in his truck. I walk up to Autumn and try to talk to her before she heads out for the day. The guys are pissed about staying late, so they fly out of there as fast as they can. It doesn't take long for it to be only us in the parking lot.

"I wasn't sure what you were planning to do tonight. Any big plans?" I ask her, leaning up against the door of her Jeep as she climbs in the front seat. She smiles at me, turning, and I step between her thighs.

"Well," she wraps her hands around my neck. Since everyone is gone by this point, nobody gets to see what's going on between the two of us. I don't want to hide Autumn, but I also don't want to push her into something in front of everybody else at work, so I'm going to try and take things slow and let her lead. "I was going to go home and have myself a nice dinner and probably a glass of wine. Then maybe read some books and plan to text this really hot equipment operator I know." She's looking at me with lust-filled eyes.

"You got another operator that you're texting that you think is hot? I see how it is." I chuckle at her, and she smiles, leaning up to kiss me.

"Yep. He's very attractive," she says seductively. She instantly makes me hard just by talking about me in this way. This woman is going to kill me.

"Well, I think that sounds like a great idea, and I'm sure that the man you are texting will be waiting for your message. Everybody knows that a text from Autumn is incredible." She laughs and pushes me backward, sliding and turning into her vehicle.

"Alright, Chief, you can chill. I will text you, though, and maybe we can determine what's going on between us officially with a phone call if you're fine with that." She looks at me one more time before she turns the ignition on her vehicle.

"Yeah, I think that's a good idea, baby. I'll call you later tonight." I close the door for her and lean on the windowsill, smiling at her. She leans over and gives me a quick kiss on the lips and is ready to go.

"Okay, I'll talk to you later." With that final goodbye, I slap the windowsill and back up, smiling at her as she drives off. I didn't want anything to happen when I came back to this town, but boy am I glad that this woman rolled into our office late like she did.

Autumn

Setting my nacho cheese and bag of pretzels down on the outdoor coffee table, I settle into the egg chair on the patio in my backyard. I love coming out here in the evenings after work to decompress and prepare myself for the next day and all of its challenges. I've barely had time to get settled, and I'm shoving a pretzel doused in cheese in my mouth when my phone rings with Brett's name flashing across the screen.

"Hey, Chief," I answer around chewing my food and swallowing. "Sorry you caught me while I was shoveling pretzels into my mouth." I laugh.

"Hey, Autumn. Oh yeah? Don't tell me that's your dinner?" Brett jokes, but there is a slight hint of concern in his voice. It makes me think of his burger and salad from dinner the other night.

"No, I had some chicken tenders and fries that baked in the oven while I did my yoga." I smile even though he can't see me.

"Well, I suppose that's better than nothing. You don't always eat the best, do you? I see your microwavable meals for lunch." Brett chides me. He's the opposite in that regard, always having a well put together lunch, and he probably eats super healthy dinners, now that I think back to his order at the restaurant.

"Hey, at least I eat something! Sure, it's not the best, but it's something. I'm not a great cook; I take after my dad." I laugh, swiping a pretzel through the cheese before popping it into my mouth.

"Well, maybe I'll just have to teach you how to cook sometime," he offers.

"Yeah, that would be great. Or maybe you could cook for me." I laugh.

"You want me to cook for you? Like on a date?" he questions. He's getting into the territory of the exact thing that we intended to talk about on this call, so I'm glad he's the one who brought it up.

"Yeah, like a date. I think that would be really nice. You know, you could invite me over and cook for me, and we could spend an afternoon together on the weekend or something," I say, being bold and suggesting to him something that I would like to do. Sometimes guys find it sexy when you know what you want.

"Well, Hotshot, I would love to do that except that currently, my residence is still my camper in my parents' backyard behind the barn. So, I don't really have a great kitchen. But I could definitely grill for you. I have a little pellet grill that I keep outside my camper, and I could whip us up some steaks or chicken or something."

"Oh, grilled chicken thighs would be so good. That's probably my favorite meal—that with maybe some grilled asparagus, since you're just grilling."

"Well, we'll have to do that sometime," Brett says. "If we decide to start doing some dates, does that mean that maybe you want to be my girlfriend?" He asks me, questioning. He sounds unsure but still laced with his familiar confidence, being bold enough to ask me the question outright.

"Yeah, I think I'd like to refer to myself as your girlfriend. That would be nice." I smile, popping more pretzels into my mouth. "But if I'm gonna be your girlfriend, I should really get to know you, other than outside of work. I know you grew up here and your family lives here, your mom owns the flower shop, your family has a farm I think, and you're just a little bit older than me. But tell me some things I don't already know. I know when your birthday is, so I wanna know some other stuff. What's your favorite color? What's your favorite dog breed? What's your biggest dream?" I say, smiling, excited to get to know this part of Brett.

I know he's an amazing operator, and he's spent a lot of time doing some pipeline work out of town, coming back just for Tony's sake. I'd heard that his dad had had a heart attack a little while back. My mom had sent a card their way—she knows his parents—and the flower shop had been closed for a few days.

"Oh, yeah. Okay, a little bit about me then, a get-to-know-you of sorts. So, my favorite color is red. I really like eagles, have a tattoo of one on my upper shoulder on my back, and my favorite kind of dog is probably a collie like my brother's dog, Amber. What about you, Hotshot? What's your favorite stuff?" he asks, chuckling.

I can tell he's smiling on the other end of the line, and he likes getting to know me this way.

"Well, I would have to say that my favorite color is definitely green. I really like macaroni and cheese—it's my favorite meal. My birthday is June 26th, and my favorite dog is a golden retriever, like my little guy, or I guess, my old guy, Finn. He's technically my parents' dog, but he's my childhood dog that I grew up with, and he's my best friend. I miss seeing him every day now that I don't live with my parents."

"You don't live with your parents?" he asks.

"Uh, no. I actually have my own house that was given to me by my grandparents when they passed away. I don't have any cousins or siblings, so it's just me. My parents were both only children, and I'm an only child, so I lucked out and got this house. Unfortunately, my grandparents are gone, but it's nice to have this piece of them, knowing that this is where they lived for a long time."

I reminisce, thinking about my grandparents. I miss them all the time, but it is true—it's nice to have this little piece of them and something to be able to remember them by. Looking at places in their house where I remember them sitting at the kitchen table or on the chairs in the living room. Everything that was here when they were alive is still here. I kept everything the same, just adding my own touches on top of what they already had.

"Well, that's really cool that you have your own place and you don't have to live with your parents. You're close with them, though, right?" he asks me, confirming what he probably saw at the Fall Festival.

"Yeah, I'm super close with my parents. I try to have dinner with them whenever I can, and I go out there a lot. But they're both retired now, and so they kind of do their own thing."

"Okay, yeah. I heard they retired a little bit ago. Mom kind of tries to keep me in the loop of things that go on in the town, even though I was away for a long time. I'm close with my parents, but not as close as I used to be. I missed a lot of years while I was out doing pipeline work, and the relationship coming back hasn't been the easiest. But we're building things back up. Living in their yard, basically, I get to see them all the time, which is nice. So, we have dinners a lot together—pretty much every night with me and them and Adam, since he still lives with them on the farm in one of the cabins out back that he and I built when we were younger."

"You built a cabin?" I ask in shock.

"Yeah. When my brother and I were teenagers, we needed to get away from our older sister, and so we would go out back. We ended up building an entire cabin. Adam fixed it up a lot in the last couple of years to really make it his own place to stay, and he's added plumbing and electricity—things we didn't add when we were teenagers, just building a shed. But he's made it look really nice now, and that's where he lives, so that he can help out on the farm. He's going to take it over someday, whenever my dad finally decides to retire—which will probably never happen. My grandparents also live on the property, just a ways off from the main house. It's good to see them as well, too. I am really close with my grandpa."

It's nice that Brett and I have the same connection of both being close to our grandparents and loving them deeply. It's one of the things that's really nice about being in a small town—you get to spend a lot of time with your family and really enjoy every moment with them. That way, when they're gone, you have all these fun memories to think back on.

We continue to talk about some of our favorite things before the conversation turns to discussion of what is going on between us. "Now, we'll have to keep things a bit secretive at work, to keep it under wraps. I don't want to flaunt our relationship around. Not that it's an issue, I don't think, but I just feel like our work should come first," I say to Brett, wanting to be clear in my intentions with this. "I don't mind spending time with you on the weekends and in the evenings if we want to have dinner together, either at your place or mine, that's fine. But I think we should be relatively low-key at work. We can laugh and joke together and enjoy each other's company, and I'm not going to avoid you at work, obviously, but we definitely don't want to be down each other's throats, is what I'm trying to say."

"I 100% agree. Work always comes first in my mind, so I think that's a good idea. We should focus on the job, and we can work together and enjoy each other's company in the process. But relationship time should be outside of work." Brett agrees with me wholeheartedly.

"Okay, good. I don't want you or anyone else to think that I got to be an engineer on this job or that anything I do is because I'm dating you. I want all my accomplishments to be on my own accord. I've loved studying engineering, and it feels good knowing that you can be a part of something so big." I say, sharing a little of what makes me love the job we're doing.

I'm glad Brett understands my wishes of not flaunting our relationship at work and keeping things low-key. I already have enough concerns about my place on the job and what people will think of me being the only woman. The last thing I want is for someone to think that anything I've achieved at my job is because I'm dating the lead heavy equipment operator, and I want to make sure Brett understands that.

Everything that I do on the job are things I've worked hard for and that I've earned rightfully in my own way. Sure, Brett's helped me fix the plans, and I'm more than grateful for that, but every learning curve that I've overcome, every new task that I've figured out how to do, has all been me putting my nose to the grindstone and making sure I learn how to do this myself. I don't want there to be any concerns about me brown-nosing.

"I get that, Autumn. Your accomplishments should always be because of how smart and capable you are. Don't let anyone try to tell you otherwise," Brett tells me, his tone reassuring and a little serious.

We chat a bit more, discussing plans for work on our three-day week next week, and Brett tells me about the dinner he's having with his family on Thanksgiving. In response, I tell him about my family dinner at the same time.

"My mom always does a huge turkey even though it's always just been me, Lucy, her, and my dad. She just loves to go overboard," I say, laughing.

"My mom also does a huge turkey, but it makes more sense when you realize it's her and my dad, my grandparents, my brother, and my two sisters and their families. There are a lot of us, so a big turkey is needed," he says, a hint of joy in his tone.

"You're excited to be able to spend time with them, aren't you?" I ask him curiously.

"Yeah, it's been a long time since we've all been together. And the reason I came back to Mayfield is because my dad had a heart attack, so it's even more important this year when I think about the fact that he almost wasn't here." Brett's voice is quiet. I can tell he's thinking about his family with so much love.

I had no idea exactly why he returned, but knowing he came back for his father's health is a big deal. "Oh my gosh, Brett. I'm glad to hear that your dad is okay, but that's scary."

"Yeah, he's one of my favorite people, and to think that I almost lost him terrifies me." Brett sharing this intimate thought with me makes my heart swell, knowing just how much he loves his parents.

"Am I one of your favorite people?" I say, trying to lighten the mood.

"Quickly becoming one, Hotshot." He chuckles.

"Well, I'm very happy and I'm excited to see where things go with us, but I should probably get inside and shower away the disgusting grime of today and hit the bed before tomorrow," I say, smiling into my phone. I don't really want this conversation to end, but there are definitely some things I need to get done before tomorrow. "I can text you?"

"Yeah, that would be great. You text me and have a nice shower." The tone in his voice is suggestive and sexy.

"Okay, Chief, keep it in your pants for right now, but you can definitely think about me in the shower if you'd like," I smirk, keeping a teasing tone in my voice.

"I will text you." I can hear the smile in his voice on the other side of the line.

"Okay," I sigh, my tone laced with joy.

"Have a good night, Autumn," Brett says before hanging up the phone.

It's a relief to know that we've defined where we stand with one another and our intentions for moving forward, both with the relationship budding between us and our actions on the job. Brett makes me feel giddy inside, and he helps boost my confidence by telling me that I have what it takes and reminding me that I have trained for this job, and I know what I'm doing.

He's smart and a strong man to have in my corner—not to mention he's excruciatingly good looking.

Brett

My family is all gathered around the table in my parents' kitchen. I sit at the corner, next to my mom. Beside me is my brother, Adam, then my sister Susan, and finally both my grandparents. Across the table are my sister Jenny, her husband Paul, and their twin boys, Davis and James. My dad sits at the other end of the table, as proud and glowing as a parent could be.

We're all crammed in for this year's Thanksgiving dinner. I know Dad's happy to have all of us home for a holiday meal for the first time in several years—I'm usually the one gone, causing him heartache, especially this year after his health scare. My mom is happy to have me home, too. She's gushed about the way I look, if I'm eating enough, and if my clothes are getting washed properly, more times than I can count since I arrived. Considering the fact that I eat dinner with them more nights a week than not, I'm a little burnt out from the care. I know she means well, though, and is trying to catch up for many years of me not being around and her not knowing what's going on in my life.

The food in front of us is steaming. Plates and bowls piled high with stuffing, mashed potatoes, green bean casserole, rolls, and more, all surrounding the massive 23-pound turkey my mom has been cooking since early this morning. It all looks so good, and I can't wait to devour it. Nothing beats mom's home cooking, and after spending Thanksgiving eating ham sandwiches in the past, I am beyond excited to dive into the food in front of me.

"Let's say Grace," my dad says, holding out his hands to the people next to him, ceasing all conversation that was going on between us. Everyone grabs hands and bows their heads for a prayer, a tradition my family has always kept for every large meal, especially holidays.

"Lord, we thank You for this opportunity to be together, and we are grateful for one another and all we have. We are blessed to have all the kids here with us, especially Brett. Bless this food and the hands that have prepared it. In Jesus' name, Amen." My father nods at the end of his prayer as we all echo his sentiment.

The food starts passing around the table, and conversation begins anew. "So, how are things going with this job, Brett? Do you think you'll be around a little while longer?" my mother asks, handing me a bowl of mashed potatoes. I know she's dying to know how long I'll be in town, and I haven't been able to give her a straight answer other than saying *awhile*. Truth be told, I know this job will go into next year, but I'm honestly not sure what will happen after it. Now that Autumn is in my life, I think

I want to stick around Mayfield to be with her but I'm not ready to reveal that to my mama just yet.

"Work's good. The guys and I are making progress on the dirt work—it should finish up maybe in the spring," I say, spooning a glob of potatoes onto my plate. "Things have been kind of slow-going, though. They hired this new engineer who definitely didn't know what she was doing. The plans were a mess back in August, but they're fixed now. I helped her with that. Seems like it was some kind of screw up with her boss that caused her to not get all the details she needed and really made her look bad."

My sister gives me a look. "Oh, it's a woman?"

Jenny has been trying to set me up with women for years—after things ended badly with my ex, who she had been best friends with, it's like she feels completely responsible for my lack of a love life. Needless to say, Jenny's meddling hasn't gone well, and the last thing I want is her butting in now. I love what I have with Autumn, and my sister will be over the moon to know that we're a couple. I have decided that now is the best time to reveal the news to everyone.

"Yeah, she's fresh out of college," I say. "She's real sweet, we've actually been spending a lot of time together, which makes sense considering I asked her to be my girlfriend." I rush out the last part and shove a big spoonful of green bean casserole in my mouth so everyone can ruminate on what I just said.

"Ahhh!" My sister screams.

"Jennifer Noel," my father warns, trying to calm her down so she's not screaming at the dinner table.

"Sorry, Daddy, it's just so exciting that Brett finally has another woman after you know who," she says, smiling and taking a sip of the wine in front of her.

"I've had women since her," I grunt. "But Autumn is different, and I really enjoy her company. She makes me think, and I enjoy watching her work. She and I get along well." I smile, thinking about the pretty blonde who takes up the majority of my thoughts now.

"Brett, honey, that's wonderful. I'm so happy for you, and I'm really glad you're helping her learn on the job. She's a lovely girl; I know her parents. Her father always comes into the shop to buy flowers for her mother," Mom says. She's always wanted me to settle down and have a family, to stay in Mayfield. I'm sure she's over the moon that I've finally decided to have a relationship with a girl who's also from here. I know she's thinking it will push me to stick around.

"So why didn't you bring her to family dinner then?" It's my grandpa, whom I've always called Pa, who asks this question.

I laugh, "Knew that was gonna be coming next. She's having her own family dinner right now; she didn't want to cancel on her parents since she's the only child they've got." I take a bite of the turkey leg that I got. Adam and I have always gotten the legs. My sisters prefer white meat to dark, so they always let us have these, and lucky for us, there's one for each.

"Well, you'll have to bring her over some other time then, I'd love to get to know her a little better," my dad says, surprising me. He's never been one to take an interest in Adam's or my girlfriends. He never really talked to Brittany, but maybe he knew she was a shitty person and didn't like her because of that.

"Yeah, I'll definitely be having her over sometime. I wanna show her around the farm," I smile, thinking of how beautiful the farm can be in spring, hoping that I can bring her around then to see the baby calves and all the blooming flowers.

From there, the chatter shifts to my sister's work as a local elementary school teacher. Davis and James are seven and in second grade currently; she teaches third and hopes to have them both in her class next year, though they hope for the other teacher. This makes all of us laugh, knowing that both of those boys love their mom more than anything, but always give her a hard time for fun.

While everyone is distracted, laughing at Pa's story about his doctor's appointment a few weeks ago, I sneak a peek at my phone and see several messages from Autumn, explaining why it's been buzzing since the start of the meal:

Autumn:

> help, my family dinner is a nightmare my mom is talking abt when she gave birth to me who talks about that at thanksgiving !!

Autumn:
> to be fair they were saying they r grateful for me which prompted my birth story i guess ???

Autumn:
> brett if you don't answer me i might die

Autumn:
> well i hope ur enjoying ur meal cuz you'll never hear from me again

I chuckle and know I'll have to ask her later what happened. I hide my smile with my napkin, but Mom catches me from the corner of her eye. Luckily, she says nothing, just smiles at me knowingly.

Before I know it, we've all consumed our fair share of food, and it's time to clean up the table. I help Mom by grabbing dishes and carrying them to the sink. She's scraping all the plates into a bowl that Adam will take out to the couple of pigs we have. Then we transition to doing the dishes, and she washes while I dry. I may not live in the house anymore, but I still know where everything goes, and I know I'm expected to help do the dishes after a big meal. My siblings have done it for years while I've been absent, so it's only fair I take my turn this year. The task is so domestic and makes me think of doing this someday with Autumn. The thought shocks me a little as I haven't thought about a future with a woman in years.

As I dry a plate, my mom asks a question I wasn't expecting: "So, you like her a lot, huh?"

I freeze, thinking fast. I know she caught me smiling at my phone, but how does she know exactly what I'm thinking?

"I like her a fair amount, yeah," I say, hoping she'll leave it alone and not ask me to analyze my feelings with her. I'm not afraid to admit or talk about my feelings, but that doesn't mean I want to discuss my fairly new relationship with my mom.

"Nice try, my boy. I know that face. You are absolutely smitten." She smiles while handing me the next pot to dry.

"Okay, yeah, ma. I haven't felt this way about any woman since Brittany, and it scares the shit out of me, especially because we work together," I say, turning away so she doesn't see my face flush.

Brittany is my ex-girlfriend, who I used to work with on Tony's crew. She was another operator that I met at Mayfield Tech. She was friends with my sister, so I knew her pretty well, and we sparked up a relationship while spending time together in our last year of high school. When we graduated, we both got hired on Tony's crew, and we worked together on many jobs at the University. I was totally in love with her, convinced that I would marry her. And of course, she was my high school sweetheart, and we both grew up in Mayfield, so every single person was rooting for us.

A year into working for Tony at the university, a pipeliner reached out to me and asked me to go work for them on a job in southern Pennsylvania. It would've been amazing work and would've gotten me into the pipeline world, but I turned it down because I wanted to start a future with Brittany. I went with my mom, we bought a ring, and I was going to propose. I put my entire career as a pipeliner on hold because I wanted to stay with her, and she had told me she didn't want to do pipeline work; she wanted to stay in Mayfield.

But a couple of days before I was going to propose, I caught her in the job trailer, fucking another guy from our crew. I was gutted. It turned out she'd had a whole secret relationship with this guy. He was from out of town, so he had zero idea that she had been with me for years.

It ruined me. I had put my career on hold for a woman who had zero intention of being with me long term. I made the decision right then and there to never choose another woman over my career.

It's the reason I left Mayfield and went to do pipeline work for years. I couldn't stand to be around the town that reminded me of her everywhere I turned.

"Honey, she's not Brittany. You need to remember that. Take a look at how she behaves and find where her passions and determination lie. From the way you talked about how she started the job, it sounds like she's very dedicated to her work. And if you're scared, just talk to her, being upfront can make a world of difference," my mom says, placing her wet hand on my bicep.

"I know, Ma, it's just hard. She's real passionate about her work and wants to learn new things every day. She seems to also be very career driven like me, but I thought the same about Brit," I shrug, placing a cup in the cupboard.

"Just be patient with yourself, Honey. Getting out there and even just asking her to be your girlfriend is already a huge step," my mom smiles at me and goes back to scrubbing the dishes. "Don't be scared to move forward with your life because of ghosts holding you back."

I nod and continue to help dry the dishes, pondering what my mom said, coming to one conclusion—there's no advice like a mom's.

Autumn isn't Brittany and never will be. Her passion for her work is clear, and she's never given me any reason not to trust her. In fact, she's given me all her trust as I helped her fix her plans. Her faith in me has been unwavering. Now it's time for me to start believing in us.

Autumn

"There's my favorite sight to ever see." I hold my arms out as Brett walks toward me. Smiling at him, just as he's about to reach me, I joke with him and grab my coffee from his hands, taking a big sniff of the delicious black liquid that's going to help me stay awake this morning. It's the beginning of December, and the weather has gone from blazing suns to Arctic chill, it seems. The cold is seeping into my bones, and hot coffee is exactly what I need to keep me warm.

"I knew it was the coffee and not me. Darn." He chuckles and throws his arm around my shoulders, kissing the side of my temple. "Morning, Hotshot. How are you doing?"

"Morning, Brett. I am much better now that you are here with my coffee." I laugh. "Are you going to be busy today?" I ask him as we walk toward his machine.

He's going to be doing some digging today, and I'm going to head over to the job trailer and work on some paperwork. I need to contact the trucking company to make sure that the trucks are coming today for the dirt that we're hauling out of here. I feel like that's all I do anymore—contact the trucking company to make sure trucks are coming to haul out dirt or bring in stone. It's one or the other, but somebody has to keep this well-oiled machine running. Since we haven't gotten to very much building yet, there aren't a lot of things for me to check. When it does come up, though, I get excited to finally do some engineering work rather than doing paperwork and making phone calls.

"Yeah, I'm probably going to be busy. I'm going to be the lead person on loading up these trucks to get the dirt out of here. Those are coming today, right?" he checks with me.

"Yes, Brett. I called yesterday afternoon, and everything was fine, so I'm sure that's still the case this morning." I laugh at him and take another sip of my coffee. Man, this stuff is so good, and I'm so grateful for him bringing it to me every day. Now that we're an official couple, we try to spend as much time together as we can while at work. We meet each other in the morning for little chit-chats before we start our day, and we catch up for chit-chats at the end of the day before kissing like teenagers after everyone leaves and heading our separate ways for the night. We also have a continuous text stream with one another, and we've even started playing 8-ball pool via text message. As usual, my competitive side comes out when we play. I've won at least half of the game we've played, and tease him about it relentlessly, but it's all in good fun. I really enjoy talking to him and spending time with him any way I can.

"Alright, sounds good. I am going to be going to work now before my boss gets on my ass about talking to a pretty lady instead of doing my job."

I laugh and push his shoulder. "Alright, Chief, get out of here. Get to work." With that, I head into the office knowing that today is going to be a long, long day.

·· ☐☐☐☐ ·☐· ☐☐☐☐ ··

I'm on my laptop in the job trailer, and I'm about to click save on the file I've been working on for two hours when my screen goes black.

"No, no, no, no, no!" I yell at my computer, slamming my hands down on the table on both sides of it.

"Fuck!" I curse. This is not what I wanted to happen. Huffing out a sigh of frustration, I put my hands on my forehead, my thumbs pressing against my cheeks, trying to will myself to calm down.

I just spent so much time on that document, and I need to send it to Mr. Matthews today. Of course, my computer just died, and my charger is at home. I don't have one here. Today has been the worst.

I've been working on paperwork, and things have not been so great. Brett and I have barely seen each other in the last few days while at work. We've been texting as usual, but I miss chatting with him throughout the day, and I especially miss having lunch with him. He's been working so hard on scooping out the dirt that needs to be hauled out of here that he's just been eating in his machine so he can keep working.

He's extremely busy, and I've been trying really hard to let him do his thing so I can focus on my work in front of me, which is much more important, but he's become my every thought. I'm constantly wondering how the digging is going and if he's laughing with James. I think about the way his eyes crinkle when he smiles, and it makes him look so cute.

Needless to say, when we don't get a chance to talk, I get a little bit frustrated. Is it pathetic? Maybe. But such is my life now—when you really like someone, then you want to spend time with them. And when you don't get to, it's hard.

Slamming the lid closed on my computer, I sit there and stare straight ahead, unsure of how I should proceed with the rest of the day. I still have about two hours left and no computer. I could run home and see if I could get my charger, but that would probably take an hour, and then by that time, what would be the point? I'm extremely frustrated, but like I said, I have two hours left, so hopefully the day will go quickly.

The next hour passes with me organizing the invoices we've gotten from the trucks that have been hauling dirt. I need to get these sorted, make sure we have all of them, and send them up to the main office that manages the paperwork and funds for Tony's crew. As I'm putting a paperclip on the latest stack, thoughts all on my handsome operator, I manage to think him into existence, and he comes walking into the job trailer.

"Hey, baby," he says, smiling at me and grabbing a water out of the mini fridge.

"Brett!" I shout cheerily, standing up and moving over to him quickly. I toss my arms around his middle and squeeze him tightly.

"Whoa, easy there, Hotshot. Don't wanna dump my water on ya," he holds the bottle in the air above both of us so that I can't bump it and dump it on us. I step back and laugh.

"Sorry, I just haven't seen you other than our quick chats in the morning, and I miss hanging out with you. Speaking of, what are you doing in here?" I ask, crossing my arms and looking at him. "You didn't break anything, did you?"

He laughs, "No, I didn't break anything. But Tony got a call that one of the trucks got a flat just down the road, so he, James, and Jimmy, the mechanic, went to see if they could get him fixed up, so I've got a bit of a break finally." He takes a long drink of water, and I watch his throat work with the movement. Even his drinking from a bottle of water is sexy.

A little bit dribbles out of his mouth and down his chin, and I want to lick it off him. Getting some courage from my lust-filled haze, I walk over to him and pull him in for a kiss. It's slow and sultry, just what I needed to push me over the edge for what I have in mind.

"So, you're saying there's like no one here then?" I inquire while smirking. I'm getting a really naughty idea in my head, and it's pretty brazen, but it could be a lot of fun. He looks at me and smiles.

"Why? What are you thinking in there, Hotshot? I can see that brain of yours working." He taps my head with his index finger. I smile at him and wrap my arms around the back of his neck, clasping my hands and playing with the bottom of his hair.

"Well, I was just thinking that since pretty much everybody is gone or busy and there's like a .1% chance anyone comes in here, we could maybe do something a little dangerous." I pull my lower lip between my teeth and look up at him, batting my eyelashes.

"Autumn, what are you saying? This does not sound at all like you." He looks at me, unsure. I chuckle, stepping back from him, trying not to lose my confidence.

"I know. It's not really like me, but I want to try something fun, something different. I've always been so serious and so stagnant when it comes to relationships and men, which is probably why I haven't gotten very far with any of them, and I just want to do something fun. I think you probably like it too, what I have in mind." I poke him in the chest, running my fingers up as he leans back and crosses his arms, looking at me.

I look down and can tell he's definitely hard in his jeans, definitely gifted in that department, and I am a big fan. I have given blow jobs before and been to third base if you want to call it that, I've just never gone all the way with anyone. I look up at him with matched confidence, cross my arms, and smile, about to lay it all out there.

"Well, I think it would be a lot of fun if I got down on my knees and gave you a little something to think about for the rest of the day." His eyes grew wide, filled with lust. I smirk at him. "I think you'd like that, wouldn't you, Chief?"

Before I lose my confidence, I reach out and undo his belt. This is my moment, and I am so excited to push this man as far as he'll let me go.

Brett

Autumn is suggesting a blow job in the job trailer at work. This can't be real. I am definitely not going to say no, but my brain is trying to think of all the ways I can prevent her and me from getting caught doing this. This is not like either of us, but Autumn makes me different.

She derails my thoughts, and makes me want to live freely and have a lot of fun. I know she's nervous, but I can guide her through this, and this could be a big moment for us. We've only traded kisses, but we've spent a lot of time together the past two weeks getting to know each other, and I'm crazy about her; that much is clear to me. If we do this, this will really take our relationship to the next level, which is fine by me, but I want to make sure this is what she wants too.

I'm standing beside the mini fridge with my forearm resting on top of it, water bottle still in hand, and she's down on her knees right in front of me—what a sight. She looks up at me through her thick lashes, lips pouting, as she unbuttons my pants. She pulls them down ever so slightly, just enough to be able to pull my cock out through my boxers and jeans.

"Are you sure that you want to do this?" I ask her, wanting to confirm that she wants this as much as I do. I know she suggested it, but her mood about it could change now that she's down on her knees. The way her eyes grow wide as she stares at the sight of my cock in her hand, she is definitely into this just as much as I am.

Knowing she is finally looking at my cock and holding it in her hands, I am so hard it hurts, and I'm just staring at this woman in front of me, knowing that this is going to be the best blow job of my life, and all she's done is touch me briefly. Her hands are like fire and ice at the same time, right at the base of my cock. She starts pumping, and I immediately lose my mind. My head tips back and I let out a deep moan.

"Oh, Autumn. I—oh—I'm—" I can't even get the words out. This is gonna make me come so quickly. She settles forward on her knees, and she's just covered by the table, should someone look in the door. Thank God we have dirt and stones outside so that I can hear if someone's walking up to the job trailer.

She leans forward and licks up the length of my shaft with her tongue, which is warm and wet. That feeling alone makes my dick jerk, and a little bit of precum dribbles out of the tip.

It's been a long time since I've been with anyone, and Autumn doing things like this to me is really not going to make me last long. I've been attracted to this woman for so long now.

We've been working together for months, and every moment I've wanted her exactly like this. Looking up at me through her lashes, with my cock going in and out of her mouth. She takes the tip in and swirls around with her tongue. I lose it again, moaning, trying not to be too loud, but man, does this feel good. She starts bobbing her head up and down, and she removes my cock from her mouth to look at me.

"Does this feel good? Am I doing this right?" She asks questioningly while still stroking my cock with her hand.

"Baby, you are doing incredible. That feels amazing. Can I sit down?" I ask her as I run my fingers through her hair and down the side of her face, cupping her chin. She smiles at me, nodding, and we move so I'm sitting in the chair, and she's tucked in front of me, almost completely under the table. Once situated, I let her go back to what she was doing before. Instantly, she's taking my shaft all the way in her mouth, as far as she can. She's only about halfway, but she pumps the rest of my length with her hand.

She's setting a good pace for herself, and if she keeps going like that, I'm going to be coming down her pretty little throat soon.

"Agh, Autumn. Just like that, baby. Don't stop. What a good girl you are. That feels incredible." Her hair is falling out of her braid with the movement, framing around her face, so I do my best to pull it back and grab it behind her head. She's making a lot of moaning sounds, and she takes my cock all the way in her mouth, as far as she can, gagging a little as she gets to the back of her throat. I feel it touch and feel her gag, and I almost come right there.

"Fuck. I was so close, baby. I'm gonna c—" Right at that moment, I hear footsteps outside the job trailer. I sit up quickly and try my best to hide her under the table. Luckily, if someone stands at the door, she should be hidden right under the table, and they won't be able to see her. But it'll be a close call.

I know she can hear the stones crunching, but she doesn't stop. She keeps going, and the thought of getting caught is making me even more excited.

"Hey Autu—oh Brett. I didn't know you were in here. Do you know where Autumn is? I need to talk to her about some paperwork for this flat." Tony stands in the doorway, luckily not coming any closer. I cleared my throat.

"Oh yeah, she, uh, just went out to the bathroom, so you could probably catch her on her way back, I think. I'm just in here grabbing a water before I head back to the hoe." I choke out the words, holding up my bottle to acknowledge that I am doing exactly as I say. I suck in a breath as she takes me deep in again, all the way to the back of her throat. It's taking everything I can to hold in the moan and hold back the orgasm she's milking out of me.

"Thanks," Tony nods, turns around, and walks back out the door, going to look for Autumn, who he most definitely isn't going to find outside. I lean back in my chair again, look down at her, and she looks up at me and smirks. She knows we almost got caught, and she likes it. My dirty, filthy girl loves the risk.

She takes me all the way back in her throat again, and I lose it. Before I can say anything, my orgasm barrels through me as I come down her throat, moaning and jerking and holding her head with my hand in her hair so she can't back away. As soon as my orgasm starts to ebb, her sucking begins to hurt, so I pull her back and look at her. Holding her hair back, I jerk her head up to look at me as she licks the last of my come off her lips. She smiles at me.

"You dirty girl, Hotshot," I say, smiling at her proudly, cupping her chin. I know she said she hasn't been with a man before, but has she given blowjobs? Because there's no way that was her first one. She climbs out from under the table and stands next to me as I tuck my dick away.

"I loved that, Brett. That was a lot of fun," she smiles and laughs as she pulls her hair back to fix her braid. Once she's good with that, I offer her my water bottle, and she takes a drink, rinsing her mouth and swallowing.

"Autumn, you have no idea how much I loved that. You are incredible." She sits down next to me, and I turn and grab her, pulling her in to kiss her on the lips. I can tell she's nervous, but she's proud of what she's just done, making me come like a teenager. "You really are incredible, Autumn, and by the way, in case you didn't catch it, Tony is looking for you. I told him you were in the bathroom, so you better go out and find him because he's expecting you to be out there somewhere." She giggles.

"I heard you tell him that little lie. Alright, I'll go find him. You better get back to work, too, Chief." She leans in and kisses me again. As she's walking towards the door, she turns around and looks me dead in the eyes.

"Brett, would you do anything I ask? Even if you almost got caught at work?" She looks at me, smiling and wanting me to say something. I look at her and grin.

"Anything you want, Hotshot. I'll do anything you want."

Autumn

"What does your family do for Christmas, little boss lady?" James asks me, munching on one of the Christmas cookies that I brought in for everyone this morning. I was up late last night thinking about how Brett and I had been fortunate enough not to get caught at work the other day. Everything about him is attractive to me, including the way he's currently dipping one of the sugar cookies with green and red sprinkles into his coffee.

We're two weeks away from the Christmas holiday, and it's snowing a lot outside. It's not often that we get snow in Mayfield, but when we do, it's gorgeous. The local meteorologists have predicted a white Christmas this year, but we'll see if that holds true. Since it's snowing outside now, rather than working, everyone is huddled in the job trailer. Not because it's warm in here, there's no heat, but because we can be out of the wind and wet, and there are sugar cookies to share.

"My mom usually cooks dinner and we eat cookies, open presents, and just spend time together with me, her, and my dad." I smile thinking of how fun it is to share gifts and laugh and spend the holiday time together. "There's also always a lot of hot cocoa and candy canes consumed."

"That sounds way cooler than what my family does. We do white elephant, so we only get one gift, and sometimes it sucks because my siblings are assholes and buy cheap gag gifts." James rolls his eyes and talks with his mouth full, crumbs falling out onto the floor.

"Don't talk with your mouth full, dickhead," Brett chides him from beside me. I desperately wish that I could cuddle up against him for warmth, but we're at work and we've been clear about not crossing that line here in front of everyone else. I imagine that everyone has their suspicions because Brett's attitude toward me has changed over the last couple of months, but we haven't confirmed or denied anything. Plus, no one has really said anything.

"Sorry!" James shouts again with his mouth full of cookies. Everyone in the trailer laughs, and it's a really nice sound. I love that I'm getting along with the whole crew now and that they treat me like one of their own. James is always joking with me, and I think he really likes me, which has helped everyone else to just follow his lead. Or maybe it's Brett's lead. Either way, I'm grateful.

"What about you, Tony? Your family do anything fun for the season?" Enrique lifts the cookie in his hand into the air as a way of pointing at Tony from across the room.

"The 'ole lady has me involved in this damn tree lighting ceremony this year," Tony grumbles, clearly annoyed. We all chuckle, but my excitement cannot be contained.

"Wait! You're the one lighting the blue spruce that's in the middle of town?" I ask, joy clearly emanating from my words. "It's a gorgeous tree this year."

Every year, the town hauls in a giant tree, typically a blue spruce, that they set up in the middle of town. It's strung with lights, and they even get a lift to place giant ornaments on it. The entire town shows up to watch the lights be plugged in, and then they run on a timer, kicking on at dusk and turning off at dawn each day until after the holiday season is over. I thought that there was a whole committee involved in setting everything up, not just a couple of people.

"Yeah, she's volunteered us to take it on this year. Wanted to try something 'new and exciting' as she puts it, so when Bev saw her at the store and asked if she wanted to be in charge, she didn't hesitate. Now I've gotta help run electrical lines for the damn tree." He shakes his head. The things that these blue-collar men will do for their women. That's true love right there. It warms my heart.

I imagine Brett would do something like that if I asked him to. He's a big softy inside, and I know he'd do anything within his power to help me with whatever I need. It's one of his best qualities.

"That's awesome, I'm so excited for that this weekend," I say, excitedly taking a drink of my coffee.

"Ha, yeah. Me too," he sounds annoyed but has a smile on his face. "So, just looked at the weather and it don't look like this snow is gonna be lettin' up anytime soon. I'm gonna call it. Y'all head on home for the day. I'll see ya here tomorrow."

James jumps up and cheers. "Woo! Alright, boys, I'm outta here. Snow mobile is callin' my name. Boss lady, can I have some cookies to go?" He looks at me, gesturing toward the box of remaining cookies on the table in front of us.

"By all means," I wave my hand, smiling at him. They don't know it, but I have a whole jar of these at home for myself. I just brought in the extras, so they can take and eat whatever they want.

"Thanks! You're a great baker. Catch you guys later!" James grabs a handful and heads out the door, leaving only Brett, Tony, and me in the trailer. I'm gathering up my stuff and putting on my jacket slowly. Brett is behind me, clearly waiting for me, but his presence doesn't rush me.

"Alright, Tony, see ya tomorrow. Have a good night." I say, throwing my bag over my shoulder and waving at him as I walk out the door.

"Later, Autumn. Later, Brett." Tony waves us off, not looking up from his cell phone. He'll lock up the trailer behind us and be on his way whenever he's done making note of the rainout. A rainout doesn't necessarily matter what type of precipitation is falling from the sky.

Coming up to the driver's door on my Jeep, I open it, tossing my laptop bag inside and turning to walk over to Brett's truck. He's standing at the open door, looking at me, smiling. I wrap my arms around him and press my lips to his.

Leaning back to look up at him, I smile. "Well, now what are your plans for the rest of the day?"

"Don't know. I was planning on having to plow snow here all day." He laughs, placing his now-empty coffee cup in the cupholder of his truck. "I'll probably end up going home and seeing what I can do to help my brother with the farm stuff. When it snows like this, it makes everything a bitch."

I laugh at his choice of words. Not having been exposed to farmwork, I take his word for it. "Well, that sounds like a really fun afternoon."

"I'm just looking forward to getting through it to this evening. You still good to go to the lights in the park tonight?" He asks, tucking a stray strand of hair under my beanie. The snow is falling all around us and on us, sticking to his beanie and his eyelashes. He looks beautiful with the pure white backdrop. The whole job site is picturesque with the untouched snow lying in a pristine white blanket.

"Yep, pick me up at seven," I say, looking down at his lips and back up to his eyes. I pull my bottom lip between my teeth. He cups my jaw with his hand and leans down, kissing me softly.

He pulls back and rests his forehead against mine. "You got it beautiful, I'll see you at seven." I turn to walk away, and he smacks my ass. I turn around quickly to look at him with my mouth wide open in shock.

"Brett!"

"Wear those sexy jeans tonight too, I wanna grab your ass more." He winks at me and climbs into his truck. I feel the heat between my thighs increase. I'm not used to being treated this way, but I sure do love it.

·· ☐☐☐☐ ·☐· ☐☐☐☐ ··

"Look at that one, it's a family of deer!" I say, pointing to the bright white Christmas light display in the grass in front of us. Brett and I are walking around the town park for the full festive spectacle of Christmas lights. Along with the Christmas tree on display, there's a whole section of the park that's lit up as bright as can be with various displays and cute characters all made entirely out of Christmas lights. There are the classic "NOEL", gift boxes, candy canes, and Santa and his reindeer, but there are also more fun and unique lights like Charlie Brown characters, penguins, and even a set of lights that are meant to be the dog family from *Bluey*, which is perfect for the kids of the town.

Various families are milling about, looking at the light displays, taking pictures, and drinking hot cocoa from the drink trailer that's situated near the park entrance. We've been walking, hand-in-hand, taking our time looking at the lights and talking about all kinds of subjects.

"Yeah, it's really cute. Just like you," Brett says, turning to me and poking me in the nose with his ungloved finger.

I roll my eyes at him. "You've said that for every one of these sets of lights."

"Well, it's true, although all of these lights don't hold a candle to how beautiful you look, especially tonight." He takes a step backward, still holding my hand and bringing it up for me to do a little twirl. I'm laughing the whole time he spins me around, and when he pulls me in close, the only thing that stops my giggling is a kiss. His lips are warm, and I'm grateful since the temperature is near freezing tonight, and I definitely didn't wear a heavy enough jacket.

"Let's get some hot chocolate," I mutter against his lips. I see a few families passing around us, but no one that I know well enough to stop and talk to. I grab Brett's hand and lead him through the somewhat blinding lights right to the drink trailer.

"They've got spiked eggnog," Brett laughs, reading over the menu. "Do people even like eggnog?"

"My parents love eggnog. I, however, have never been a fan. That shit's gross," I slap my hand over my mouth because I realize there are a lot of small children around, so I should probably watch what I say.

Brett leans in and puts his lips against my ear. "Better watch that dirty mouth, Hotshot, wouldn't want any of the kids to hear." My face turns fiery red at his words, not just from the cold. He wraps his arms around me from the back as we stand in line waiting for our turn.

"Two hot chocolates, please," I say to the girl taking orders while holding up two fingers. Before I have a chance to pull up my card on my phone to pay, Brett is handing cash to her and placing the change in the tip jar. "I was gonna get that!" I protest.

"No, you aren't. You're never gonna be buying anything when we're on a date. My momma raised me better than that. If word got back to her, I'd never hear the end of it." Brett smiles, tugging my hand to pull me over to the pickup side of the trailer, away from the growing line.

We get our hot chocolates as soon as they're ready and walk back to his truck. It's chocolatey goodness that warms me to my core and smells just like Christmas. Brett opens the door for me, and I climb inside. I don't bother to buckle up, just holding the cup in both of my hands, using it to warm up my frigid fingers. As soon as he gets in the driver's side, he turns the truck on to crank the heat. I adjust the vents so they're pointing right at me, warming me up instantly. I also turn the heated seats to the highest mode they go.

"If you were so cold, you could have told me, and we would've come back sooner," Brett points out, watching me.

"I wanted to finish looking at all the lights. It's okay, I'll warm up quickly." I take a drink of my cocoa. "I should've dressed warmer, but of course, I opted for cute instead of warm when choosing my outfit tonight," I laugh.

"Aut, you could dress like a marshmallow with 20 layers, and I'd still think you're cute." He reaches over and pinches my chin with his thumb and forefinger. The way he looks at me is with true sincerity, and I know he's telling the truth. I could be at my ugliest and Brett Stewart would think the sun is shining right from me; I don't doubt that for a second.

"Thanks, baby," I say, testing out the term of endearment.

"Aw, my nickname upgraded," Brett jokes.

"Ha. Ha. Very funny." I roll my eyes at him. Before I have a chance to say more, I yawn. Brett watches me and smiles, placing his cup in the cupholder.

"Alright, sleepyhead. Let's get you home." He puts the truck in gear, and I settle into the seat, feeling the warmth of the heated seats and the vents surrounding me. The best warmth I feel, though, is when Brett reaches over and rests his hand on my thigh. Spending time with him tonight was the best, and I really enjoy these little moments we get outside of work. I look over to see him focusing on the road, and I study his features. The last thing I see before sleep overtakes me is a soft smile on his handsome face.

Autumn

"It's pretty loud in here!" I shout over to Lucy, who's standing beside me, dancing to Drunk Skunk. They're a local band that's becoming increasingly popular, and they're playing at Bobby's tonight to ring in the new year, so we thought we'd go out. I even invited Brett to come with us. We've traded a kiss with our coffees every morning at work since establishing our relationship, and we try to spend as much time together outside of work as we can. We don't go out to public events a lot, but tonight is a big night.

Bobby's Bar is having a big celebration and doing our own little version of the New York City countdown, where he'll famously drop some beer bottles while standing on the bar top. It's something he's done every year for as long as I can remember, and it draws a good crowd of the younger townsfolk. A lot of the older townsfolk have complained that it's too much and that the kids get too rowdy, but Bobby cuts all drinks off at one a.m., and he keeps doors open until three to give people a chance to sober up before going home.

"Yeah, but they're playing awesomely!" She puts her hands up in the air and twirls her hips. She said earlier that she'd like to leave here tonight with someone and have a little fun to ring in the New Year. She's had plenty of her little fruity drinks, but I'd never let her go so far that she couldn't decide for herself. If I didn't think it was right, I wouldn't let her go.

Brett is standing next to me, drinking a beer and taking in the music, but he's not really dancing. He's just a stick in the mud in the middle of this crowd. I'm so glad to be able to spend tonight with him and ring in the New Year with a kiss from my boyfriend for the first time, but I wish he would let loose a little bit.

"What do you think about getting some food and moving to somewhere that's a little quieter?" He grasps my arm while he's talking in my ear, and his touch sends electricity throughout my entire body like it always does.

"Yeah, that sounds great. I could go for some mozzy sticks!" He turns away as soon as I answer him and grabs my hand to guide me through the crowd. Before it's too late, I grab Lucy and the three of us are forming a train of people trying to get back to the bar tops that have been moved to the side to accommodate the dance floor.

Once we reach the table, I climb into the chair and set my beer down. "What'll it be for you ladies?" Brett asks to gather our preferences before going over to the bar to order food and more drinks for us.

"I think I'll do an order of mozzy sticks, a pub burger, and a small fry. Oh! And another beer," I add the last part, lifting up my almost empty bottle and drinking the last dregs of it.

"Got it. And for you, Goth Princess?" He turns to Lucy. He's been calling her that ever since we picked her up tonight, and she thinks it's hilarious.

"An order of pretzel sticks—with the cheese, a Reuben, and another peach margarita." She emphasizes the *with* so that Brett doesn't forget her cheese, which she's extremely serious about.

"Sounds good, I'll be right back." He says before walking off toward the bar. I stare at him when he goes, imagining the way he looks with no clothes on. Lately, I have been having a lot of fun dreaming about all the inappropriate things we could do to one another.

"Girl, you have got to stop drooling over him. It's getting on the table!" Lucy shoves my arm and smiles at me.

"I am not drooling!" I retort, shoving her back.

"You so are! But that's okay, if I had a hot boyfriend like him, I'd be drooling everywhere too. You know, you guys should fuck and get it out of your system," she says before drinking the final drops of her drink. "Seriously, go over there now and walk past him to the bathroom and see if he'll follow. I'm not saying you should have sex in the bathroom here since I don't think your first time should be in a disgusting bar bathroom, but you can at least get him alone and emphasize what you want and plan something for later."

I look at her, completely unsure. "You're being totally serious right now, aren't you?" She just looks at me and shrugs.

Feeling a jolt of confidence, I decide I'm going to do it. I'm going to corner Brett and tell him that I want to do this with him. "Alright, I'll do it," I say, nodding at Lucy, and before I lose my confidence, I walk away from her and toward the bar before she can stop me.

Winking as I walk past him and giving him the come here gesture with my finger, I know what I'm doing is dangerous, and I'm having way too much fun. I make my way to the bathroom, secretly hoping that he'll understand what I'm after and follow me.

Letting the door close softly behind me, I stand in front of the mirror and check myself out. Tonight, I look hot. I'm wearing a strapless band tee that I cut myself and a denim skirt that accentuates every curve of my body. This is usually the skirt I wear if I want men to notice me. Despite having a lack of experience when it comes to relationships and actually getting down and dirty with men, I'm good at flirting, and I've spent my fair share of time in bars watching men lust over me while I move on the dance floor. I reach into the top of my shirt and pull my boobs up just a bit to really emphasize them. They're not overly large, but I've always been proud of them–one of my greatest features besides my brain.

I lean on the sink in front of me, staring myself down. "You are absolutely insane, woman. He's not going to follow you in here. And if he does, what are you gonna even do!?" Trying to give myself a pep talk, I drop my head low with a huff.

"Yeah, Hotshot, what are you gonna do?" I hear the door creak behind me, and my head shoots up to meet those oceans of blue eyes in the mirror.

"Brett..." My voice comes out breathy, and I gasp as he comes up behind me and pulls my hair off my shoulder.

"Just waiting on the food, baby, got a little bit of time before it's ready." His voice is sultry and relaxing, and I find myself melting into him.

"Oh, do we now?" I ask him, leaning back into his touch, feeling goosebumps form over my body with his kiss to my neck. "What are we going to do with the time?" I know I'm egging him on, hoping and praying that this gets me somewhere. I can't deny the man does wild things to my body, especially when he's this close to me. I intended to come in here and only get him to see if he would follow me to talk, but his touch has me wanting more.

He turns me around and backs me up against the sink. He cages me in with his arms. "I promise you; I can have your legs shaking before our food is even ready." He smirks, and his face inches closer and closer to mine. My brain is turning to mush, and all I can think about is how badly I want to kiss him.

My body moves without any thought, and I grasp him by the back of the head and crash his lips into mine. He tastes exactly like he always does, like bourbon and dirt, but this time there's a hint of honey as well.

Our mouths move quickly with one another, never against, always in sync. Kissing Brett is nothing like any of the other guys I've kissed throughout my life. Brett fuels a fire deep within me and sends electric pulses through my body every time his tongue darts out to travel across my lip.

His hands roam over my hips and waist, and he picks me up and sets me on the countertop between the two sinks. He moves down to grasp my thighs, which are mostly exposed due to the shortness of this skirt.

"Autumn. These fucking clothes are incredible. You know exactly what I think of you when you're wearing stuff like this, don't you?" He travels across my jaw, down my neck, and stops at my shoulders. He softly kisses my collarbone and looks back up to meet my eyes.

"Perhaps I like knowing what you're thinking for once." I share the thought before I have time to think about the words coming out of my mouth. Brett's face flashes with shock, but he quickly corrects and focuses his steely gaze back on me.

"Well, I will gladly tell you what I'm thinking right now." His hands slide up my thighs and edge under my skirt. His touch is like fire on my legs, leaving burn marks wherever his hands pass. "I'm thinking that I want you to lean back and let me eat this pretty pussy of yours."

My eyes go wide, and I can't hide the shock on my face. I feel myself tense up ever so slightly. He must feel it too because he pulls his head back and squeezes his hands where they are on my thighs. "Would that be alright, Hotshot? I want to know how wet you get for me." He comes back in for a kiss, and I find myself immediately melting into it.

Our tongues go back to battling for dominance, and his hands push the material of my skirt up so that my black panties are now exposed. He brushes a knuckle across the area I so desperately want him to touch. "Brett...please." I can't help the slight moan that comes out.

"Please what, baby?" He mumbles onto my lips as he begins trailing down my neck again.

"Please touch me." My hands are uncontrollably roaming across his back and arms, exploring the extensive muscles he has from years of manual labor and operator work.

"As you wish, Hotshot." His finger pulls my panties to the side, and he runs them through my center, pausing to apply pressure right to my clit. The man knows exactly what he's doing; he found that with absolutely zero thought.

The moan that escapes from my lips is feral, and I clamp down on my lip to avoid making too much noise. Brett has locked the door, but we are still in the bathroom in the back of the bar.

As he slips a finger inside of me, I gasp. "Brett. Fuck, yes." My head falls back, giving him easier access to my neck, where he licks and sucks. He'll likely leave a mark on my overly sensitive skin, but in this moment, I do not care.

He moves down and kisses the top of each of my breasts before yanking down my top and exposing both of them with a single motion. I didn't wear a bra with this shirt since it's strapless, and in this moment, I've never been happier about that decision.

He takes my pert nipple into his mouth, sucking and licking the darker colored flesh. His tongue feels like heaven. As he moves to the other breast, he slips a second finger inside of me, and I can't stop the moan that breaks free from my lips. "Oh Brett, oh God."

"Baby, there ain't no God in this bathroom, only me." He grabs my hips and, in one fluid motion, slides me to the edge of the counter and drops down to his knees. "Look at you, baby. This soaking wet pussy, all for me."

He sets his lips on me and licks right up my center, flicking his tongue on that extremely sensitive bud he's been rubbing with his thumb. I've had a few men drop down and eat my pussy, but it has *never* been like this, and he's only just started.

One of my hands flies back to support my body on the counter while the other winds its way into his hair and gives a little tug. "Brett, fuck. Yes. Do that again." He repeats the same movement as before, flicking my clit with his tongue in a way that sends shockwaves through my entire body. If he keeps doing this, it won't take me long to come; I'm already soaking wet for him.

"You're going to come all over my face, Hotshot, and I want to hear you say my name when you do it."

The words he's saying don't even have time to register in my head before he's moving his mouth on me in ways I've never felt before. His tongue is hot and warm, and it feels incredible moving through me. I feel the familiar curling sensation in the base of my stomach, and I know I'm close.

"Please, Brett, I'm going to come." I whimper and pull his hair harder.

"Fuck baby, yes. Come on my tongue." As he says those last words, I reach my peak and I feel my body clench and release in a world-ending pleasure. Brett pulls his head back, and I shoot a stream of liquid all over his face and tongue, which he sticks out to catch all he can.

"Oh my god...Brett!" My legs are shaking and I'm squirting everywhere, something I've not done before with any man, only my vibrator. The smirk that appears on his face is absolutely feral, and his tongue darts out to lick his bottom lip.

When I finally stop shaking and coming, he stands up, pulling my skirt back down, and kisses me. I can taste myself on his lips, and it excites me. "Autumn, that was the sexiest damn thing. I've never had a woman squirt on me before."

"Well, I've never squirted on someone before. I've only been able to do that with my vibrator." I nervously tell him while sliding down from the sink and standing to fix myself. I pull my top back up and place both of my breasts back in their respective places.

The smug look that Brett has on his face is one for the books. Before he has a chance to make any cocky remarks, I put my hand up to stop him. "Don't get a head full of hot air, Chief. We wouldn't want you to float away."

With that, I ensure my outfit is put back to where it should be, and I turn to exit the bathroom. "You might want to clean up in here before you leave, you got a little something." I gesture in a circle around my face to reference the remnants of our little fling that he's got all over his face. "I'll go out first and grab our food, and then you give it a minute or two that way no one suspects anything scandalous is happening in here."

"Oh, baby, they probably heard you all across the bar," Brett says with a smirk, wiping his face on the back of his hand. I feel my cheeks turn bright red, and I turn and walk out the door, letting it shut behind me as I walk over to the bar.

"Autumn!" I turn to see Colin, my coworker from Arch, walking towards me. I don't really like Colin. He's smug, and cocky.

"Oh, hey, Colin. I didn't know you liked Drunk Skunk," I turn to see our food and drinks sitting next to me on the bar top.

"I'm here with my girlfriend, Ashley." He jabs his thumb over his shoulder. "I saw you were here with that guy from the WhitewaterU job, Brett, isn't it?"

I look down at my fingers nervously, "Uhh, yeah. Brett. How do you know him?" I look back up and meet him in the eyes in a challenging gaze.

"Mr. Matthews was discussing the project with me. He's the lead operator, isn't he?" Colin gets a smug look on his face as he crosses his arms. He has this cocky attitude about him, like he's plotting something. Suddenly, fear courses through my whole body, and I go rigid. He's going to tell Mr. Matthews about me being here with Brett.

"Oh, yeah. He is. We're actually here with a whole group of people." I try to stumble over my words to ensure Colin doesn't figure out this is a date. "My best friend Lucy is over there waiting for me now." I nod my head in their direction, and Lucy catches my eye with a look of concern. I see Brett has made it back over to the table as well.

Colin huffs and looks over towards them. Seeing the two of them together, his grin falters ever so slightly, but I still don't think this is going to end well for me. "Ah, I see. Well, I'll see you around Autumn."

With that, he turns and orders his drink from the bartender. I grab our drinks and food and head back to my friends. I fear that this can only end one way, and I don't think I'm going to like it very much.

Autumn

"You can't be fucking someone on this job, Autumn!"

The way he says fucking is like a cold bucket of water over my head. Mr. Matthews is pacing behind his desk in his office after having called me in here first thing this morning. I'd had about two weeks of complete bliss, thinking that Colin wasn't going to say anything about what he saw at the concert. Turns out my hopes were misguided, because he clearly let Mr. Matthews know about it.

"Is this little rendezvous of yours the reason you've been having problems—missing meetings and important details at this job?"

My back goes straight, and I feel defensive. I would never, ever let a relationship get in the way of my job or my ability to do it.

"Absolutely not, Mr. Matthews. Brett is actually the one who realized the original plans were not going to work because of the 811 mess-up. He saved the project from very early on. We've been working together to ensure that everything is successful. Since then, we have been working together on the job, and Brett has always informed me of things going on, and vice versa. I promise that any interactions Brett and I have are not affecting my ability to do this job."

I feel the need to not only defend myself but to defend Brett. He hasn't done anything wrong, and Mr. Matthews is going on and on about him as if he's this horrible person.

Brett has been super amazing and super helpful to me this whole job. He has always been in my corner in the way that most people haven't—the way that people at Arch Engineering haven't, the way that Mr. Matthews hasn't. Brett has always been supportive of me. And yes, he did think I was in over my head with this job, but he has been nothing but helpful, pushing me to do my best. The same cannot be said about my boss here. I would never tell him that outright, though.

"This ends now. You are not to have a relationship or any kind of interactions with this man who works on your job. Do you know how bad this looks for the company—having an employee sleeping with another employee on the job site? Autumn, that is not a good look."

Mr. Matthews is scolding me, shaking his head as he sits down at his desk, arms crossed over his chest.

"You need to stay away from Brett. Any interactions you have need to be solely about the job—the work that needs to be done. And you know what? Actually, all interactions that you need for this job should either go through me or Tony. You don't need any direct interactions with this operator. Any guidance you have to provide, or thoughts or feedback you have to give, take them to Tony or bring them directly to me, and I'll share them with Tony. This way we can avoid any future 'confusion.'"

He says confusion with a mocking tone, as if anything going on between Brett and me is misguided—as if he would even know what's going on between the two of us.

I'm not afraid to admit that I love Brett. We've been spending so much time together, and he's been the best boyfriend I've ever had. He's a perfect example of how a man should treat his lady—bringing me coffee, helping me with the job, making sure that I have information that's been hidden from me and kept from me. Somehow, we had a meeting last week that I had no idea was happening. Luckily, Brett did, and he told me about it beforehand, so I knew. He's the only person on the job who's come to my defense, who's made sure that I have the details I need, made sure that I have the information I need to do my job successfully. He's the only person who's been in my corner the whole time.

But this job is most important to me. I worked my ass off in college to get this degree and to get this job. I'm not going to let that get screwed up on the very first job I have.

"Yes, Mr. Matthews. I understand. I will cease my communication with Brett regarding work matters unless I directly need to talk to him for some very specific reason that Tony asks me, or something like that. I don't want anything to get in the way of me being able to do my work, so I will focus only on doing the job that I need to do."

I cower in my corner, sounding so resigned. I'm disappointed. I was so happy to finally have things going well for me—my job was going well, I finally found a man who could treat me right, it seemed, and who was giving me the support I needed to do my very best. And now it's being ripped out from underneath me.

"In addition, I'm going to put you on a probationary period for the rest of this job and dock your pay for this month. If you can get through the rest of this job without any more issues, without missing any meetings, then you can stay here at Arch Engineering. But if you can't—if you miss important meetings, if you miss important details—we may have to discuss your employment here."

Mr. Matthews' voice is stern, and I know he means business. Shock must flash across my face, because he continues.

"I don't want to be this way, Autumn. I want this job to go successfully, and I want you to do a good job at it. So, I need you to put forward your very best effort."

"Yes, sir, Mr. Matthews. I will do everything I can to put forward my best effort from here on out, and I apologize sincerely. I will make sure that I prioritize this job over everything else." I am struggling internally with this whole situation, but my job is the most important thing to me right now, despite how important Brett has become. I was honest about that with him from the beginning; my job will always come first.

"You're dismissed."

I walk back to my desk and sit in my chair. My head falls into my hands. How could this have happened? I know it was Colin who told Mr. Matthews about what he saw on New Year's at the bar. It seemed like Mr. Matthews didn't know the full extent of my relationship, but clearly, he knows that Brett and I have something going on between the two of us.

I hate Colin for what he's done. He's always trying to one-up me, always trying to push me back down behind him. We started here at Arch at the same time, and he's always gotten the better work. He's always been short with me, not wanting to ever develop any kind of decent working relationship. Clearly, Colin dislikes me, but I have no idea what I've unknowingly done to make him feel that way about me.

I pull out my computer and try to type up an email with some notes about our discussion that I can send to myself. I try to keep an interaction log of every time something happens between me and Mr. Matthews so that I have a record of our discussions and things we've talked about. I've done this since the beginning of my time here. It's important to me to have this backing, as a young engineer, especially a young, female engineer. People don't always trust me, so I want to make sure that I have all the details correct while they're fresh in my mind from every meeting we have.

I'm absolutely gutted that I'm going to have to end things with Brett. My heart is breaking into a thousand pieces, and it's going to shatter even more when I have to tell him what's going on. Do I tell him the reason why I'm breaking things off with him? I'm sure he'd understand, but I don't know if he would accept it. Brett has never pressed my wanting to keep separate at work, but if I tell him that my boss is saying we can't be together, he might tell me to just grow a backbone and stand up to him. I'd love nothing more than to do that to save my relationship, but this job is important to me. I can't lose it; I don't know where else I would go.

My brain is turning too quickly, and I can't gather my thoughts. I know is that this is going to be tough, but maybe I can come up with everything I need to say on the drive to the job site. I grab my keys and my bag, walk out to my car, and climb in. I know that the next ten-minute drive is going to feel like the longest one of my life.

Brett

Climbing out of my dozer, I look up and see Autumn coming towards me. Her head is down, and something about the way she's carrying herself is off.

"Hey, Hotshot. You, okay? I missed you this morning." When she's almost to me, I try to reach out to grab her, but she backs away. Confused, I give her the space she's looking for and try again. "I got your coffee, but it's sitting in the job trailer in case you want it. It might be cold by now."

She looks... not happy, and I'm not really sure what's going on. "Everything okay?" I question, concern racing through my body. Is something wrong? Did something happen to her parents? Lucy? My mind is going to every possible bad scenario I can think of, worrying that someone she loves is hurt.

"Hey, Brett. I'm just going to do this right away because it might hurt less, I don't know. We need to stop dating. I think that we should maybe focus on work rather than what is going on between us. I just don't want our relationship to cause issues with us getting our work done. I know we started out on the wrong foot, and we've grown together, but I think we should cool things that are happening between us and maybe just take a step back. You need to focus on your operating, and I'll focus on my engineering, and we can just get the job done. I think that's probably for the best."

She sounds so sad to be saying this, and I can see in her face that she doesn't want to be telling me this.

"Autumn, what is going on? Why are you coming to me, saying this? Are you unhappy? Should I do something? Do you not want to be with me? I thought we had something really special between us."

I am confused, and I need to know what's going on with her. I need to know why she's not okay, because that much is obvious.

"No, it's not that. It's me, actually. I know that's the stupid line—the whole it's not you, it's me thing—but I think I need to focus more on work. I've been missing some meetings, as you know, and missing important details and information. I think I've just been distracted and need to focus more on my work rather than on what's going on between us. I don't want to miss anything anymore, and like I said, this job is important to me since it's my first one. So, I feel like I really need to do a good job, and I need to impress my boss. If I keep missing meetings and stuff, I'm going to get in trouble. I just came from a meeting with him where we discussed the future of the project, and I think the best way to avoid any future issues is to just stop distracting myself with thoughts of you all the time."

She's rambling and very clearly nervous. I can see faint tears running down her face, but she's trying hard to hide her pain. I want to tell her to shut up. To beg her to fight for what we have. I want to tell her that I'll help her make sure she gets her work done. But I've been where she's standing now, losing track of everything in my work because of a relationship, and I don't want to do that to her.

My heart shatters as she talks, and even though I disagree, I respect her wishes. "Oh. Well, okay. If you wanna slow things down, then that's fine. We can cut back on the texting, or... not really sure what you want me to do," I offer, trying to provide a remedy to the situation that prevents us from completely breaking up.

"I think it's best if we just don't text unless it's work-related. And maybe stop getting me coffee in the morning. I'll be okay, and we'll move on. Most of my communication will probably come through Tony now. I'm just going to coordinate with him most of the time, and then I might be spending more time at the office rather than in the job trailer. That way, I'm not here to bother anyone or cause any issues when I can do things from the office at Arch."

She's closing in on herself, and I can see it. I had worked so hard with her to get her confidence up, to get her to feel like she can do this job and do great things. She was fitting in so well with the team—laughing, getting along with the guys, hitting them with their jokes right back—and now she's just pulling back into her little shell. Somebody has done this to her.

There's no way Autumn woke up this morning and decided she needed to focus more on her work. What happened? I don't understand.

"Autumn, did somebody say something to you about me? Was it someone here on the job site? Because if it was one of these suckers, I'll talk to 'em."

"No, Brett. Everyone on the job is so nice to me now; it wasn't anything any of them said. I just kind of had a realization that I needed to focus more on my work rather than any relationships. I'm gonna go ahead and go now. I just wanted to stop by and let you know that you'll probably just be hearing from Tony now instead of me." She's trying to hide a sob as she turns and walks away. I barely get my words out before she's too far to hear me.

"Okay. Well...do what you need to do, I guess, but I thought I meant more to you than that." I see her tense up, knowing my words have hit their mark, but she keeps walking. I am confused, heartbroken, and slightly angry watching her walk away with complete sadness radiating from her. She's crushed, and I don't know what to do. Frustration runs through my body, and I ache to hold her and make it all feel better.

I know in my heart that Mr. Matthews is the issue here. Autumn is more than capable of doing this job—despite my beliefs at the beginning that she wasn't. Getting to know her has been the best thing I've ever experienced. She is smart, funny, caring, and she gets the work. In a blue-collar job, it's hard to find women who understand the work and what all goes into it.

I'm gonna do everything I can to prove that Autumn can do this, and that she just hasn't been given the right information. I've gotta get my girl back.

The thought crosses my mind like a whip. My girl. Yeah, Autumn has snuck her way into my brain these last five months. She fills my every waking thought and my dreams when I sleep. I have to show her how capable she is. And I know just how to prove it.

Pulling up my text conversation with Knox, I send off a quick text:

Brett:

> Hey man, how's that information hunt going? I gotta know—do you have any updates?

Sticking my phone back in my pocket, I stew on the situation. I know it's very likely that something happened, and Mr. Matthews somehow found out about Autumn and me. Not quite sure how, but I know I have to take this guy down. He's hurting Autumn. He's crushing her dreams, and he's squandering her work performance and ability to be the best she can be in her engineering field.

Autumn is incredibly smart, and she knows what she's doing. Even better yet, she gets along well with the crew. Getting along with the crew is half the battle on some of these jobs. I've known engineers on jobs who don't get along with anyone, and guess what? They're hated. The job doesn't go well because none of the pipeliners or hands give a fuck about what the engineer thinks. They don't care to follow his or her direction, and they lose that respect.

Autumn garnered that respect here. All of these guys like her. They follow her lead and her guidance just the same as they do Tony or me. It doesn't matter that she's a woman. Sure, she got off to a rough start, and I helped her get where she needed to be, but she picked herself up and pushed forward despite all the challenges she faced. She earned that respect back, and she started over. She wasn't afraid to buckle down and do the work, to show these guys that she's capable. She gets along with us. She goes out to dinner, out to the bar, and she can drink her way around Enrique—which is a lot.

Autumn finally fits in so well, and I hate to see her revert into herself, not putting forward her best foot because someone is holding her back. If he's threatening her, and I find out, there will be hell to pay.

My phone dings with a text message from the man I've been waiting on for a couple of hours.

Knox:

> Hey, man. Uh, yes. Starting to get information. Looks like your girl's email was hacked and updated. I found the previous draft where she had it. Looks like it was logged in from another laptop located at Arch Engineering. So could be a boss, could be another employee—it's hard to say. Also hacked into the boss's phone. Found the phone number that he has listed for an 'Autumn

> Harris.' Turns out it is connected to no one. The phone number is incorrect. It's not Autumn's phone number that you gave me, so he's been texting the wrong number. No wonder he hasn't been getting any responses. I'm going to continue to gather some information. I'll share everything with you once I have it.

I look at my phone in shock. I knew it. I knew this man was keeping stuff from her. Now if only I had a way to prove that his laptop was the one from Arch Engineering that hacked into her email... which Knox probably can.

He's an incredible hacker. He used to be in Special Ops in the military, but after a bad op, he retired. Now he lives in the mountains outside of Mayfield in a small cabin and does some hacking and dirty work for people when they need it. The man's loaded with his retirement from the military, so the hacking is just extra fun for him.

I'm gonna keep gathering this information, and I'm gonna use it to prove that Autumn is being targeted at her job by her own boss. Surely there's some kind of charge that can be filed here. I'm going to get to the bottom of this. And I'm going to win back my girl.

·· ☐☐☐☐ ·☐· ☐☐☐☐ ··

When I'm leaving work that evening, my mom calls me. It's perfect timing as I was going to find her after work anyway.

"Hey Ma, everything okay?" I ask, concern in my voice that something is wrong with Dad.

"Sweetheart, do you have time to stop by the shop? I got some new ceramic vases in, and the boxes are super heavy. I would ask Adam, but he and your father are trying to get the last of the cattle checked by the vet today before the snow that we might get next week." She says, calming my racing heart with each word. Knowing that everyone is okay and she just needs muscles is a relief.

"Yeah, absolutely. I'll be there in ten, okay?" I assure her.

"Sounds great, Honey, see you in a bit." She hangs up the phone before I even have a chance to say goodbye.

Chuckling, I throw it in the cup holder of my truck. I swear my mom has a sixth sense for when I'm feeling down, she would always call me on days I was especially missing home without her even knowing. Hearing her voice was always a relief to me and a reminder that home wasn't so far away when I could just call her.

As I drive to the flower shop, my mind is on Autumn and what happened today. She broke things off with us without a valid explanation other than that she wanted to focus on her work, which I understand, but I don't see why we have to be over for her to do that. Hasn't she been focusing on her work for months now?

I roll the window down to let cool air blow on my face. It's mid-January, and the temperatures have been around freezing for a couple of weeks now, making work outdoors on the job site suck.

This is the time of year that Mom's flower shop begins to ramp up for Valentine's Day in a few weeks, so I understand why she got new vases in. I was so excited to be able to treat Autumn for Valentine's Day, but I guess we won't get that now.

I still can't figure out her change in behavior. She was completely fine last night when we talked on the phone, but when she arrived at work this morning, she was totally different. She had even texted me first thing that she was going to stop at Arch before coming in. Something had to have happened with John while she was meeting with him at the office. It's the only explanation.

My blood begins to boil. If I find out that he did anything to her, I'll kill him. Wanting to get to the bottom of it, I pull into the parking lot for the shop and I text Knox:

Brett:

> Hey, man, can you find out if any emails were sent to Autumn that reprimanded her, or if any documents in John Matthews' computer reference a write-up?

I usually only ask for general updates and not something specific, so I think Knox will know something's up. If Autumn had gotten in trouble with John, there would be a paper trail, I hoped. It's possible that he did something to her that wasn't written down, but if that was the case, I have no idea how I'd ever find out. Before I can think more on that point, a text comes in.

Knox:
> Ah, let me guess, your woman broke things off with you?

Brett:
> What. Happened.

The fact that he texted that in response means that something happened at the office this morning. My heart rate picks up, frantic to know what he said to her.

Knox:
> You would be interested in this email.

1 image attached

I open the picture he sent me of a screenshot depicting an email. Reading through it quickly, I realize it's a policy change. A no-fraternization policy change. Autumn got in trouble for being with me, and John made this new policy. I don't even respond to Knox; I just climb out of the truck and slam the door.

There's no way this policy existed before this morning. I would have known. I read through all of the documents for every job. I've never heard of a no-fraternization policy with any company. This is ridiculous.

Pulling open the back door to Mom's flower shop, I walk out to the front showroom and call out for her. "Ma?" It smells wonderful in here with all the scents invading my nose. The scent of various flowers always reminds me of my childhood, when I would spend days here helping my mom.

Mom keeps the flower shop stocked up with all kinds of beautiful arrangements that she makes herself first thing each morning. I walk around the room admiring the beautiful bouquets of roses, lilies, and baby's breath that are more commonly purchased as well as some of the native bouquets that contain things like coneflowers, bluebells, and violets.

The colors all pair together so nicely. I walk over the section of cut flowers that sit in little jars of water, where you can build your own bouquet. I grab a light pink rose, the only one left in its jar, and twirl it between my fingers. I wonder what Autumn's favorite flowers are. She's probably a lily person, bright and beautiful, taking up lots of space with their shape, just like Autumn brightens a room with her wonderful personality.

The thought of Autumn being in here looking at flowers brings a slight smile to my face and a pang to my heart. There's so much I want to do with her; it kills me knowing that she wants to distance us.

"In here, Honey," I hear her voice come from her office in the back. I place the rose back in the jar and walk back the hallway. "Glad you're here," she says as I stop and stand in the doorway.

I can tell my body is tense from all the stress of today and from the news I just found out, but I try to let it go so I can focus on my mom. However, she looks up from her desk and takes one look at me, stopping short.

"Honey, what happened?" She asks, taking her glasses off and setting them on the desk.

"She broke up with me. She said it was so she could focus on her work, but I just found out that her boss created a no fraternization policy, and Ma, I know she got yelled at because of me." My heart breaks into a million pieces looking at my mom. That's the moment it hits me like a ton of bricks. Autumn got yelled at by her boss because she's been spending time with me.

"Brett. This is not your fault. Nor is it Autumn's." Mom stands and walks over to me, pulling me in for a hug.

I wrap my arms around her tight and squeeze. "Ma, I was so focused on her not hurting me that I didn't even think about what being with me could do to her." I feel the panic rush through me. Autumn didn't want to end things with me—she had no choice. It makes me feel better about her calling things off, but it leaves me in a confused position. "What do I do?" I pull back and ask my mom, holding onto both of her shoulders, looking into her eyes.

"Well, if it's a work policy, there isn't much you can do." She sounds sad for me.

"No, no. There's got to be something, I just have to find it." I feel a newfound energy coursing through me. "But I will figure it out later tonight. Right now, I'm here to help you." I say, smiling at her. "Now, where are these vases?"

Autumn

The music is blaring in my Jeep as Lucy and I pull into the driveway in front of my parents' house. We're here for my mom's birthday party, and we are already several minutes late thanks to the fact that Lucy had been fighting with her computer trying to save a copy of the presentation she was working on for one of her classes.

The weather is cold today. It's late January, and although we haven't had a lot of snow the last couple of weeks, we have had our fair share of cold weather. Today, it's currently 40°F, and the icy temperatures are a perfect fit for my icy mood.

I unbuckle, climb out of the car, and walk into my parents' house. After everything that happened between me and Brett today, I stood in my room debating if I wanted to come tonight. But I had promised my mom I would, since it was her birthday after all.

"Mom, Dad, we're here!" I call, taking off my coat and hanging it up in the hallway. I kick off my boots, trying not to get snow inside the house. Lucy does the same behind me. Finn is running around our feet, excited to see us. I give him a quick pet before he moves over to Lucy, preferring her to me as he always does.

"Hello there, handsome boy," she coos, squishing his face between her hands.

"In here, girls! We're getting dinner ready," comes my mom's voice from the kitchen.

It wasn't going to be a huge birthday party, just enough for me, my parents, and Lucy, I think. I don't have any true siblings, just Lucy, so there typically weren't any others, unless my mom invited her friends.

Sure enough, walking into the kitchen, I see that my mom had indeed invited them. Both Susan and Jane are sitting at the counter with glasses of wine while their husbands, Josh and Peter, talk with my dad over in the dining room.

"Mom, you better not be cooking your own dinner," I say, going up to her and hugging her with a kiss on the cheek.

"Oh no, honey. The girls and I are just standing here enjoying some wine while your dad and the men are setting the table and getting everything ready. I haven't lifted a finger. I didn't even pour my own glass of wine," she chuckles, lifting the glass.

"Good. Let's celebrate this beautiful birthday lady." Lucy shouts, taking her turn for a hug.

I walk into the dining room to find my dad, leaving Lucy behind.

"Hey, Dad!" I say, giving him a big hug. My dad's hugs are always the best and so calming. I have been waiting for this all day after stewing over everything that has been going on.

"Hey, Cupcake. How are you doing?" My dad kisses me on the top of the head as he holds me in the tightest hug I've had in a long time.

"I'm okay, Dad. Is there anything I can help with?" I lean back and look up, waving to the other two gentlemen in the room.

"Yeah, you could grab some plates off the China cabinet and help me set the table. I'm supposed to be working on that, but you know how I get with setting the table and making sure we have all the correct silverware," he laughs.

My dad isn't always the best at those little things, but he sure is funny, and he loves my mom so deeply—the kind of love I want to have. The kind of love Brett gives me. The thought of him makes my heart hurt, and I shake my head to prevent myself from crying.

I start setting the table, and Susan walks in, carrying some more glasses for wine as well as glasses for water. Together we set each place. My dad made my mom's favorite dinner: stuffed chicken breast, mashed potatoes, and steamed broccoli. He also told me earlier in the day that he was grabbing an ice cream cake from Dairy Queen—my mom's secret guilty pleasure. Secret being a loose word, since we all know it's her weakness, even if she tries to hide it.

As we eat dinner, conversation flows. We talk about all kinds of things: life, Lucy's experiments, preparations for spring at the campground that Susan and Peter own, and Finn's usual shenanigans as he begs for food from everyone at the table before settling down beside Lucy's chair.

When the conversation turns to my work, I try to keep things minimal. Obviously, Lucy already knew everything, from me dumping all my heartbreak on her on the drive over here, so she helps pull the conversation away when it gets too close to things I don't want to share. Mom and Dad know about Brett, but I haven't had a chance to tell them that I'd broken things off with him yet.

After dinner, I go into the kitchen with my dad to help carry plates and get the cake ready with candles.

"Are you sure you're okay, Autumn? It sounds like things aren't going right at work. You don't sound happy. Everything okay with the job? How about with Brett?"

My dad's words hit me in the gut. He knows me better than anyone. Of course, he'd sense something was wrong.

"It's just... I broke things off with Brett this morning." I shrug, trying not to cry. I have never had issues telling my dad about relationships or anything in my life—he's always been my number one supporter and confidant. For some reason, I've always found it easier to go to him than to my mom. Maybe because I typically value logic over emotion.

"Do you want to talk about it?" he asks nervously, putting a hand on my shoulder. "If you don't, it's okay. Maybe not right now, but perhaps after supper. We can leave Lucy with your mom, and we can chat. I could give you some advice."

"You know what, Dad, that would be nice." I smile up at him. He gives me a soft grin back, nodding.

Without another word, he grabs the cake, lights the candles, and carries it into the dining room. As he steps through the doorway, everyone bursts into singing *Happy Birthday*.

Once the cake is eaten, Lucy and I are finishing up the dishes. I ask her if she can spend some time with my mom so I can talk with Dad.

"Of course. I got you. I love talking to Momma," Lucy says, kissing me on the cheek before trotting off to join my mom in the living room.

I walk out to the enclosed back porch, where my dad is already sitting with a glass of whiskey, waiting for me. He'd not only poured a glass of wine for me and had it waiting on the table, but he'd also started the outdoor stove so that the porch would be warm.

"Thanks, Dad," I say, taking a sip.

"Always, Honey. Now, what's going on?" He waits patiently for me to gather my thoughts so I can share what's happened with him.

"So... you and Mom know that I've been seeing Brett casually outside of work. I would definitely say we have a relationship, have since November, but it hasn't been anything too serious since it's only been a couple of months. I mean, I haven't even brought him here to meet you yet," I laugh.

"Yes, we know. Your mother wanted to stay and talk with him at the Fall Festival back in October, but I don't think you two were together at that point." He smiles and nods his head, listening intently.

"That's the guy. We have been spending a lot of time together at work, talking in the mornings or after everyone leaves at the end of the day, texting all hours of the night, and we even went to the New Year's Eve bash at Bobby's together." I smile, thinking back on how much fun I've had with Brett over the last few months.

My dad notices my grin and gives me a moment to think before I continue.

"Well... someone from Arch Engineering saw me at the bar with Brett. I didn't think anything of it, but this morning, Mr. Matthews sat me down in his office. He basically told me I couldn't have a relationship with Brett and said if I didn't end things, I'd lose my job."

My dad raises his eyebrows, listening carefully, shock clear in his features.

"So... I ended it. I told Brett we had to keep things professional. But Dad, I think I *love* him. It's going to kill me to see him at work every day and barely talk to him. We had something so special between us, and now it's gone. I don't know if it's worth risking my job, but... I just don't know what to do. Telling him that we had to be done this morning was the hardest thing I've ever done." The tears start flowing down my face as I let myself cry freely for the first time all day. My heart is hurting, and I don't want to pretend I'm okay anymore.

Dad sits in silence for a moment, thinking. "Did you tell him that you are ending things because of your job?"

I sniffle. "No, not outright. I told him that I need to focus on my work, so I don't miss things anymore, but I didn't tell him that Mr. Matthews said it was him or my job." I pull my sleeve down to wipe the snot from my nose.

"Well," my dad says slowly, "if you like him and you two work well together, then I don't see why you couldn't keep it professional at work. The rest, though—you've got to be careful. I know it's hard to have relationships on the job. Look at your mom and me. We worked together for years, but luckily, we were married before, so no one was really worried about us. I know it's hard, but John is probably just looking out for the job, thinking about what could happen if things went badly."

His logic makes sense, even though it isn't what I want to hear. But that's my dad—always levelheaded.

"Yeah," I say softly. "That actually helps. I think I've been letting my emotions cloud my brain. We might be able to still be friendly and keep it professional at work. Seeing him a little is better than not seeing him at all, even though it will feel a bit like torture, I'm sure." I laugh.

"Of course. Start there. Be friends, get through the job, and maybe things will be different when the work is done," he points out, giving me a warm smile.

I smile back at him. "Thanks, Dad. Really. I don't know what I'd do without you. I love you."

"I love you too, Sweetheart." He hugs me tight before I go back inside.

Later that night, after Lucy and I left, and I get settled back at my place, I sit down on my couch with my contracts spread out across the coffee table—both Arch Engineering's paperwork and the agreement with the company Tony's crew works for. I'm starting to move forward by searching for anything that mentions fraternization between employees. I want to make sure there's no policy in here that I missed since Mr. Matthews was so stern about everything this morning.

With a glass of milk and a plate of Oreos, because apparently the ice cream cake wasn't enough sugar, I read over every line. Nothing. No clause, no policy.

Technically, that means I'm in the clear. Legally, nothing is stopping me from being with Brett. But still... Mr. Matthews had been so adamant. Too adamant. And the only reason he even knew that I was with Brett in any capacity was because Colin had run his mouth. Why would he go to Mr. Matthews and tell him what he saw? We could have just been out with a group of friends, I mean, we pretty much were. It just didn't make sense.

Finally, exhausted, I decide to check my email before bed. Scrolling through quickly, I almost miss it—an email from Mr. Matthews that came through early this morning after I left his office. The subject line: *New Policy Update.*

My stomach drops. I already know what it will say before I even open it. Sure enough, four lines in:

> *"There will be absolutely no fraternization between fellow employees of Arch Engineering, between contractors and employees of Arch Engineering, or employees of contract companies for which Arch Engineering is hired."*

He's done it. Mr. Matthews created a brand-new policy this morning just to spite me. It hadn't existed two weeks ago. But it sure as hell did now.

Brett

"So, you gonna tell me what's been going on between you and the little engineer?" Tony looks at me while shoving a French fry in his mouth. Always the guy with the best manners.

I take a long drag of my beer, trying to think about what I want to say. I know Autumn is nervous about anyone with authority finding out about us being together, which is why she broke things off. I'm not sure how she'd feel if I told Tony. Ultimately, I decide that he already knows, so I sigh.

"Well, we did have something going, but she ended things about a month ago." I shrug, trying to sound nonchalant about it because the last thing I want is Tony to know how much I'm hurting. I was hoping that the break would get better with time, but every time I see her, it's like the wound is ripped open again. Which is so hard when we work together every damn day.

"Ah, knew something had you hurtin'. It wouldn't happen to be because of that asshole Matthews, would it?" He knows how John Matthews is—walks around like a big man with a tiny dick.

"Yep. Apparently, he found out that we were dating and spending time together outside of work and told Autumn that there was to be absolutely no fraternizing with me. So, she cut things off, ended it all." I'm broken and numb inside. Autumn wanted space, and I know she was just scared of her boss and what could happen with her job, especially since he launched that new policy Knox told me about.

"Oh, that explains the email I got a while back then," Tony chuckles. "Sent it out to all the employees at Arch and all our employees and contacts, too. Turns out they created a brand-new no-fraternization policy."

"Yup," I say, popping the "p" knowing that he did that simply because of us. "That fucker. He's been treating Autumn like shit. I'm gathering proof of it—all those meetings she's supposedly missed, all those important details? I have a fellow looking into it. I'm pretty sure it's because of him. I can't confirm yet, but I'll figure it out. I just can't believe he created a policy just to spite Autumn."

She's been avoiding me at work, trying to stay as far away as possible, which I understand. I've been giving her space. I know she's scared, and the last thing I want to do is push her further than she can handle. I'm being patient and going slow. Quietly, I'm gathering my details in the background so I can take John down—down to the pits of hell where he deserves to be.

"Yep, sounds like you did a little number on that one there. She used to be so cheery at work, teasing James for all his shit. Now she just mopes around all day, I can hardly stand to be with her for too long," Tony eyes me. "She's real heartbroken over this, I can tell." He takes a bite of the burger in front of him. We agreed to go out to Bobby's after work, just the two of us. He wanted to talk to me, and I assumed it would be about Autumn, but it feels good to get it off my chest with him.

"I hate knowing how much she's hurting, but I don't think she's really upset with me. If anything, she's upset with John and this whole situation. When we first started talking, I was so scared that she was going to use me like Brittany, but Autumn isn't like her at all. I shouldn't have assumed. She's always placed her job first but has never once indicated that she'd do anything but work hard on her own to get where she wants to be." I say with sincerity. Since the whole Brittany situation went down while I was on Tony's crew, he's familiar with it.

"She's not Brittany, that's for damn sure. Girl's a hell of a better worker. But she's young and this is her first job. According to John, she's nervous, but I wanna see her succeed. I know she can, she's smart, and she sure as shit knows what she's doing. I like watching her with the crew. Anyone who can handle James is a winner in my book. She's real flexible and learns on the fly. Hard to find that in an engineer nowadays, especially a young woman. So, I'm supporting her any way I can—and if that means keeping you away, then that's what it means." Tony nods.

I know what he's getting at, trying to tell me that I need to focus on the work and get it done as fast as I can so that I can get laid off, and then there will be no policies lingering between us, preventing us from getting what we want. "I saw you with Brittany; your actions toward Autumn are nowhere near the same. We'll get you both through this, man."

"I understand, Tony. I also wanna see her succeed. She's impressed me in the last few months, watching her on the job site. And she's kind, nice, and damn, she's so pretty." I smirk. "I mean, have you seen her? Well, don't tell me you've been looking at her. But she is attractive, Tony. She's everything I could ever dream of if I made my own perfect woman. I gotta do what I can to get her back. But yeah, I know—now that means waiting until the job's done."

"Yeah, Brett," Tony says, nodding. "You gotta wait till the job's done."

·· □□□□ ·□· □□□□ ··

That night, I'm in the barn helping my brother, sweeping up feed and making sure the cows get their silage.

"Man, I don't know what's going on with these guys. They're sick as heck. Some kind of weird bacteria, I think. Dad wants me to get it checked out at the university." Adam shakes his head. "I think I'll wait and go this fall to that world bacteria conference—you know the one? They'll probably have something there about what to do. We've been working with the vet to try and keep it under control," he continues, "and everybody's being treated for what we think's going on. But nothing's certain."

"Dad said you've seen a bunch of cows get sick the last week or two," I point out. "Think you can wait until fall, or do you need to do something now?"

"I think they can wait till fall. Like I said, the vet's got them on a treatment program now, and they're starting to get better. I just don't want to keep seeing them get sick. Hopefully, it dies off soon. We've been seeing fewer get sick, so maybe it's just a passing bug."

"Alright," I nod.

"Listen, I'm gonna go ahead and go inside now. Gran and Pa wanted to see you. Maybe you should pop over and let 'em know you're alive." Adam sets his fork down before turning back to me one last time.

"Yeah, I'll head over there." I laugh and wave at him. "Have a good night, Adam. See you tomorrow."

He nods and walks off. I head toward my grandparents' trailer at the back of the farm property. When Mom and Dad took over management of the farm when we were kids, Pa let them move into the main house, and he and Gran set up in the trailer. They've lived there ever since. I try to stop by at least once a week now that I'm home, but I haven't felt like going anywhere these last couple of weeks, and I've been staying close to my camper.

When I get there, Pa is sitting on the porch in his rocking chair, coffee in hand, with another empty mug beside him.

"Hey, Pa," I say, sitting in the chair next to him.

"Hey there, Brett. Your gran's inside. She was getting eaten by bugs, so she's getting a shower and going to bed. Tired tonight."

"That's fine. I can see her tomorrow." I cross my legs, settling into the chair beside him. "How you doin'?"

"Oh, I'm tired, but I'm old. What do you expect?" he laughs. Pa's always been funny—that hasn't changed. "So, are you gonna tell me about her?"

I blink. "Tell you about who?"

"The woman who's got your brain tied in knots. I know that look—you look forlorn, like somebody left you behind. You've been moping around the farm for weeks, barely coming to visit. I know that feeling. When your gran and I first dated, she left me not long after to go gallivanting with other boys. She came back, though. Those two years we were apart were the hardest of my life."

I laugh. "Well, since you know so well, yeah, there is a woman. But we aren't together right now. She doesn't want to be—for fear of losing her job."

"What'd you do to the poor girl?" Pa's eyes widen. "You didn't hurt her, did you? I'll be kicking your ass."

I throw my hands up. "No! I swear, I didn't hurt her. She hurt me. She came up to me at work—we work together—and told me we couldn't be together anymore. Said we had to be strictly coworkers. I know in her heart that's not what she wants, but what can I do? Then her company went and released a no-fraternization policy, brand new, just because of us. Now

I really can't get her back until I'm off the job. So, I'm just... chugging along, day by day."

"Brett, I'm gonna tell you something." Pa leans forward. "I just told you about your grandma and me. We spent time apart, but we came back together. When I tell you this, I mean it—you have to keep showing up for that woman. Every day. Put your best foot forward. Be kind. Be a friend. Even if that's all you can be right now. She'll be back. Trust me on that."

He pats the back of my hand. "I'm 85 years old, and I still show up for your gran every day. Bring her flowers, pour her a glass of wine, make sure she gets her shower when she's had a rough day. Her priorities come first. Whatever she wants, I push for. I defend her. And I know if you do the same things, it'll work out for you too."

He smiles, then stands. "Now, I'm gonna go show up for your grandma in her shower right now, so you go on and get outta here." He chuckles, and I wince, laughing to myself. "Keep in mind what I said, boy. Show up for your girl. Be there for her. Even when she says she wants you away—that's when she needs you most."

Pa heads inside, and I sit on the porch, thinking about what he said. He's right. All I have to do is keep showing up for Autumn—even if she doesn't know she needs me to.

Autumn

This work week has been extremely long, and I'm hoping that it's over soon. Tony wants to sit and talk with me about some updates on the job—sounds like we're getting close to the dirt work being finished, which is exciting to be moving onto the next stage of the project. Next, we need to think about getting a crane in here for building purposes: getting the foundation poured is the first step, then setting blocks, setting walls... before we know it, we'll have a building. It's really exhilarating to see progress being made on a job that I brought from an idea to reality.

Stepping into the job trailer as I type some thoughts on my Notes app, I don't look to see who's in there, just assuming it's only the boss. "Hey, Tony," I call, finally glancing up, placing my phone into my back pocket, and taking my hat off.

It's only Brett inside. "Oh. hey, Brett," I say nervously.

I haven't been nervous around Brett for months, but all of a sudden, since the breakup, I have been. He has respected my request and hasn't been bringing me coffee in the morning, and he's been giving me the distance I asked for. He only asks me questions that are important for the task at hand—work-related stuff—when he can't ask Tony.

It's a strange shift, but I'm thankful for it because I'm still very much attracted to Brett in every sense. He's kind, funny, and watching him laugh with the guys shatters me inside. Not to mention, he's the most handsome person I've ever seen in my life.

And while Brett continues to show up and be helpful, I've shut down. I don't feel like joking with the guys or going to the restaurant anymore. I barely even go to the bar with Lucy. I just want to stay busy and focus on my work. I put my head down and power through. I only chat with folks when I need to and spend a lot more time at the office down at Arch than I used to. It's just easier to be away from here—where Brett is—because just being near him is ungodly distracting, I'm worried I'm going to say something I shouldn't.

"Hey, Autumn, Tony isn't in here," Brett chuckles, and I smile slightly in return.

"I was just grabbing some flags, and I'm heading back out now, so I won't keep you," he says and walks out of the trailer.

As he leaves, I try to peek after him—only to be caught by Tony. "Hey Autumn, let's chat," he calls, pulling my attention away from Brett's fine ass wandering away.

"So, it seems like we'll have the dirt work done in about a month," Tony begins. "We need to get the crane ordered now so we know when we can set it here. We have to get the mats and everything we need to set it on. Also, I need to ensure I have an operator." I frown.

"Brett isn't going to be the operator?" I ask, curious.

Tony shakes his head. "Oh... he could be, he just won't. He refuses to get his crane certification, and therefore, I can't have him on this job. We're stuck with needing a crane operator—so I think we're going with ol' James, the fun guy. Long as his cert is up to date. Can you find out?"

"Oh boy," I mutter.

"Yeah, James is a handful, but he can operate a crane, so I'm fine with that. It's easier than trying to find someone else and bring them in," Tony continues, rolling his eyes.

He goes over logistics and details, but my mind is elsewhere. Brett isn't going to stick around. If Brett leaves, he's not an employee here; therefore, being with him wouldn't be fraternizing or breaking the policy. A spark of hope ignites in my chest. I just need to make it through this next month.

Tony keeps talking, giving me everything I need to contact the CAT company and get the crane out here. If not, I'll contact Doosan for an alternative, but that's okay—it's probably cheaper anyway. I gather my supplies and head back to the office to organize myself. I can't stay here with the buzzing excitement of knowing Brett might be done with work soon—I need to get away from him and get my thoughts straight before I decide what I want to do.

·· ▢▢▢▢ ·▢· ▢▢▢▢ ··

A few days of phone call after phone call to get the crane details organized, and I'm feeling like I've finally reached my breaking point. Sitting up in my chair, I feel my back crack and decide I need to get out and stretch my legs. It'll be good for me to find James so I can ask him about his cert anyway. It's easier to ask him rather than call the hall and check through their paperwork; I'll be on hold for hours.

Outside, I look around and find James walking toward the second excavator we have on the site. I call to him to get his attention before he climbs inside.

"Oh, hey, little boss lady, what's up?" He asks, smiling at me and putting his sunglasses back on his face.

"Tony wanted me to ask you if your crane certification was up to date. We need to get an operator sorted, and he was hoping not to have to bring in someone new." I say, crossing my fingers behind my back, that he'll say everything is good.

"Ah shit, I know it's out of date. I wanted to get it redone before I started this job, but the class at the training site was full, so they couldn't get me in, so I'll have to wait until summer." He makes a nervous face. "Tony's gonna hate me, ain't he?"

I laugh, "Only a little, it'll be okay. It's me you have to worry about because now I gotta find an operator." Shoving him with my hand, he catches himself and puts his hands up.

"Alright, alright, you can have your way with me. I insist," he laughs and wiggles his eyebrows suggestively.

"Fat chance, James." I roll my eyes at him. "Get your ass in that hoe and get back to work before I decide to go find Tony and give him the news in front of ya."

"Yes, ma'am!" He shouts and salutes me before turning to climb into his machine. I laugh and shake my head. That man is quite the character.

Walking back to the job trailer, I see Pam, the truck driver, standing outside her rig smoking a cigarette. I walk over to her.

"Hey Pam!" I shout, waving to get her attention. Now that I'm done holding him hostage, James is getting ready to load dirt into the bed, so the sound of the machines makes it quite loud out here.

"Hey there, girl!" Pam shouts, cigarette hanging out of the corner of her mouth. We've interacted a handful of times, and every time she has been a hoot.

"Is this your last load?" I ask, glancing at my watch, noting that it's 4:30.

"Probably. Little Jamie here takes forever to load me, so we don't get as much done as I would like, but that's not really my problem now, is it?" She laughs and coughs as she blows smoke out of her lungs. "Man, these things will really kill ya."

I laugh because I never know what will come out of her mouth next. "Yeah, I suppose they will."

Settling in next to her, we watch James for a couple of buckets, but my attention is drawn to the excavator operator across the site. I miss him, and it kills me to be here with him every day knowing that we can't be together. Knowing the dirt work should be done soon and he'll soon be off the job has been the only thing getting me through the day.

"You gonna go over there and undress him, or you just gonna eyefuck him from here?" Pam asks, lifting her hand with the cigarette toward Brett's machine.

I turn and look at her wide-eyed. "Oh, come on, everyone on this crew knows you two were together and that fuckwad John over at Arch ruined it. There ain't a soul here who wasn't cheering for you two. Especially after what happened to that poor guy before," she says with all the confidence in the world. I'm getting the idea that dislike of Mr. Matthews is more of a common thing than I realized. But something she says catches me off guard.

"Wait, what happened to him before?" I ask, curious.

"That girl the whole town thought he was gonna marry went and screwed the steward while on the job site. Ruined the poor boy's brain and chased him clean outta town for years." She says, taking another puff on her cigarette and turning to look at James. "Hey! It's full!" She shouts at him, walking toward him, waving her arms before reaching for her radio to let him know to stop putting dirt in the bed.

What she said shocked me. I didn't know Brett had been hurt by a woman on the job before. It explains why he was out of town for so long, but makes me feel like a total idiot for what I've done to him in this whole situation. If I had known, I wouldn't have started anything with him. I should've kept my distance from Brett to protect both his heart and mine.

As I'm heading toward my vehicle, I hear someone yell. "Hey Autumn!" I turn to see Brett smiling, and he's jogging toward me.

"How did your meeting with Tony go this morning?" he asks, smiling.

"It went well," I reply. "We discussed needing the crane soon, so I've been working to straighten out those details and get it ordered."

"Ah, that's great. Who's he getting to operate?" Brett looks happy. He takes his gloves off and shoves them in his back pocket.

"Not sure yet. James was supposed to be it, but his cert isn't up to date, of course," I laugh. I haven't found Tony yet to tell him that we need to look for someone else, so I'm not really looking forward to that conversation.

"Tony will probably have you hire Alice if she's available." Brett laughs, crossing his arms in front of me. "She's quite a handful, but she's a really good crane operator and great teacher. You'd like her." That makes me smile, and soon we're chuckling together like old friends. I'm really glad things aren't too awkward between us and that we can still work together. I can feel myself easing up a little as we talk. Brett just treating me normally helps me relax.

"Did Tony tell you how long we have left on the dirt work?" He asks, getting a more serious tone and expression on his face.

"Yeah, he said it should be all finished in about a month." I shift my papers from one arm to the other. I feel like the conversation just verged into dangerous territory, and I'm nervous to see what Brett will say.

"That's great." He leans forward and gets very close to me to whisper in my ear. "Think about what that means for us." And with that, he backs away and waves. "See ya later, Autumn."

I stand there open-mouthed and in shock, because he clearly still wants to be with me after everything that went down between us. Why else would he have said that? And the mention of this brings so much excitement to my veins, I may just start counting down the days.

Brett

Standing in line first thing this morning at the coffee shop, my phone lights up with a text from Knox. I had texted him a few days ago, and he said he would get back to me as soon as he had more info.

Knox:
> Got those docs you mentioned, my man.

Brett:
> Nice, thanks. Could you send them to me here?

Knox:
> I'll send over more details I have later. Found proof that it was your guy who edited Autumn's email, too. Still working on how to get that.

4 pictures received

Brett:
> Owe you one, buddy.

Knox:
> More than one, lol.

I scan through the photos I got from Knox. He managed to get the full original blueprints from the 811 company that were sent to John Matthews at Arch Engineering, with all the appropriate details for the utilities. Complete, along with proof that the document was edited and a portion of it was cut out before being emailed to Autumn. This is impeccable proof that I can use to show John has been hiding information from her, possibly even sabotaging her.

If Knox can get proof that John edited her email and sent it to Johnny, I'll be 100% set to take him down. Ideally, I could get John to admit he doesn't like Autumn or that he did this. Maybe I can have a conversation with him, man-to-man, and see what happens.

"Morning, Brett! The usual?" Sydney chimes, pulling my attention from my phone.

"Ah, morning, Syd. Yeah, and can you add the second coffee to my order too?" I nod, tapping my card on the reader to process the payment.

"Things looking up for you with the mysterious 'A' again? You haven't gotten that drink in a little while." Sydney chuckles as she pours two cups of coffee, adding the cream and sugar to Autumn's.

"Things are stalled at the moment, but a very smart man reminded me that if you want to get the girl, you gotta keep showing up for her." I smile and take the coffees from off the counter where she slid them to me.

"Ugh, well, whoever she is, she is so lucky," Sydney swoons, emphasizing the *so* in her college-girl accent. Sydney is a great barista but definitely has those valley-girl vibes. She'd do well out in the big city once she's older.

"Have a good day, Syd." I laugh as I walk out the door, the bell chiming above me.

As I drive to the job site, I think about all the things I could say to Autumn. I could pour my heart out, tell her how I really feel, and let her know I'll do anything to stay with her. But the truth is, I want this job, and I want to still work with her. If that means sacrificing anything with her to protect her and not mess up her job, then I'll suck it up. I'm still going to do as my Pa suggested and show up for her. I'll start to bring her coffee again, help her with plans when she lets me, sit in the job trailer with her, have lunch, and put forth my best effort to just be her friend if that's all I can be. Knowing that I only have about a month left gives me something to look forward to through it all.

Arriving in the parking lot, I see Autumn is already here. Hers is the only other car in the lot, as usual. I climb out of my truck, carrying both coffees, and head toward the job trailer.

"Morning, Autumn," I smile, walking in the door and holding out her cup.

She looks at me, confused. I know I haven't gotten her coffee in a long while, but like I said, I'm just going to keep showing up for her.

"Thank you, Brett... maybe you should give that to Tony instead," she says, trying to push me away.

"Nope. Tony brings his own coffee—his wife makes it for him every morning. This is for you. Ain't no harm in a friend getting coffee for another," I nudge the cup toward her again. She hesitantly reaches out and takes it. I sit down in the chair next to her.

"Okay... well, thank you," she says. "I haven't been having coffee, I've been having tea, so I'm surviving. But this is so much better." She inhales deeply, a slight moan escaping her lips. "This smells heavenly. Thank you for this. I am very grateful."

"You got it. I'm going to keep bringing you coffee from here on out. It's the least I can do as your friend and your nicest coworker." I laugh, holding up my cup and toasting hers. "So, what's on the agenda for today?" I ask.

She smiles and looks down at the papers in front of her. "Well, I'm finalizing everything that's going on, and I believe the crane's being delivered today, so we're going to be getting that set up," she says, flipping through them.

"Okay, cool. So, the dirt work's just about done anyway, right? I think there are just a couple of trucks to haul out, and then it's mostly setting the building—starting with pouring the foundation, right?" I ask, sitting across from her with my forearms resting on the table, holding my coffee.

"Uh, yes. It appears that way. The dirt work is pretty much done—you're right. About five truckloads of dirt to haul out, then it's just working on the building. I think our crane operator is starting today for training since the crane's being delivered. We wanted to get her started early. From my understanding, she's a great operator and should get through training quickly," Autumn says, emphasizing she.

I notice the pride in her voice. Autumn has always been proud to be a woman in this field, and I know she likes connecting with other strong women on site. "Okay, cool. It's Alice, ain't it?" I ask casually.

"Yep, just like you guessed," she replies. I nod silently.

Alice Rupert. I know her. She's a steady operator and takes young engineers under her wing. Good. Autumn will have support while the dirt work wraps up, and I'm no longer here to guide her through.

Just then, Tony walks into the trailer.

"Morning, Brett," he says, nodding. "The first dirt truck is supposed to be here at 7:00 a.m. sharp, so you might want to get your machine ready."

"Yes, sir, Mr. Bossman," I say, standing and saluting him, heading for the door. He starts laughing, shaking his head at me. "Catch you around, Autumn!" I call as I step outside.

The day flies by. I load trucks, supervise the crane delivery, and make sure it's set up safely. Alice shows up, teasing me and embarrassing me in front of Autumn—but it makes a good impression on her. I'm glad they seem to be getting along already.

At the end of the day, I see Autumn leaning against her Jeep, arms crossed, staring at me. I walk over. "Hey, Hotshot.

What's up? You clearly want something," I ask, leaning against the front of her Jeep.

"You didn't tell me you knew Alice personally. I thought you just knew of her as a crane operator," she laughs, leaning against the hood.

"Oh yeah, we've crossed paths at the Union Training Academy and worked a couple of job sites together. She's a good lady," I say, smiling. "A good one to have in your corner."

"Yeah, she seems super nice. I already really like her. But... I wanted to chat with you. You can't bring me coffee, you can't have lunch with me, you can't do all the things you've been doing because I need you to keep your distance. I told you before I can't risk losing my job and being near you. It makes me lose my head. I can't do this."

Autumn starts rambling, flailing her arms, clearly lost. I cut her off, looking her straight in the eyes. She's trying to push me away, just like Pa said she'd do.

"Autumn... I'm not keeping my distance from you. The dirt work is almost over. I'll be back in those panties before you know it."

Autumn

I'M SITTING AT MY desk in Arch Engineering, and I absolutely cannot focus today. My brain is still reeling from when Brett told me that he would be back in my panties soon—a sentence that had sent my thoughts spinning.

I haven't had lunch yet, so I start thinking about going out to grab something to eat from the coffee shop. They sometimes have little premade wraps that are pretty good. I'll grab one of those on my way to the job site and eat it in the job trailer.

I start gathering my things, trying to think about how my life ended up here. I'm working a job I love, but at the risk of losing a relationship with the man I love. Everything feels topsy-turvy. I like working for Arch Engineering and doing my engineering work, but at what cost? It's something I need to think about. I'll keep pushing Brett aside to keep this job for now—it's my first—but once I finish this one, I need to figure out what I want to do.

I don't love the policies at Arch, and I don't love the way I'm treated here. Mr. Matthews really bothers me. We don't get along well, and he favors Colin. We clearly do the same level of work, but Colin gets all the good feedback, and I get the brunt of the stick. I'm often asked to bring coffee and donuts to meetings and handle secretary duties that aren't part of the job I signed up for. I like the comfort and safety of working under a firm, but I'm not sure this is the right one for me.

I don't really want to start out on my own—I don't have the skill set, the bandwidth, or the client backing—but I need to consider my future. Maybe that means looking somewhere else, another town, another engineering company, maybe even moving toward the city. The problem is, I love the small-town life. I love getting to know everyone around me, having a small crew, and being close to home. I do want to travel and see the world, I don't want to be stuck in Mayfield forever, but I'm torn.

I grab my keys off the desk and pick up my bag, heading to my car. Passing by Colin's desk, I see him sitting there, looking like he hasn't done a lick of work all morning, with an empty takeout box on his desk. He's pretending to work, making himself look busy while I toil away, working my ass off and facing challenges he'll never dream of. It's frustrating—but I remind myself: I'm doing better by working harder.

Once I arrive at the coffee shop, I walk in and the bell chimes. Sydney, my favorite barista ever, is behind the counter.

"Hey, Sydney. How are you?" I say, looking at the premade wraps in the deli case. They're handmade, locally sourced, and rolled up neatly with price tags. I grab the last remaining Italian sun-dried tomato basil wrap—definitely my favorite.

"Oh, hey Autumn! I'm good, how are you?" Sydney smiles, bringing my wrap to the counter.

"I'm doing okay. Just this," I say, placing the wrap on the counter. "Oh, and I'll also do a coffee with two creams and two sugars."

Her eyes go wide. She squeals. "Oh. My. God. You—OMG! You are—" She's shaking her hands, jumping up and down like she just realized something. I'm confused.

"What are you talking about, Syd?" I ask, pulling out my wallet.

"Okay, so every morning Brett—you clearly know Brett—he comes in here and he gets two coffees: one black, and one with two creams and two sugars. One time, I asked him who the second coffee was for, and he said it was 'A.' He's never denied that it was a *her*. In fact, yesterday he said things were back on with him and 'A,' and he's going to keep 'showing up for her' because that's 'how you get the girl.'" She mocks his voice, trying to make hers sound deeper, and giggles at herself.

"Oh... wow." I'm starting to piece things together.

"Yes! You're 'A'! You're working with him at the Whitewater University job, right? He comes super early every morning to get you your coffee." She pours my coffee into a to-go cup and slides it across the counter.

"Uh, yeah. Brett does get me coffee from here every morning," I say, feeling my cheeks heat.

"Oh. My. God. He is totally head over heels for you. That guy is in love! He's never ever late and so reliable. Ugh, girl! You are so lucky!" Sydney laughs, wiggling her eyebrows.

I grab my coffee nervously. "Yeah, uh, well, thanks, Syd. I'll see ya around." I start walking toward the door.

"Have a good day! Say hi to Brett for me!" Sydney waves.

As I drive to the job site, I'm still processing. Brett gets me coffee every morning, but he actually talks about me to the barista? If I had known, I would've told him not to—Syd is the biggest gossip ever. But it's cute. He likes me. Considering he was there yesterday telling her he'd continue showing up for me, that explains him bringing me the coffee again despite my insistence not to, his desire to sit with me in the job trailer, and being nice after work. He's respecting the space I asked for while still being my friend. I'm grateful.

Once I park my Jeep and head to the job trailer, it's empty. I text Tony to see if he can stop by for lunch. A knock at the door frame pulls me out of my thoughts—Brett is standing there, half-eaten lunch in hand.

"Hey, there you are! I didn't think you'd be here for lunch. I was going to eat in my machine, but then I saw you walking over. Thought I should eat with you," he rambles, setting his lunch on the table. His meal is wholesome and balanced—then there's me, my premade wrap, and coffee.

I take a look at his meal and then look up at him. "I guess we can't all be put together," I say, laughing.

"Yeah, I know. But, Autumn, I have fantastic news for you!" Brett starts.

"Brett…" I begin. He sounds far too excited for anything, and I hope he's not trying to spring something else on me today. I'm having too many emotions run wild after what I learned from Sydney.

"Wait, wait, let me say this. It's really important news." He looks at me, waiting for confirmation.

"Okay, yeah, alright," I nod.

"I'm getting laid off today!" Brett says, excitement all over his face.

"Wait, you're excited about getting laid off?" I ask, confused.

"Yes. There's someone on this job I like, but I'm limited in what I can do. Now, with being laid off, things will change—we can spend more time together." His hope is written all over him.

I smile widely at him. It's the first sincere smile I've been able to give him in months. "Now I got you. That wouldn't happen to be a blonde engineer for Arch Engineering, would it? Because I can call Colin to come over if you want," I tease, shoving him on the shoulder to make him laugh.

Brett laughs a hearty laugh. "Yeah, go ahead and do that. Definitely call him." He's definitely in a better mood, and it's transferring to me. Today is starting to look up.

I laugh. "All I gotta do is make one quick phone call, and your wildest dreams can come true."

Brett and Frank both got laid off yesterday, which was great. They didn't want to transition to other machines, so Tony let them go. Luckily, we have Alice and James, who can operate literally anything.

I love Alice, and getting to know her has been so fun. Since she started on the job, she's become one of my closest friends and quite possibly my "replacement Brett" on the job. She's been the one who's been in my corner and always reminds me that I can do this job.

She's also been there for me to listen to my complaints every time I get into it with the safety guy, Bob. He's the one guy on this crew that I cannot seem to get along with. We just don't work the same. I get that sometimes there will be people like that on jobs, so it's kind of nice that I'm getting this experience of people who like me and people who don't like me. It's preparing me for any future jobs.

I'm sitting in the job trailer when Alice walks in and sits down in the chair next to me. "Hey, girl."

"Hey, Al. How's it going?" I ask.

"Oh, you know. It's fucking going. Just taking a break, thought I'd come in here and see my favorite girl. How are you holding up? Heard Brett got laid off yesterday."

Surprisingly, when Alice first started here, I opened up to her pretty quickly. I told her everything that went down with Brett. She's the only one on the whole crew I've told, so she knows I've been kind of a mess the past few weeks. Luckily, she's been really supportive and helping me keep my head up so I can focus on work.

"Yeah, he did. Today he's doing some stuff on his family's farm. We've been texting on and off." Brett was done with work yesterday afternoon, but we didn't get a chance to talk after because he had to go help his brother with a cow emergency. Something about a heifer caught out on pasture, so I let him go and said we'd talk later.

"Are you guys back together?" She asks tentatively. I know she's been rooting for Brett to get laid off for the last few weeks, so that we could get back together. I had told her how adamant I was about waiting until he was off the job to try to have a relationship again. The wait was long and torturous, but I think it was better to do it that way than risk getting in trouble with my boss.

"We haven't had a chance to talk about it yet, but hopefully we can soon." I cough into my hand in turn to blow my nose into a tissue. My allergies have been awful today, and I feel like I've been run over by a train. I've been coughing and blowing my nose so much I think I've gone through a whole box of tissues.

"Girl, why are you here today? You look terrible, you sound terrible, it's clear that you're sick as hell. You'd better take tomorrow off." Alice says, overdramatically leaning back from me so I can't cough on her.

I laugh and shrug. "There's work to be done."

"There's always work to be done," Alice argues. "You take one day off, rest and get better, and the work will be here when you get back."

"I really don't think I'm sick. I'm pretty sure it's just allergies. This spring weather really gets to me." I say, wiping my nose with yet another tissue.

"I don't care what it is," Alice says. "You need to take care of yourself, and who knows, maybe if it is just allergies, then you can spend some time with your man. Ya know, get him back. It's been how long now since you guys have been together? Take the day, spend a little time together, have a lot of sex, and get better. Then you can come back to work freshly fucked and happy." Alice cackles. She's a lot older than me, and her advice is to always just have sex and the world will be better again. She doesn't know that I've never had sex before, but the advice is still appreciated.

"I suppose I could take the day off and spend it with Brett tomorrow. I haven't taken a day off since I started." I shrug. "Alright. I'll text Tony and let him know I'm gonna be off tomorrow. I'm sure he'll be fine with that."

"That's right, you take care of yourself, and you win back your man!" Alice cheers, fist pumping into the air. She's right. I'm going to take some time to recuperate and enjoy spending time with my man.

Brett

I KNOCK GENTLY ON the door, hoping I'm not being too loud or waking her up. After a few phone calls, Tony let me know that Autumn didn't come to work this morning. She told him she was sick and needed the day off. I hope that's not true. I hate the idea of her being sick and all alone. I wish she had texted me about it. Regardless, I mentioned it to Mom, and so she whipped up some soup and tea. I'm holding both containers in my arms when the door swings open.

"Autumn." I gasp, my voice rough and desperate. "Tony said you're sick today."

She giggles. "Yeah, I had some allergy issues yesterday, but thankfully, they're remedied today. I'm actually glad you're here. I was going to call you and invite you over to hang out anyway. I wanted to talk about us."

"Oh, thank goodness." The relief washes over me. "I want to talk about us, too. But also, I have proof!" I say, and confusion mars her features.

"Proof of what, exactly?" She lets the door fall open and waves her arm to invite me inside. She's wearing a little black robe, paper-thin. I can see her nightgown underneath—not a grandma one, but lacy and sexy, hugging all her curves. My hands itch to touch her, but I know we need to talk first.

"John has been keeping information from you. Tony shared all the emails between John and him with me. John had all the correct dates and times for the meetings. If we get your emails and texts, we can prove he withheld information on purpose. He's even been texting a fake number, pretending it's you—but we have it." I spill everything, slipping off my boots while she holds the soup and tea.

"Wow. Brett. I don't know what to say. Uh, come in. Is this soup? And tea?" She wraps the robe tighter and slowly walks to her kitchen counter. I see a steaming cup of coffee on the counter; she must have made a whole pot this morning since she intended to invite me over.

"Yeah, that's from my mom. I told her you were sick, so of course she had to whip up soup and some flu tea. But anyway, I think we have everything we need for proof to take John to court, if that's what you want, of course. I've been working with someone I know—a friend of my little brother Adam's, actually—who does some covert and discreet hacking. I don't know if anything that we have is legal in that regard, but we have enough that we got legally for a lawyer to question the rest. Then they can go through and find the rest of the information legally, and you'll have everything you need." I place my arm on the island in front of me and look up at her, where she is still standing, trying to take this all in.

"Knox has helped me prove that John edited the blueprint files, deleting the segment from the 811 map that caused you to mess up the plans on the first day. And he's been texting a fake number, claiming it's you. And I believe that one, because John showed me conversations where he texted you and you never responded to him, and that didn't feel like you." I chuckled slightly, knowing that Autumn always texts back.

"Oh. Uh, yeah. Every time Mr. Matthews texted me, I always answered. So that's definitely not right. And if he's sending me notifications about meetings via text, I definitely didn't get it." She sits next to me, grabbing her coffee and taking a small sip.

"This is overwhelming," she says, "but I feel a lot of relief. I know now that missing all of those details and meetings was not my fault, and it hasn't been my fault."

"Do you want to go forward legally with this? We have all the information—we can confront John." I sit in the chair next to her, taking her shoulders to make her face me. "Autumn, are you okay?"

She looks at me with sad, puppy-dog eyes, warring with herself. "I don't know, Brett. I just...I think this job is hard. I don't feel like I can be successful. I'm afraid I'm letting people down. I've wanted to do well, but I keep making mistakes. I missed a form for the concrete delivery yesterday, almost causing a huge delay that would've been costly."

I open my arms, and she leans into me. I take a deep inhale of her hair. She smells like home.

I tilt her chin up. "Autumn, you are more than capable. I know it's hard, but you're one of the strongest people I know. Do you know how I know?" She whimpers, shaking her head. "Tony says the job is going extremely well. He's happy with the progress—that means you're doing a great job. The crew likes you. Enrique and James are obsessed with you—they get along with you so well. You weaseled your way right into our group, and you did it flawlessly. You're a wonderful woman and an incredible engineer. I'm so proud of you."

I want to kiss her and make her feel so much better, but first, we need to talk.

"Aut," I stop pulling back to look into her eyes. "What about us? We need to talk about it." I say, worry on my face. I know she's fallen into me, and she's grateful for the information, but that doesn't mean she wants to be in a relationship with me again. A lot has happened in the last few weeks, and things could have changed.

"I still want this, Brett. If you want this, there's nothing I want more than to be in a relationship with you that doesn't revolve around work." She chuckles, looking up at me. I breathe a huge sigh of relief, and I know she can feel it.

She wraps her arms around my neck, standing on her tiptoes to kiss me. She deepens the kiss, and I swipe my tongue along her lips, asking for entry. She obliges, and I dive in further. She tastes like coffee and cinnamon. I am going to make this moment unforgettable—right here, right now. I'm going to show her just how much I want this with her.

I moan, and she turns her head to the side. I kiss along her jawline, down her neck, licking, biting, sucking, pushing her into a frenzy. Our hands roam under shirts. Before I know it, she breaks the kiss, grabs my hand, and starts leading me down her hallway toward her bedroom.

Entering her room, I see a soft, modern vibe: pale greens, complete organization, deep oak furniture, and a matching green-and-white rug. She leads me to her bed. We sit side by side. She pauses, unsure.

I lift her head gently, meeting her gaze. I lean in, kissing her passionately. Autumn begins pushing me back onto the mattress. As soon as I'm flat on my back, with her straddling me and trying to remove my shirt, I pause, grabbing her wrists to hold her still.

"Autumn, I know you haven't done this before. Are you sure you want to do this?"

She looks into my eyes, and her answer is two words that undo me completely:

"I'm sure."

Autumn

What am I doing? I have no idea how to do what I'm about to do, and panic ensues in my head. I am going to have sex with Brett, and I am so excited about it. But I'm also so nervous. What if I'm bad at this? What if I don't satisfy him?

I look down at him lying under me on the bed. I've just told him that I want to do this, and he's looking at me like I hung the moon. He cups the back of my neck and pulls me down to kiss him. His tongue traces my bottom lip, and I part my lips to allow him entry. He swipes his tongue through my mouth, and a small groan escapes him. I like that he's vocal in bed; it lets me know that he's enjoying this as much as I am.

"Let's get this off of you." He tugs at the bottom of my nightgown, lifting it over my head. He tosses it off the bed somewhere on the floor. Usually, I care about messes, but in this moment, Brett could trash my whole house, and I wouldn't care as long as he keeps looking at me like that and touching me the way he is. He's running his fingers up the sides of my body, and I can feel the goosebumps forming.

"Autumn," Brett gasps and grabs my breasts with his hands. "You are fucking perfect. Look at these tits, they're beautiful." He sits up, letting me fall backward on the bed until he's on top of me. He drops his head to my breasts and takes my right nipple in his mouth. He sucks and licks softly, and my head tilts back in ecstasy.

"Oh my God, Brett. Wow, don't stop doing that." I moan loudly while running my hands up his body, along his arms, through his hair, pretty much anywhere I can touch him. I feel him chuckle against my nipple before placing a gentle kiss on it and moving over to the other. This one he sucks and licks just like the other, but before he pulls his head back, he takes the nipple between his teeth and gives it a little bite. I gasp and moan, pulling tight on his hair.

"Brett!" I yelp. "Oh!" He picks his head up to look at me.

"I didn't hurt you, did I?" He looks nervous, afraid he's hurt me.

"No, I just wasn't expecting that, but it felt amazing." I pull him down to kiss me again, and I pull his shirt up, breaking our kiss only momentarily to slide it over his head. I run my hands all over his body. He is fit but still has some chubbiness to his body. He feels perfect under my hands and fingers, and he has charming amounts of body hair all over his chest, abdomen, and back.

He reaches down to the hem of my panties and pulls them off of me, tossing them somewhere in my room over his shoulder. I start to laugh.

"What's so funny, Hotshot?" He laughs, nipping and kissing at my thighs.

"Oh, just admiring how much of a mess you're making in here." I smack him on the shoulder and push him backward. "Time to get yours off."

I unbuckle his belt and unbutton his jeans, pulling them down his thighs, revealing his plaid boxers. His legs are also hairy.

"You are one of the hairiest men I've ever seen." I smile at him. "I did not think that I would find body hair sexy, but this is doing something to me." Rubbing my hand down his chest, he growls.

"Yeah, well, you rubbing my chest hair does something to me, too, Autumn. I'm very sensitive there." He says, grabbing my wrist and pushing me back on the bed. He kisses down my chest and abdomen, stopping right at the bottom of my stomach. He looks up at me one last time for confirmation. Once I nod, he places his nose right over my pussy and inhales like he cannot get enough of the scent of me.

"Fuck, Autumn. You smell so damn good. I cannot wait to eat this pussy." He hovers just over me, and I can feel his hot breath on me.

"*Brett*," I moan with a gasp. "Please!" I'm not above begging to get him to touch me.

"Please what, baby?" He blows a cool breath across me, causing me to shiver.

"Please touch me, lick me, I don't care. Just do something!" I'm desperate to feel him on my skin. Before I have time to think again, he runs his tongue completely up my center. I gasp and pull back from him, only for him to grab my ass and pull me forward.

"Oh no, you don't. You're staying right here, and I'm devouring this pussy." He says before continuing to lick and suck directly on my labia, finding my clit underneath it all with ease. Brett makes a complete meal out of me, licking and sucking, lapping up all of my juices with his tongue. I feel the tightness in my belly growing as he places a finger at the edge of my entrance and wets it with my arousal and his saliva mixed.

He pushes slowly inside of me and pulls back out, placing a second finger with it before pushing both back inside. Once his fingers are all the way in, he curls them with precision, hitting that magic spot that he found before that caused me to squirt all over him in the bar bathroom. He continues to suck on my clit while curling his fingers inside of me, and my orgasm builds fast.

"Brett, I'm gonna come." I barely get the words out between gasps; it feels like heaven with him fingering my pussy. He picks up the pace, sucking harder with his mouth, and when I feel like I'm about to pass out, my release hits me, washing through me with such hot electricity. I feel the release as my pussy squirts all over his face. Brett takes it all in open-mouthed, catching what he can and wearing the rest like a reward all over his skin. He stops fingering me and instead rubs his fingers over my clit quickly, causing even more to squirt out from my body.

"God baby, you are perfect. That is amazing, I fucking love it." He praises me.

"Brett, I know you love that, but I'm gonna need you to fuck me *now*," I emphasize, desperate with the need to feel his cock inside of me. He pauses, unsure, looking around, and I place a hand on his arm. "No condoms, I want to feel you. I'm on birth control, it's okay."

"Okay, Hotshot. Whatever you need, Babygirl." He kisses me quickly before getting himself situated. "I'm going to go slow, and you need to tell me if I hurt you at all. I'm not exactly small for someone to be taking for the first time."

I smack him on the shoulder for his cocky comment, but I know he's right. His cock is big. It filled my entire mouth and then some when I gave him the blowjob at work. If he can use that as well as he can his fingers, my pussy is definitely going to be wrecked.

He places his head at my entrance and slowly begins to push inside. The sensation is tight and full, with a little bit of pain. But the pleasure that courses through me as he pushes in and out just that little bit is overpowering all other feelings.

"Brett, please," I beg. Clawing my hands on his back, pulling him into me as close as possible, I moan loudly when he sinks deeper inside of me.

"Fuck Autumn. You're so tight, it feels so good. I gotta go slow or I'm gonna come. I just need a minute." Brett gets all the way inside me and pauses. I've never felt this full in my life, but the sensation is painful with glorious pleasure.

"Brett. Move." I say more sternly, beginning to move my own hips, desperate for the glorious friction that I need between us. He begins to slide in and out, muttering praises of "good girl" and "that's it, baby" in my ear while he's pressed tight against my body.

He leans up, bracing his one arm on the headboard, using the new angle to take in all of my body. Everything feels so good, and he's being so gentle and slow, and it feels like heaven. If this is what sex with Brett is like, I never want to do anything else for the rest of my life. What could top this?

"Brett, that feels so good. You're gonna make me come again, baby." I saw, running my fingers through his hair and down his arms.

"Good, I want you to come again on my cock this time before I come." He grunts out, picking up the pace of his thrusts. While looking me directly in the eyes, he reaches down with his other hand and begins to rub my clit. The pleasure that evokes in my body is unreal, and I know my orgasm is seconds away.

"Fuckkkkk," I say, moaning loudly as I begin to squeeze his dick.

"Yes, baby. That's it. Come on, this cock." He says, and as soon as I hear him say cock, my body explodes. I close my eyes, feeling the sensation running through my entire body, releasing the breath I held while my orgasm was building, my breathing is shallow and fast, and before I have time to think, I feel Brett tighten above me and grunt as he comes inside of me with one final, sloppy thrust.

He presses his head into the pillow next to me, taking a minute to recover. I feel him kiss me behind the ear and up the side of my face until he meets me on the mouth.

"Autumn, you are the most incredible woman I have ever met. That was amazing. I want to do this with you for as long as you'll let me." He looks at me with worry in his eyes, his vulnerability in this moment very clear.

"Brett, baby. You aren't doing the dirt work anymore. I'll do this with you as long as you'll have me," and I kiss him into oblivion.

Twenty minutes later, we go for round two until we both fall asleep wrapped up in each other's arms.

Brett

I WAKE UP IN a room I don't quite recognize, the sound of a shower running pulling me from sleep. It takes me a second to get my bearings until I remember what happened last evening. I lay there, smiling. Autumn and I had sex—and it was everything.

Now, she's in the bathroom getting ready for work. She has to go, and I don't. I get up and walk over to her bathroom door, opening it and stepping inside. I strip off my clothes and peel back the shower curtain. I catch her smiling at me.

"Good morning," she says, her voice lustrous.

"Good morning," I reply, stepping into the shower. "How are you feeling this morning?" I ask, concerned she might be sore after everything that happened last night.

"I'm more than great," she says, smiling at me. "A little sore, but nothing I can't handle." She begins rinsing the shampoo from her hair under the shower, water flowing over her body. My dick stands at attention.

"Would you care for a repeat of last night, or are you too sore?" I ask, checking my watch. We have a little time before she needs to leave for work.

"Well, if you're offering," she says, smiling, throwing her arms around my neck. She begins kissing me, and I'm instantly kissing her back, running my hands all over her body. The water running down her skin makes everything slippery, and I try to be patient with her by going slow, but she's running the show this time.

Breaking our kiss off, she turns me around to block the water and bends her knees, getting down on the shower tiles on the floor. She grabs my cock in her hand, and she starts pumping slowly while looking up at me through her lashes. I block all but a little trickle of water from getting on her.

Her skin is glistening, and she looks more beautiful than I've ever seen her. She takes the head of my cock in her mouth and sucks slowly, bobbing her head quickly. It doesn't take long before I'm feeling like I'm going to come, and I need her to slow down because I want to tell her I want to come on her pretty tits.

"Autumn. I'm going to...I'm going to come," I grunt out. "And I want to come on those perfect tits of yours. You think I can do that?"

Without removing my cock from her mouth, she nods. She pulls her head back ever so slightly and begins sucking on just the tip while pumping the rest of the shaft with her hand.

I'm getting closer, and it's only been a minute, but Autumn does things to me that no other woman ever has, so of course, she gets me there in a matter of seconds.

Before I know it, she pulls back, and she starts stroking my cock with her hands in quick movements. I feel my orgasm building, and I brace my hand on the wall, putting my other one in her hair at the top of her head. With a grunt, I let it all out as I come all over her tits. She keeps stroking, and this orgasm is going to give me a heart attack.

Once I'm completely emptied, I grab her wrist, so she stops pumping because it starts to hurt. I pull her up to me, turning her so that she can rinse herself off with the water stream. She washes away all of my cum, and I push the middle of her back between her shoulder blades to bend her forward.

"Are you ready for this, baby?" I ask, placing my head at her entrance.

"Mmhmm," she nods, biting her lower lip. With the aid of the water, in one quick thrust, I'm inside of her. She gasps, quickly turning into a moan, and I begin sliding in and out, feeling the lubrication from how wet she is and from the water flowing down our bodies. It's so smooth and it feels amazing.

Just like last night, she's so perfect for me. She starts squeezing my dick inside of her, and I feel her orgasm building. I reach around her front and start rubbing her clit with my fingers. I know her body will react well to this because she loved it last night when I was doing it. It doesn't take her long to come.

"Oh my god, Brett!" She begins yelling my name and moaning quite loudly. I keep thrusting inside of her, letting her ride out her orgasm as long as possible. Slowing down before pulling out completely, I trail kisses all along her shoulder and back. As she comes off the high from her orgasm, I finally slide out of her, turn her around, and kiss her face softly.

After we are done, Autumn gets out, gets dressed for work, and throws a bagel in the toaster. She will be going without coffee this morning, which I don't love, so maybe I'll swing by and grab one to bring to her at the office.

As soon as the bagel is done, she slathers cream cheese on it, grabs her work bag, kisses me goodbye, and says, "Okay, I'm off to the office. I don't want to be late, and I have to text Tony. I'll see you later. Can I trust you to lock up the door before you leave?"

I salute her. "Absolutely. I'll make sure all your doors are locked and everything is turned off." She smiles, kissing me again.

"Okay, have a good day." With that, she walks out the door.

It's now time to implement my master plan. I'm meeting Knox in town at the coffee shop before heading over to Arch so he can hook me up with a wireless mic I can wear under my shirt. He's got a whole recording setup so I can capture my entire conversation with John. I plan to confront him and see if I can get him to admit to any of his foul play to give Autumn the extra confidence boost she needs to take this mess to a lawyer.

I turn off all the lights, make sure the toaster is unplugged, and walk out, locking the door behind me. I climb into my truck and drive to the coffee shop.

I walk in the door of the coffee shop and spot him sitting at a small table. I stop by to talk to him before ordering my drinks. "Hey man," I say, shaking Knox's hand and pulling him into a hug, slapping him on the back. "Thanks for all your help with this. I owe you. Once I get this data, I'll get you that $500 we agreed on."

Knox nods. "Sure thing. I trust you."

"Let me place my order quick, and we can chat." I walk up to Sydney at the counter. "My regular two coffees, please," I tell her, receiving her signature squeal and smile, then meet Knox at a table.

"Okay, here's the mic and the wires," Knox says. "This little box goes inside your jeans waistband. Run the wires across your chest and put the mic here in the middle. There's body-safe tape, but it'll probably pull some chest hair." I wince at the thought, knowing it's likely that I won't use that.

"Do I have to press anything to record?" I ask.

"Just flip this switch," he says, pointing. "Turn it on in the parking lot, go inside, and it'll record everything." He sips his coffee, satisfied.

"Thanks, man. Appreciate it," I feel the adrenaline start to kick in, knowing I'm really going to do this.

"Here's your coffee, Brett," Sydney calls. I grab it and head back to Knox.

"Anything else I should know?" I ask, finally taking the mic from him.

Knox shakes his head at me. "Nope. Just do your thing."

·· ☐☐☐☐ ·☐· ☐☐☐☐ ··

The drive takes five minutes. My brain races with thoughts of Autumn, last night, this morning, and how much I care for her. Over the months on the job site, I've watched her grow into a strong engineer. She's marvelous to watch, and I'm proud of her work ethic. Not to mention, she's beautiful and funny, and I absolutely adore her.

Once parked, I hide in my truck, attaching the mic, making sure the wires aren't showing. Once everything is set, I grab the coffees and head inside. There are only three offices here, so it's not hard for me to find Autumn's—pictures of her and Lucy, her parents, and college friends line the walls. She's not in there, so I set her coffee down and head out to find John.

I pass the other office with pictures of a scrawny blonde guy, Colin. Autumn has mentioned him before. Mr. Matthews seems to favor him, even though they started at the same time. At the end of the hallway is a big office—would make sense that this is John's. I look in, see him sitting, and knock on the door.

"Hey, good morning, John. You got some time to meet? I have some stuff I want to chat about."

"Hey Brett, how are you? Absolutely, let's chat. What's going on?" He smiles, shaking my hand, then sits at his desk. I take the chair across from him, careful not to ruffle the microphone wires.

"I got laid off from the university job," I start, trying to sound nonchalant. "I wanted to talk to you about Autumn and her work there. She and I worked a bit to fix those plans she messed up at the beginning of the job."

"Ah, yes. Autumn has had many difficulties on that site, I believe most involving you," he says, crossing his arms.

"Ha, yeah. I was shocked you had such a newbie handle such a big project. I would have thought you'd check her plans before she brought them in," I share with him, willing him to spill something that I can get on recording.

"Oh yes," he sighs. "She has been difficult to work with. I don't always have a chance to review her items before she shares them with others. The last I had checked, things were going okay with the team she was working with but then somehow that mishap occurred. I also heard there were advances made toward you, which I apologize for. I immediately implemented a strict no-fraternization policy, and Autumn was reprimanded and docked pay."

I hide my shock—Autumn didn't mention that she was docked pay.

"Good. That's what I like to hear," I say, feigning concern. "I don't know if women really belong on the job site." I push him a little harder, trying to get him to admit something.

"Brett, we don't know each other well, but based on that comment, I'd say we'd get along fine. Keep this between us, but

I do think women don't belong in engineering. They're too emotional."

I laugh. "Yes, women are moody, can't focus, and mess everything up. They can't even keep track of a simple schedule to make a meeting on time," I appeal to his ego, trying to get him to admit he didn't tell Autumn about meetings.

He leans forward, elbows on the desk. "I'll let you in on a little secret, I didn't tell Autumn about those meetings. The only way to have grounds to fire her was if she screwed up. I texted a fake number saved as Autumn Harris. She missed multiple meetings, and it made her look bad."

There it is—he admitted it. He withheld information to create grounds for dismissal.

"Yeah, wow, that's pretty smart on your part. Most of us from the crew can't even believe Autumn got an engineering degree with the way she behaved on the job site. But anyway, the real reason I came in was that I wanted to tell you that I appreciate all the work you do, and if you ever know of any openings on a crew... let me know. If I'm laid off, I might take it. I might be sticking around Mayfield for a bit longer, so I'm exploring all avenues for operating jobs I can. Figure you probably have a good sight on what's comin' down the line," I nod, stand, and shake his hand.

"Of course Brett, I know your work ethic is second-to-none. I appreciate you stopping by. Tell your mom I said hi," he nods at me as I walk out the door. I will absolutely not be telling my mom he said hi.

Outside the door, I pause. I now have proof for Autumn to take to a lawyer. Pulling up my shirt, I turn off the recording switch, hoping that everything is saved.

As I walk back past the offices, Colin—or I think that's his name—steps out. "Uh, hey, man. She isn't here. She just ran out crying. Not sure what's going on."

The color drains from my face. I run out the front door and look left and right, finding her sitting on a bench in front of the building. "Autumn!" I yell, walking up to her.

"Get the fuck away from me, Brett! You don't want to be near me now! I'm a woman and might be too stupid for you to be around!"

I know immediately what she overheard.

Autumn

I COME BACK TO my desk from the bathroom and see a familiar coffee cup sitting there—one from the coffee shop in town. Popping the lid off, I see the steam rising, still warm. And it's exactly how I take it: two cream, two sugar. Only one other person knows how I like my coffee. Why is Brett here?

I take a sip, feeling it flow through me, energizing me. Since he's been laid off, I don't get my coffee in the morning from him. It feels nice and comforting, especially after the wonderful morning we had. I've been smiling ever since I left the house, and I can't stop. The birds are chirping, the sun is shining—it's a beautiful day in May, and everything seems to be looking up.

If Brett dropped off my coffee, maybe he's still here. It's warm, so I decide to look for him. Where would he be? Maybe talking to Mr. Matthews. I don't know why, but that's the only logical place I can think to check.

I walk down the hall and see them sitting in his office with the door open. I try to hide so they don't see me, eavesdropping—and what I hear stops my heart cold.

"Yeah, wow, that's pretty smart on your part. Most of us from the crew can't even believe Autumn got an engineering degree with the way she behaved on the job site. But anyway, the real reason I came in was that I wanted to tell you that I appreciate all the work you do, and if you ever know of any openings on a crew... let me know. If I'm laid off, I might take it. I might be sticking around Mayfield for a bit longer, so I'm exploring all avenues for operating jobs I can. Figure you probably have a good sight on what's comin' down the line."

Brett is in his office... talking shit about me. After the night we had. After the morning we had. My heart shatters in my chest.

Did he use me to get off? Was that his plan all along? Was his niceness on the job just a setup? My gasp is silent.

Tears start streaming down my face. I can't stop them. I start running, past Colin, brushing against his shoulder without even looking back. He turns and calls after me, but I don't care. I go outside and sit on the bench. The sobs come uncontrollably.

I can't believe Brett of all people would do this. He never once struck me as the type to talk about women like that—or talk about someone he cares about like that—or at least, someone I thought he cared about. I cover my head with my hands, drop it into my lap, and let the tears flow. My heart continues to break.

"Autumn!" I hear him yell, running toward me.

"Get the fuck away from me, Brett! You don't want to be near me now! I'm a woman, and I might be too stupid for you to be around!" I yell, sobbing.

The concern on his face turns to fear. He comes over and sits next to me, pulling something from under his shirt that looks like wires.

I'm confused, choking back a sob. I suck in a breath and hiccup. "What... what the heck is that?"

"This," he says, "is why I was here. Why I brought you coffee. Why I was there for you last night... and why I'm here for you right now, Autumn. This is proof."

I'm even more confused.

"Last night, I told you everything I found—what my friend Knox found. But we needed solid, undeniable proof that this was actually John's doing. So, I came up with a plan with Knox. I didn't tell you until I could first show you that it would work: get into John's office, have a conversation with him, and get him to admit what he did to you. Anything I said in that office was a lie to lead him on, to guide him into admitting what he did. And Autumn..."

Brett grabs my shoulders and looks at me, smiling. "I got him. I got him to admit that he withheld information from you to affect your work performance—just so he could have grounds to fire you."

I'm still hiccupping and sobbing, wiping away tears. "You got him to admit it?" I ask, hope shining through.

"Yes, baby. I got him to admit it." He pulls me into a hug.

My sobs are different now—full of relief and outrage. My boss withheld information from me, affecting my performance, all because I'm a woman. This is sexism and discrimination. I curl up into Brett, grabbing onto his shirt, and sob through a snotty inhale.

"What do we do now?" I ask him.

Brett takes a deep breath, his calm presence grounding me. "Now, we work with my buddy Knox to gather everything. We get you a great lawyer, and we sue. I don't know what you want out of this—money, which you deserve, especially since you took a pay cut after everything that went down with us—but we do whatever you want. You need to do this. You need to quit this job."

"If I quit, I won't have money," I choke out.

"I'll help you. I swear I will. I have money. I can move in with you if we need to. We'll work on this together. I'll do anything to help you."

I lean back, sitting up on my own. He grabs my hands in both of his, forcing me to look into his eyes.

"We are a team now, if you'll let me. We are stronger together. I will protect you, defend you, care for you, and push you to be the best you can be. And if that means taking out the fuckers who hold you back, that's exactly what I'll do."

I take his hands in mine and lean into him, kissing him with slow, deep passion. This kiss is meaningful—it says I'm with him, I want to do this with him, I need his support, and I will be his support. We are a strong team together.

When I lean back, Brett smiles at me.

"When you walked into the job trailer with those failed blueprints," he says softly, "I didn't know that recreating them together would be creating blueprints of love, Autumn. But I'm so happy that we did."

Autumn

Two years later

I CARRY THE PIZZA box inside and set it down on the small island in the kitchen of our camper.

"Brett, I got the pizza we ordered," I say, seeing him pop out of the fridge.

He has two beers in his hand and sets them on the island, giving me a big kiss.

"Okay, I got the movie and the fort all set up, and I'm going to go ahead and get all the food ready. You go get a shower," he says, smacking me on the ass.

"You got it, baby," I say, laughing, and I head up the small set of steps to the tiny shower located at the front of our rig.

Brett and I are currently living in our fifth-wheel camper. We upgraded his old camper to something bigger when I moved in and began pipelining with him on the road. Now we have a weekly movie night—pizza, snacks, and cozying up in the living room to watch whatever we're in the mood for: a feel-good flick, an action movie, or whatever calls to us.

Sometimes I like to think about how lucky I am to have Brett and how far we've come since we met. We met on a rocky start, on a job site of all places. My boss at the time, Mr. Matthews, was a sexist pig who tried to tell us we couldn't be together. I try not to think about him too much, but it's nice to reminisce about the fact that I crushed him when I sued.

As soon as I told a lawyer about the sexual discrimination I'd experienced, and after we had proof of his admissions and all the files Knox collected, I knew we'd be successful. We took our case to court instead of settling with Arch Engineering, and it blew up. Local news covered it extensively—a big sexual discrimination case—and it got a lot of attention. We put Mr. Matthews out of business, and he had to pay out so much that I was able to take over Arch Engineering.

Now, I'm the lead engineer there, with a small crew of all women. I operate the company remotely while taking on pipeline engineering jobs, allowing me to travel with Brett. We've become a package deal quickly, and everyone knows that if you call requesting Brett on the crew, you have to have a space for me as well. It's nice knowing I have some semblance of job security in a field that's constantly changing. We're always moving from one job to the next as we finish what we're working on.

As for Arch, since I operate remotely, I needed to hire a lead person who could represent my interests while I'm out on the road. Surprisingly, I found that Colin was the best fit for the job. He is the only man I have working for me currently. Yes, the crew is all women, but that doesn't mean I wouldn't hire men—it's just that few have applied. I've earned a bit of a reputation around Mayfield as a "man-eater," which is fine with me. I have my man, and that's all I need.

Colin admitted that he was the one who turned me in for having a relationship with Brett, but he didn't know about the full extent of Matthews' discrimination. He profusely apologized and keyed me in on how Mr. Matthews was telling him lies about me to try and get him to dislike me. We've discussed everything that happened between us in detail with lawyers present, and we're in a much better place now. I would venture to say even friends, and honestly, he's a smart engineer. I trust him explicitly, given that he operates my company while I'm out on the road. My goal with all the engineers on my team is for them to have someone on their team like Brett—someone who supports them no matter what. I keep open lines of communication with everyone and encourage them to ask questions, be vulnerable, and learn from the experienced workers.

Last fall, we finished the engineering building. Brett stood right beside me while I cut the big red ribbon at the unveiling. He helped with the dirt work on the job, and it was a big moment for us both. Thinking back on how far we've come, I'm so proud of all that we've been able to achieve and overcome. Life tried to push us apart, but we persevered, as love always does.

After my shower, I throw on my sexiest pajamas—a little tradition—and go to the living room. I find my big, burly man, soft and gooey on the inside, sitting on the couch in our little blanket fort he built for me, with the popcorn and pizza in front of him.

Brett acts tough on the outside, a go-getter who will do anything for anyone. But for me? He's a softy. The best cuddler I've ever found. I snuggle up next to him, and he hits play on the movie.

I'm so grateful that life forced me to spend time with him, to get to know him, because he really is a great guy. Life has a funny way of pushing you in the right direction, even with thousands of obstacles in your path.

Acknowledgements

Writing a book and dumping my thoughts was the easy part. Making it readable, professional, and ensuring that it made sense was the hard part. I couldn't have achieved this dream without so much support, guidance, and feedback.

So many times, I wanted to give up. I didn't think I could finish, I didn't think I could publish, but Thomas, my dear, you believed in me wholeheartedly and you still do every day. I'm forever grateful for you, without your support, guidance, and copious amounts of information, this story would not exist beyond my imagination. I spent hours brainstorming and dreaming about these characters, running ideas past you, constantly asking, "Do you think this could happen?" And you put up with me for all of it. So my first and biggest thank you is of course to you. Thomas, you are my biggest supporter. I love you. Thank you for believing in me.

Thank you to my parents as well for teaching me the power of hard work and determination. Because of the life lessons you instilled in me as a child, I was able to keep going. I was able to create Autumn, a character who despite being shoved down time and time again, stood strong and got the job done.

I would also like to thank my wonderful beta readers. You helped me refine my ideas, make sense of what I was doing, and made sure my words made sense to others. Tiffany, Anna, Melissa, and Diana, you are amazing.

These next three were officially my editors, and they gave HUGE feedback for my story and helped me more than they'll ever know. To Rosemary, Meg, and Casy, thank you, thank you, thank you. There is not enough gratitude for your feedback and knowledge.

Lastly, cheers to any women who are out there kicking ass in a male dominated field. You rock, and you are powerful. Even when life tries to chew you up and spit you out, you persist.

About the Author

S.A. Bierly is an American contemporary romance author born and raised in central Pennsylvania. She grew up on a family-owned, third-generation, dairy farm, so blue-collar work is deep in her history. She married her high school sweetheart, a blue-collar worker himself.

S.A. Bierly has a career in science by day and when not writing, she can be found spending time with her family and her two dogs, or reading spicy romance and fantasy novels.

www.ingramcontent.com/pod-product-compliance
Lightning Source LLC
LaVergne TN
LVHW091709070526
838199LV00050B/2328